Jericho Brotherhood

Enough
Release
Deny

Brotherhood Bonds

Bail Out
Shake Down

To Jeff, who reminded me of the magic of love and gave me back the desire to write again.

GET AWAY

JADE CHANDLER

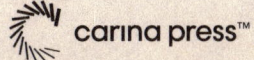 carina press™

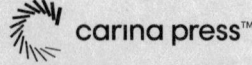

carina press™

ISBN-13: 978-1-335-01621-8

Recycling programs for this product may not exist in your area.

Get Away

Copyright © 2019 by Jade Chandler

www.CarinaPress.com

Printed in U.S.A.

GET AWAY

Chapter 1: Delta

I left the red convertible Porsche 911 curbside before walking into the casino. Dressed in a long-sleeve button down, dress pants and Chuck Taylors, no one would ever associate me with Jericho Brotherhood. The less intel my enemy had, the better I did.

I barely noticed the overdone lobby of the Remington as I moved straight toward the elevator and the high-roller poker game that started in thirty minutes.

I stepped onto the elevator, swiping my key pass to the exclusive high-stakes floor. As the elevator moved up, I stared out at the Las Vegas strip through the glass wall of the elevator. The skyline didn't inspire me, it only represented dollar signs. I'd made good bank from the tables in Vegas, and I planned to keep on taking the suckers' money at the poker table tonight.

The door opened and the squat promoter I'd been dodging came my way. "Ren, my brother, how's it hanging?"

Better than it ever has for this balding douche. I smirked at him but kept walking toward the check-in table.

"Those looks, your skills—the promotional deals

would be worth thousands." He had to almost jog to keep up with me.

"Fuck off, Smitty. Never going to go pro." Those guys were all flash and sizzle—besides, no one would want a biker to promote their brands. And I wanted cash, not fame.

I handed over my ID to the man in a tuxedo behind the check-in table. I hated this moment with a passion. My skin prickled with the exposure as the man read my name. Terrence Owen Holt, Jr. He checked it off on a sheet then smiled up at me. "Thank you Te... I mean Ren." He stumbled over the greeting at my cold stare. "Mr. Holt, welcome to the Remington." He gave me a weak smile.

No one ever called me Terrence—one of these lackeys had made that mistake once. No one else had made that mistake since. I was Delta now. Before the army had given me that name, I'd used Ren. My old man had cursed me with his worthless name, and I hated it almost as much as I hated him.

"Ren, glad you could make it." Jerry, the gaming manager, held out his hand to me. He'd tried comping me rooms for the week, but I'd refused. I never stayed where I played—it was one of my many rules. His job was to distract me, but I wasn't that stupid. I avoided his hotel, the honeys already flashing their goods in high-dollar dresses, and the booze that flowed like a river in this place.

I shook his hand. "Jerry, nice spread." I shoved hands in my pant pockets and surveyed the room. I spotted the other players in seconds. I'd researched most of them, focusing on their weaknesses. One player was missing.

Know the enemy—another rule of engagement.

"Where's Allers?"

Jerry glanced away, nervousness flashing across his weasel face. "Got sick…isn't coming." He rubbed hands on his black pants. "I found a replacement."

Fuck me, I hated wild cards. "Who?"

"Frank Ricci." Jerry looked away, uncomfortable, then he motioned a petite blonde bombshell toward him.

The girl sauntered over with a regal sexuality that probably had men bowing and scraping to buy her a drink. I had no use for pussy in Vegas—I was here for the game.

"Glory, this is Ren, one of the players tonight."

The blonde with a face that was too perfect, too symmetrical, too cold gave me a smile that was as practiced as the way she'd made up her face. It sure didn't reach those bright blue eyes.

"Hello, how ya doing tonight?" The Southern accent made me pay attention. I'd bet a thousand that she was from southern Oklahoma, my home turf.

"I'm great, sugar. Getting ready to win a lot of money." I crossed my arms and assessed her. She was an ice queen who wore her pride like a crown. In this town where women flocked to men, she'd stand out, be sought out, because she didn't chase.

She sipped the dark burgundy wine she held and scanned the room, not a bit interested in me or the others. Maybe we weren't rich enough for her.

I heard the door to the suite open a second before she lost all color, turning so pale the veins were a light blue web in her neck. She stepped back, a small O on her lips, and dropped her wine. As if in slow motion, the wine sloshed up and over the side as it fell from her slack fingers. Cherry-red nails, I noted, even as I snaked my hand out to rescue the glass before it marred the cream carpet.

The red splashed my hand as I caught the glass— a cabernet by scent and temperature. Give me beer or whiskey any day. I glanced back to see her face a mask now, although her color was still off.

The man, who had to be Frank Ricci, stood inside the door staring hard at the ice queen. There was complicated emotion swirling in that guy's eyes. He stared with a passion that was too possessive. Lovers maybe?

Her nervousness was all too real, so maybe an ex-lover then. That fit the way he stared, and she glanced everywhere but at the newest member of the poker game. I saw an opportunity for intel and took it. While she was distracted, I curled my arm around the middle of her back and guided her away from the scene.

She complied, leaning into me just a bit. Ricci had definitely unsettled her. I led her out a glass door and onto the empty balcony. The same majestic view of the city greeted us here. I turned my back on the view and let Glory stare out at it.

"Can I ask you a personal question?"

She bristled and glanced behind her.

"Where are you from in Oklahoma?"

Her face lit up with surprise, then she smiled her first genuine smile of the night. "My accent is that obvious?"

That smile sucker-punched me in the gut. The ice queen had melted, leaving a sexy beauty in her place. When Glory gave me that smile, it was hard to remember my name. My cock twitched to life, and I reminded myself pussy was not my goal tonight.

"I'm from a speck of nothing called Barden, Oklahoma. I've been here four years, but I can't shake the accent." She nodded to me. "You're from Texas?"

What were the fucking chances? In this city of millions, I run into a girl from my hometown—well, it had been since I joined the Jericho Brotherhood six years ago.

"I was born in Texas, but you won't believe this, I live close to Barden now. It's a small world." I grinned wide but her smile dropped away. The ice queen returned.

"Did Avery send you to check on me?" She fisted hands on hips. "You have to be one of *them*."

Fuck. Fuck. Fuck. This was all backfiring on me. My plan to find out about Ricci had uncovered my secrets. Secrets she had no obligation to keep. Not that it'd be the end of the world if the fellow players knew I was a member of the club. I wasn't ashamed, but I did love misdirection—it gave me an edge at the tables.

"Stay the fuck away from me. I don't want or need *your* kind of help." She stalked away from me. Anger snapped in each step of those tall, red heels. She was through the door and out of my sight in seconds.

I didn't move because I was too busy calculating the odds and figuring out the best way to play the hand Glory might deal me. Tonight there was a two million dollar pot at stake and I wanted a big share of that. Did Ricci coming or Glory knowing I was a biker change how I played? Most people assumed I was some kind of business whiz kid. And I let them. Would they challenge me more if they understood I was an outlier, not at all like them?

I scanned the people congregating near the bar and considered the best strategy. In the end, I decided to hold steady—I was good at reading others and I would rely on that to tell me if I needed to change strategies. I'd put hours of work into researching, watching, and finally constructing my strategy for this game. It would be stupid to abandon that plan until there was a definite reason to change.

I returned to the suite and grabbed a bottle of water from the bucket near the bar and strolled toward the playing area. I swiveled my gaze side to side, catching sight of all the players except Ricci. Damn, where was he? And for that matter where was Glory? A few more steps and I found them both. The bastard had Glory trapped in the far corner of the suite. He boxed her in with two arms, blocking any escape.

"Ricci," I called in a loud, slurred voice, hoping he'd think me on my way to hammered. "What you doing with my girl?" I knocked into him, dislodging his arm, so she could escape. I held my hand out to the queen.

She quickly grasped it and tucked herself into my side. Fear flashed in her deep blue eyes, but that was the only sign I saw that anything was wrong in her world. She was a damn fine actress.

"Sugar, I've been looking for you. I come all the way to Vegas to see you and you disappeared." I leaned down and planted a slow, wet kiss on her lips.

Ricci stared from me to her and back. "You from Barden then?"

I raised an eyebrow. So he knew Glory—pretty well by the possessive glint in his eye and the way his fist clenched and unclenched.

"You know it, I come to see her all the time—this girl is special to me." I'd just changed the strategy for the night because of this woman. What the fuck? Yet adrenaline coursed through me at the thought of letting go of my plan and figuring out a new one on the fly. It's what the military had trained me to do.

"This is the punk biker you told me about?" He wrinkled his nose and looked down at me.

I wasn't the tallest guy at five foot ten, but no one looked down on me. "You watch your next words very carefully." Not even the cash at hand would stop me from teaching this boy a lesson if he dissed me or my club.

"Yeah, I told him everything." Glory nestled closer to my side. "So you best leave me be." Her cold words to Ricci made no sense to me.

She hadn't told me shit about Ricci or how she knew him, but I bet I knew the story here. She'd dumped this guy, and he thought intimidation would bring her back. It was a situation I'd seen a million times as a military cop before I'd received a Bad Conduct Discharge—the Big Chicken Dinner as soldiers referred to it. Add to that my ability to read even the smallest tick or gesture, and the situation crystalized for me—the situation was serious. The idea that this guy would even make Glory frown pissed me off.

I didn't understand the pathetic suckers who kept pushing after it was over. Worse, the idiots who thought they could use intimidation or violence to make the women toe the line. My father had been just that kind of prick.

"Do we have a problem? We can settle it right fucking now?" I let the violence inside me flow into my voice.

Ricci wasn't stupid. He slid right past us and didn't look back. I pulled Glory tight to me, squeezing her ass through the tight red dress she wore. The scent of peaches tickled my nose as I bent toward her.

"You better kiss me so he knows it's real," I murmured in her ear before sliding my lips to meet hers.

She stiffened but didn't pull away when I planted one

on her. Her tense body tightened like a snake coiled to strike. Her lips stayed firmly clamped shut. Stubborn and feisty.

Her body softened by the smallest degree then heat flooded through me when she opened up for me. I poured that heat right back into our connection, needing to possess her.

She rubbed against my cock, tangling her arms around my neck, finally giving as good as she got. I needed all of her, a taste wasn't even close to enough.

The five minute bell rang and broke the spell she'd woven around us. Fuck, what had she done to me? I'd totally forgotten about the mission—the poker game. All I wanted to do was take her to my room and fuck her until she screamed my name.

I stepped away—nothing came between me and the game.

I pulled a black card from my pant pocket and slid it between the shimmery material and her bare flesh of her neckline. "Call me if you need anything. We always help our own."

Her mask was back in place and I couldn't tell what she thought. That was unusual. As I walked to a table, I sent a quick text to JoJo and Rebel. I needed the score on Glory before I made plans to get her naked.

I sat at the green felt poker table where most of the players were already seated. I shut down my emotions and focused on getting into the right headspace. I leaned back in my chair and met Ricci's challenging gaze. He was bringing his grudge to the table, and that was my advantage.

"Time to shuffle and deal," the dealer announced as the clock rolled over to midnight.

Texas Hold 'Em was a game of odds and people—equal parts art and science. I played many kinds of poker but this was my favorite.

I peeked at my two cards. Jacks—a nice pocket pair that was all kinds of dangerous, but my favorite hand. I came out strong with my bet, then watched the enemy react. The players thought they'd mastered their tells, but I could read even the slightest change in their expression and body.

Danvers, our old CO, and still a good friend, told me I read micro expressions, whatever the fuck that meant. He was a good guy but he was in his head too much—I followed my instincts. And they said that Ricci would follow me down to the last draw, so I had to make sure I had the best hand in the end. Luckily, Ricci wore his cards on his face. I'd separate that fool from every damn dollar and then take his girl home for the night.

Chapter 2: Glory

My lips were scalded by our kiss. No one had ever made me come alive like that in my twenty-eight years. I thought Mark, my high school boyfriend, was the man meant for me right up until he joined the damn Jericho Brotherhood. But our chemistry was a shadow of what had pumped through me during that one kiss.

Ren sat with his back to me at the poker table. I could barely take my gaze off his wide shoulders—the man was built with solid muscle. His messy short golden hair looked as if he'd just rolled out of bed. Add the disreputable scruff on his jaw, and he was too damn hot for his own good. And, unfortunately Mr. Hot Stuff knew it.

I hated cocky guys—all attitude and show. Ren was that kind of guy. Being too beautiful for my own good all my damn life had taught me about that type. Those guys were as deep as a puddle and about as appealing.

He drew in the pot on the first hand, and Frankie radiated anger. I hoped Frankie lasted until late in the game so I could escape without him bothering me.

"You girls go freshen up. Be back in thirty." Jerry patted my ass as he walked behind the four of us.

I bit my tongue and turned toward the suite door.

Down the hall was a lounge where we could touch up our makeup and relax before we had to go play hostess again.

"I can't believe Frankie showed up here," I told my friend Celeste as we swiped into the room. The other two girls had headed for the elevator to sneak down to the smoking area in the basement.

She frowned at me. "His uncle owns this place... Didn't you know that?"

"What?" I squeaked.

When Celeste, my roommate, had suggested I join her at the Remington, I'd done it in part because I wanted to escape Frankie, who'd made a complete pest of himself since we'd broken up last month. When someone—I suspected Frankie—had started leaving dead roses on my car and sending me morbid poems, a new job seemed like the quickest way to lose the admirer. Celeste had suggested here, and I'd come. Why hadn't she told me about Frankie's connection to the casino?

Three weeks at the Remington with no dead roses or bad poetry, so I had considered that a win. Now, it looked like I'd gotten myself in a worse situation.

"You know Frankie is connected to the DeLuca family—they own this place." Celeste stared into the mirror, reapplying her lipstick.

"I knew his uncle was in the mob, and that he steered clear of that." I couldn't believe this. "Why didn't you tell me about his connection here? You know I wanted to get away from him."

"Hey, everyone is connected in Vegas. You can't escape a man like Frankie at any casino." Celeste rolled her eyes. "You are too naïve for Vegas, darling."

I worried my lower lip, then stopped. I hated when I

did that. "Maybe or maybe not." I wasn't willing to concede the point.

"Who was the hot number you lip-locked?" Celeste's East Coast accent sounded nasally to me. And she only let it show when she wasn't working. When there were high rollers around, she was all class and sophistication.

"A guy from my hometown—one of the bikers I don't like."

"You liked that kiss, girl," she squawked.

I sat at the vanity and opened the makeup box I'd left here. No way was I using the crap the casino provided. I had standards—expensive ones. And I didn't believe in applying other girls' bacteria to my face. But I was in the minority.

Celeste shook her head at me. "Girl, you need to get your priorities in order. Take that biker home with you and earn some cash." She tsked. This wasn't a new argument. We'd been roommates for two years now.

"I do it my way." I had received a nice bump in salary when I'd joined the Remington. And working the special events boosted my wages more, but I drew the line at the special bonus. Jerry and his crew offered the biggest incentive for the girls who would give the players anything they wanted. Celeste called it partying, and she did it every chance she could. I refused to be a whore. I mean if you were paid twenty bucks or a thousand, you were still selling yourself. And I hadn't come to Vegas to be a prostitute, not even the high-class kind. Not that I cared what she or the others did, it just wasn't in me to bend that way.

"Well you better watch out for Jerry and Frankie tonight—they'll both be trying to change your mind."

Celeste brushed out her fake eyelashes and fluffed her teased auburn hair.

"I can avoid trouble." I lined my lips and reapplied my favorite MAC lipstick.

"Trouble is your middle name." She stood and stretched. "I'm going back to watch the action. I might just snatch up the biker dude. He had to put down a half mil to play tonight—he's got scratch." She winked at me. "Ready?"

I shook my head. "I'll come back when my time's up. The longer I stay away from Frankie the better."

The door shut and I moved from the row of vanities to the leather couch. I curled up and stared down at my phone, planning to read another chapter in my romance. Instead I clicked open the list of players tonight and found him. His picture didn't even begin to capture his sexiness. Terrence Owen Holt, Jr. *Call him Ren* was noted under his name. Age thirty-two. From Oklahoma City, Oklahoma. Entrepreneur? was listed under profession. And that was all Jerry had on him. They didn't know jack shit. Hell, I knew more about him, and I'd just met him, but Brotherhood boys were cut from two molds: military or misfits. Ren shouted *military* with his short hair and the way he held himself ready for whatever came.

I swiped the message icon on my iPhone and clicked on Avery. She was my best friend in the world, and now an old lady to Rock, a member of the Jericho Brotherhood. I had known I would leave Barden for years, but I had stayed until my two best friends joined the club. I would never do that, so I'd packed up and followed my dream to Vegas. I'd always loved dance and theater, but Oklahoma was a wasteland for those kind of arts. As a

kid I'd taken every kind of dance possible, and Mama
had signed me up for every pageant in Oklahoma and
Texas. It only made sense I'd end up a Vegas showgirl
in a chorus line with a sequined costume, dancing my
nights away.

I was earning a living doing what I loved. While I
hadn't taken the town by storm, I was definitely holding my own, and it wasn't because of my goddam face.
Here every dancer, every girl who worked the strip was
breathtaking.

Unlike home. As I'd grown, I'd turned into that un-
touchable kind of beauty that made most people treat me
like some china doll. Mama hadn't helped any with her
passion for beauty pageants and get-rich-quick schemes
that hinged on my looks and her brains. They never
panned out.

Tell me about Ren, a biker in your brotherhood. He's
in my casino, playing high stakes poker. I hit Send and
the message flew to my bestie.

The door opened and the other two girls tottered in
with glassy eyes and the scent of weed and cigarette
smoke hanging on them. Both had been dancers for ten
years at the casino, and they only worked the parties now.
I'd never seen them at a single practice or show. Celeste
had explained that the dancers referred to them as Jerry's
Reserve. They were wild girls who Jerry pimped to the
less picky high rollers. As long as I never had to do it, I
didn't care what they did.

Without a glance my way, they each sat down at the
vanities. One sat at my station and I hurried over to grab
my makeup. Just as the skinny black-haired woman
grabbed for the lid of my makeup case, I laid my hand
firmly over it. "This is my makeup."

"Bitch, it's all the same shit. Take another makeup case home," she snarled at me.

"No, it is my *personal* makeup." I slid the case toward me and pointed with my chin to the bag of cosmetics the casino provided. "That's what you're looking for."

"Aren't you special." She sniffed and smiled over at her companion. "Too good for the Remington's stuff. Aren't you the princess."

I didn't bother to respond because they weren't even worth a retort let alone a frown. I'd known from a young age girls could be vicious bitches. And that hadn't changed with age. It's why I cherished Avery and Celeste. Neither of them were threatened by me.

The two girls glanced my way before leaving. In five minutes I was due back in the suite. The first break in the game would be in fifteen minutes.

I stood and slipped back on the red heels that had cost half a paycheck, but they didn't kill my feet so I considered it money well invested.

My phone buzzed in my handbag. I picked it up and saw Avery's pic on my phone. She'd texted me back. His name is Delta. One of Rebel's bounty hunters. Rock says he's a pussy hound. Is that a good or bad thing? I vote good thing for my girl if you want to get laid. And who doesn't? She included a whole lot of eggplant and other sexual emoji. Avery liked emoji too damn much.

I grinned and stuffed the phone back in my purse. Delta—one of the bounty hunters along with my third cousin Rebel. I was related to too many of the damn bikers anyway. And in my opinion, that kind of family wasn't a good thing.

I hurried down the hall and into the suite right on time. Jerry gave me the stink-eye, but I ignored him and took a seat at the bar. This vantage let me see Delta's profile. No doubt he'd hate any name but his biker one—it was one of the things Avery had told me.

She'd told me a lot about bikers, and I had to admit part of me loved the life she described. But in the end, they were a cult of misfits who lived on the very edge of the law and the wrong side of respectability. And what's more, I wasn't meant for that tiny town and a dead-end job. I needed the bright lights and challenges Vegas offered—it was who I was. And Barden just didn't have what I needed, no matter how much I'd thought I loved Mark or was tempted by the other bikers.

I'd wanted Mark to follow me to Vegas, to embrace my dream, but it wasn't meant to be. And dammit, I deserved to be somebody's number one consideration. I wasn't second to anyone, especially some cult.

A player stood up and walked away, pulling my attention back to the game, which had an intense vibe at the moment. Even the players not in this hand all watched the play unfold. Delta was aloof and looked relaxed compared to the others, but then he didn't give much away. The pile of chips in the center was huge—easily several hundred thousand. I bet it was the first big pot of the night. Frankie, of course, was in the hand. His stack of chips was much smaller than the other players'. If he kept this up he'd be the first out.

The room had an artificial quiet to it with the sound of shuffling chips the only background noise. One of the veteran players considered Delta and Frankie again, then dropped his chips on his stack and folded. He stood and walked away from the table, muttering something.

Play moved to Delta and he didn't hesitate a second before pushing in three stacks of chips.

"Goddammit, Ren—you *are* a cocky SOB." Sid, another regular who was known for his mouth, pushed in a small stack of chips.

Delta must have raised. The other player pushed in his chips and that left Frankie staring down at his meager pile. Frankie was normally the aggressive player who bullied others. That didn't appear to be working tonight.

"Fuck it." Frankie mumbled and pushed in all of his chips.

Frankie had been a royal pain in my ass the past few weeks, and I enjoyed seeing him squirm. He was in over his head at this game, that was obvious from his lack of chips.

The last card flipped up—a ten of spades. The five cards out on the table were a four of diamonds, an ace of spades, a jack of spades and a seven of diamonds. One last round of betting was set to the side since Frankie couldn't bet more. Frankie showed his cards first. "Aces up, for a triple, boys." He grinned wide but there was fear under the smile.

The next guy threw in his cards and muttered, "Fuck."

The next guy threw his cards face down, meaning he'd been beat.

Ren flipped up a king of spades and a seven of spades—a flush.

"You fucking prick—you bet that shit." Frankie stood up and knocked his chair to the floor. "You're a rotten player, no one plays those fucking cards." He sputtered and shoved the chips—a full-on temper tantrum now. "You're a fucking cheat, that's what you are."

The guys at the table scooted back and two looked to the official for help. There were rules in poker—I'd worked enough games to know that. And calling another player a cheat was against the cardinal rule. It had serious consequences.

Delta did some maneuver and was across the table in a flash. Frankie was down, arm curled behind his back, head smashed into the table. "You better resolve this before I do." Delta looked every inch the brawling biker in that moment—deadly dangerous.

Jerry hurried forward with the two officials in the room. "Let him go."

"When security is here to detain him." Delta looked hard at Jerry. "He doesn't get the family pass on this one."

Jerry turned white and put his phone to his ear. Seconds later two bulky guys with guns at their waist came rushing in the room. Delta let Frankie go and stepped back. "If I'd known you let family play, I wouldn't have even come to this game, but this shit isn't going unchecked."

Jerry glanced at the other players, who were all nodding along.

"You can't run shoddy games, mate," Aaron, a weekly player at this game, moved next to Delta. "We're playing a big boy game, and if this bloke ain't ready for it, then he should go suck his uncle's wanker."

Delta grinned at the Australian. I'd always liked Aaron but I loved the way he stood by Delta now. Two of the other players moved over beside them.

Jerry gulped and put the phone back to his ear. "Review the tape on the last hand. We have an allegation of cheating by Frank Ricci."

"I will have you fucking fired, Jerry," Frankie snarled.

Security restrained Frankie.

"You're fired too!" He spit at each of the guards.

They didn't look impressed.

A waitress brought drinks, but the players didn't budge from the small groups they had formed. A tense knot of silence held the room captive. Accusing a man of cheating in a formal game of poker at the Remington had two outcomes. If the accuser was right, the accused would be stripped of his cash and banned from the Remington, and all Vegas casinos in practice. If the accuser was wrong, the accuser would be stripped of cash and banned from the Remington, and usually other casinos. No one wanted this kind of problem in their casino.

Frankie was so fucking screwed. And Delta was as calm as could be. If I hadn't seen him turn deadly, I wouldn't believe it now. He appeared totally relaxed, harmless even. But I'd seen the flash of who he really was when he'd put Frankie down.

Jerry listened when his phone rang then sighed, heavily. "Frank Ricci, you are banned from the Remington poker tables for life. And banned from this casino property for one year."

"No fucking way! I own this casino. You're the one out of work!" he bellowed and tugged on his arms.

A phone rang from Frankie's pocket.

"Let him get that." Jerry sounded more weary than anything.

With a smug look Frankie retrieved his phone. He held it up to his ear and the smug smile dropped from his face. "Yes, sir." Then a moment later. "I understand, sir." And finally. "I understand, sir." And he swiped off his phone.

Frankie's eyes met mine, and he gave me a cruel smile. "Grab your coat, baby, we're going out tonight."

I glanced at Jerry and saw in an instant I was on my own. Jerry would let Frankie have me in order to soothe the brat. Fear sliced into me—I wanted nothing to do with him. He'd take out his rage and shame on me. I raced through alternatives to get out of this tight spot. The card Delta had given me poked my breast. And an idea struck me—one I knew would work.

I smiled at Jerry. "I'm happy to do that but I will have to cancel the private party D—" I corrected myself. "Ren booked with me."

Delta winked at me before Jerry turned to him.

"You have plans with our Glory?"

"I do." He crossed his arms and dared Jerry or Frankie to push him further. "That a problem?"

Frankie stalked toward the door, but he shot me a look filled with hate. Adrenaline pumped through my system. I was safe for now, but the way he'd stared at me couldn't be good for my future here. Maybe I should look for a new job, although I hadn't been at the Remington very long and that would look bad. But I didn't need to be on the bad side of Angel DeLuca, Frankie's uncle and owner of this casino. Maybe I should've just gone with Frankie after all.

Once Frankie left, a buzz started in the room. Delta stalked toward me, and I wanted to duck for cover. His eyes flashed with something dark even as he smiled down at me. "Stroll with me on the balcony." He looped his arm in mine and turned me toward the glass door.

I had no choice but to follow him. And honestly, I owed him since I'd used him to escape Frankie.

On the balcony, he walked up to the railing and looked out at the night skyline. "What's your situation, Queenie?"

The nickname irritated me, but he'd saved me from Frankie. "What do you mean?"

"The Frank Ricci situation."

I sucked in a breath. "He's my ex and he doesn't like being my ex. I came to work here thinking he'd be less likely to harass me. He told me he rarely even plays here."

"And you thought, why not work here where my ex prick can control my life?" Delta's harsh tone made my back stand up straight.

Maybe it wasn't my best move, but he didn't have to be an ass about it. I blew out a breath and reminded myself not to lose my shit, again. "Look, I shouldn't have gotten you involved. Sorry."

"Too late for that, sweetheart. I was involved when I found out your hometown." Delta's icy blue eyes assessed me and maybe found me wanting.

I wanted nothing to do with the Brotherhood. "I don't need your help."

"Oh Queenie, you need me." His voice dropped into this sexy timbre that made me want to squirm.

Since I'd agreed to be his sexual partner when I'd told Jerry we had a date, no doubt my boss would collect the two grand. Delta would let me back out if I asked, but I didn't want to be that girl. So I sucked in a breath and straightened my spine. "I doubt that."

Chapter 3: Delta

Queenie gave me a glare that dared me to do my worst. Damn, she had moxie, and I liked it too damn much.

"You won't doubt long." I turned her toward me and kissed her the second time that night. Peaches filled my nostrils and her soft body pressed into me. Damn, she had me hard again.

The balcony door opened and someone cleared their throat. "Five minutes, Mr. Holt."

I stepped away with a reluctance that shouldn't be there. What was it about this blonde that made my blood run so fucking hot?

She was beyond beautiful but that wasn't it. Her defiance turned me on. In fact, she might have as much attitude as me.

We walked into the suite again. "You wait for me, right here."

She frowned and started to argue.

I placed a finger on her lips. "Frankie might be waiting out there." I flicked a hand toward the hallway. "I can't protect you there."

Her brow creased more but she nodded.

"Say it."

"I'll stay here." She spoke with a sullenness that amused me. Definite 'tude.

I walked back inside with no desire to play anymore. But if I left now, there would be rumors and then more subtle challenges next time I played. Nope, I wasn't letting the dickhead even dent my reputation.

I sat down to a table that was lighter three players—Frankie had been forced to leave, but two other players had also left. Poker players were superstitious, and confrontations brought bad luck.

I noted the players who left, then focused on the ones who'd stayed. The chump's move would be to come out dominant, trying to win every hand just to prove some nonexistent point. They had witnessed me win by luck on the river the hand before, so I wasn't going to tempt the others with more bluffs, so I settled in for the slow, conservative play.

Three long hours later, I pushed away from the table. "That's the night for me. Color me up." Two attendants came forward and I watched as they counted my chips—a million and fifty thousand dollars.

And that was a new high for me—I'd gone from barely having twenty bucks to my name after JoJo and I left the army to a fucking millionaire. I'd never won more than $200k before. This had been my first invitation to the big games.

Glory sat curled up on the couch, eyes closed. Damn, she looked sweet asleep. I wanted to hold her close and protect her from all the assholes—problem was that I was an asshole too.

I walked past her with the slip of paper certifying my winnings. In the back corner, a big, burly guy took it and asked for my wire transfer number, then sent my money straight to my bank account.

Money safe, I turned to my girl for the night. She glanced at me with sleep-heavy baby blues.

I stared down at the girl who'd raced out of Barden as fast as she could get gone. Rebel had texted me the essentials. A town girl, she was related to Jericho, our Prez, and good friends with both Pixie and Sharpie. Glory Atkins was a biker chick at her core, but she'd stayed far away from our life. Maybe I should just escort her home without demanding my reward for saving her ass.

If I was a decent guy, I'd walk her to the door to her place and leave her be, but I wasn't, and what's more, we both had an itch I planned to scratch tonight.

"Ready to ride?" I held out a hand and she clasped it. "I want to make you scream my name."

"You paid for it." The bite in her voice pissed me off, but I wasn't getting into that here.

"Glad we agree, princess." I pulled her into me and placed my hand in the small of her back.

I could feel the anger building in the stiff way she walked out the door. We stepped inside the elevator and she turned to me, ready to tell me off again. I shook my head and looked to the corner of the elevator where a small camera taped us.

We made it to the Porsche and drove away from the Remington.

"You have some fucking nerve," she huffed with arms crossed. "I don't owe you shit no matter what you paid."

"Agreed."

"And if you think I'm putting out because you paid cash to that slimeball, you are mistaken."

"I agree with you." I smirked at the way she just kept going, not even paying attention to what I said.

"You fucking men are all the same." She whipped her head to me. "What did you say?"

"I said you're right. I don't expect you to fuck me because of what I paid Jerry."

She gave me a confused nod.

"I expect you to fuck me because you can't help yourself."

She snorted. "Right!" She gave me a teasing grin. "You think a lot of yourself."

"A drink, a kiss and you decide," I challenged her.

She showed me that real smile I'd seen earlier. "I'll be showing you the door."

When I was ready to go, after I'd fucked her until she quivered in my arms, totally sated, then I'd leave through the door she was so eager to show me.

"Where do you live?"

"Let's go to your hotel room." She winked. "I can get a taxi from there."

"I want to be sure Frankie isn't around, then we can go back to my place."

"Fine. But I have a roommate."

"I like an audience. She can join us if that's the way you play." I riled her up on purpose. I loved her fire and needed another taste of that heat.

"That's going to happen, oh, let me see—" she gave me a sweet smile that was all sarcasm "—about never. I don't do that."

"And what do you do?"

Color flushed her cheeks. "If you were that lucky, what I do would make your eyes cross and your dick crave me the rest of your goddam life."

"I can't wait for that."

"You won't be that lucky."

I turned into her apartment complex, which was away from the strip and in a decent part of town. "Which building?"

She pointed to the third one in the row. "Why are you even here?"

"In Vegas?"

"No, with me. Is this because of Avery?"

"That's Rock's old lady?" I parked the 911 in an empty slot.

She nodded.

"I wasn't looking for you, but I couldn't leave a friend of the club in trouble."

Her long legs were toned and tan without the help of sheers. She had the slim athletic grace of a dancer. I focused on the spot where her leg met the shimmery hem of the short skirt. I wanted to slide my hand up her thigh to see if she wore panties. Make her come right now in the Porsche. But that wasn't the deal I'd made with her, and she'd hold me to that. If my kiss didn't melt her resistance, I'd be booted in a flash.

She gave me a frosty glare. "The club and I aren't friendly." She slammed the door behind her when she exited the car. The red dress framed her ass perfectly, and her rising temper only turned me on more. Damn, I loved a hellion.

I pulled the keys from the ignition and followed her across the parking lot, and appreciated my view as she climbed the steps to the second level, then placed a key in the first lock before moving down to a second dead bolt.

"You had trouble here?"

She gave a quick shake of her blond mane. "But one

of the girls a building over was raped, so we installed the second lock."

Damn. She needed to move somewhere safer, but in a city, a woman alone was always a target. Inside, she quickly disarmed a high-quality alarm that hadn't come with the place. She wasn't telling me everything, but then why would she? We'd just met and she wasn't my biggest fan—yet.

She dropped her bag on the couch and stepped out of her shoes, leaving them where she kicked them off, right where she'd trip on them later. I scooted them next to the end table and scanned her place. The living room was small but stuffed with things, colorful knickknacks and too much furniture, not nearly as stylish as I figured she'd be. She was physical perfection, and I expected the same in her living environment.

Discarded chip bags, two glasses and other debris littered the surfaces in the living room. A counter connected the small galley kitchen to the living room. The kitchen was clean even though the counters were stacked with boxes of food and an assortment of pans. I leaned on the living-room side of the counter.

She had started music while I'd checked out her place. Rock with a happy beat played low. "There's no room in this place." She opened the cabinet and brought down a bottle of Johnny Walker blended scotch.

Johnny and I were close buds.

"But this is pretty clean for us." She shrugged and poured three fingers of the amber scotch into each glass. "Ice?" She sipped her own straight scotch as she assessed me.

"Ice." I nodded. *Always leave them guessing* was another of my rules.

She sniffed, opened the freezer, plunked two cubes in my whiskey and sashayed my way. I pulled her into my arms before taking the scotch.

She grinned up at me. "The drink." And held her glass out for a toast.

"To a long night together." I clinked her glass.

She tried to back away but I held her firm. "Drink up, Queenie." I tossed back the liquor in my glass in a single drink, set the empty glass on the counter and held out my hand.

She stared at me a long minute before reaching out to clasp my hand.

I tugged her close to me. "A dance?"

Her eyebrow shot up. "You dance?"

"I have many talents."

She laughed. "Humility isn't one of them."

I swayed with the music.

"Tell me you can do more than this."

"What do you have in mind?" I held her closer and did the grind. "Dirty and sexy?"

"The swing?" she challenged.

The song changed to a slower one. "Or intimate and personal."

We moved together, our bodies swaying, and hands skimming over the other. Damn, she was perfect.

I clasped her close and we moved in synch—I got lost in her and the sensual way she touched me. She led and I followed. We melded together and then moved apart. I twirled her around the small room and she gave a breathless laugh. I bent down and kissed her—tasting her—losing myself in the moment.

I inhaled her arousal mixed with that fruity scent of hers. She wanted me but didn't want to give in to what we both craved. I lifted her, lips locked, and made my way to the couch. I sat, breaking our kiss.

She sighed and stared down at me. When I tugged, she sat beside me. I leaned into her and kissed her again. She ran hands across my chest. Damn, she was sexy and alluring. I needed more. Unable to resist the temptation of those shapely legs, I ran my hand up her calf, skimmed over her knee and cupped her thigh.

She sucked in a breath with the glass poised at her ruby lips.

I slid my hand to her inner thigh and slid it under the edge of her hiked-up skirt until I reached damp lace panties. One question answered, anyway.

She gulped down half her drink. Her wide eyes focused on me. Fuck, I wanted her.

Her mouth parted in a slight O as I traced the line of her panties, then she opened her legs wider. Did she realize she'd done that?

I ran my thumb up her seam, feeling the full lips of her pussy. I circled my finger over her sex then slipped a single finger under the edge of those panties to feel the wetness I needed.

She closed her eyes as my rough fingertip touched hot, sensitive flesh. I didn't want to leave that hot pussy, but I had to do it. *Keep her off balance.*

Her eyes popped open when I removed my hand from between her legs. Questions were reflected in her gaze.

I tasted her on my finger. Her sweet tang filled my mouth and made my cock stand at attention. I needed to devour her pussy.

Every nerve in my body was on edge. My heart raced and I needed deep inside her right now.

She placed her glass on the couch next to us and bent

toward me, coming in fast, but I wasn't having that. When her lips hit mine, I held her close, not settling for the drive-by kiss she planned.

Another jolt shot through me, just like the other times. I swept the hair from her cheek and the fine strands reminded me of silk. Every inch of her outside was soft but inside she was made of steel. She moaned when I nibbled her lower lip and pushed deeper. Heat flared between us and I couldn't keep my hands still another second. I moved up her thigh and sought her warmth again. She ran a hand down my cheek and then cupped my neck as she greedily sought more.

That's my girl—I needed her worked up.

When I pushed against her folds, she parted her legs farther, giving me better access to her sweet center. I planned on worshipping her pussy with my mouth soon, but now I hunted for the slick heat I'd brushed against earlier.

I slipped the strip of lace to the side and ran fingers through her seam, reveling in her wetness. I thumbed her clit with quick strokes. She bucked and moaned in my lap, bouncing against my hard-on. This was the sweetest torture ever. Thrusting two fingers into her core, I drummed a quick beat with my thumb on her nub. She writhed and tried to pull back but that wasn't happening. So wet and ready, she was seconds from falling over and I was taking her there.

She dug those red nails into my shoulders as she crested and I pushed my fingers deeper. She cried out in pleasure. Her tight pussy clenched around my fingers and I couldn't wait for that to be my dick, needed it to be now. But I wasn't some careless kid—I could wait.

The sweet vulnerability of the moment slid past my

defenses. I wanted more of the open girl before me, but this was a onetime deal. She wasn't the casual kind of girl and I wasn't the relationship kind of guy. I brushed hair from her face again.

You can take the girl out of the small town, but not the small town out of the girl.

Her eyes flicked open. "That wasn't—"

The doorbell rang over and over and over. Some dipshit kept it pushed in.

Glory bolted upright and the dazed look vanished. I'd punch the motherfucker just for that.

"Who?"

"Gloreeeee!" the dipshit shouted as he continued to ring the fucking bell.

"That's Frankie," she groaned and started to stand.

"I will deal with him."

She shrugged. "He's been a pain."

I pulled off my shirt and removed my loafers and socks.

Glory appraised me with one eyebrow cocked.

"Sexy, I know." I winked, then headed to the door.

She rewarded me with a laugh—clear and bright and full of promise.

I flung open the door and glared at the dipshit.

"Glor—" He broke off mid shout. "Oh, dude, sorry. I got the wrong place." He started to stumble away, but I hauled him back toward the landing.

"That's right, dude. Glory's place is never the right place for you."

The booze fog lifted a little as recognition played across his face.

"You, you're the fucker who got me banned and who..." He trailed off and cocked a fist.

I let go of his shirt.

He swung, missed, and fell on his ass. As he tried to stand, I put my foot to his ass, giving a small push, and he tumbled down the steps. He lay sprawled on the walkway, out cold. Stupid fuck.

I closed and locked all three internal locks before turning back to my woman.

She stood with my shirt and shoes, holding them out for me. "Now it's time for the door."

Chapter 4: Glory

He'd dealt easily with Frankie, but then he'd made everything appear easy. Once he was gone, I'd have to make the harder, long-term stand if I wanted the prick to leave me alone.

He turned toward me. The God of Sex wouldn't look more tempting than Delta standing barefoot in my living room in black dress pants bulging from his erection. Damn, he was big. I reminded myself he needed to go and thrust out his clothes.

He gave me that sexy half grin and closed the distance between us, but he didn't take his clothes. His arms wrapped around my middle and he claimed my mouth in another mind-stealing kiss. No! I couldn't let him win again. Last time he'd had me moaning in orgasm, so I had to stay strong.

"I need—"

He swallowed my words and robbed my ability to speak.

His tongue darted in my mouth with expert caresses designed to drive me wild. It was working. I dropped his shoes, then his shirt. Pressing into him, I wound my arms around his neck, falling into the kiss.

Nipples erect and body quivering, I dug deep for the

resolve I needed. He was too good and that was trouble. He needed to go.

My body thrummed with the need to touch and taste as he played my body like a master musician. I wanted to see what else he could do, but I wouldn't. Couldn't. I'd left Barden and the Brotherhood in my past, and I wasn't going back. Ever.

I stepped back, arms out as my last line of defense. "The door." I wished my voice was stronger instead of a breathy plea.

He cocked that stupid eyebrow and smirked. We both knew he could have me with just one more of those intoxicating kisses.

He stepped back and the smirk stayed in place, letting me know this was his choice as much as mine. "Never thought you would be a coward."

I opened my mouth, trying to decide on the best bomb to drop on the arrogant SOB. "You don't—"

"I don't have to go." He stepped toward me. "You don't want me to go." Another step.

I didn't want him to go. Honestly, I wanted another orgasm, but that was wrong.

Why is it wrong to take what is offered? I argued with myself. No one had ever made me feel like he did.

And that's why you can't risk it. Another voice broke into the debate.

"Pride is a lonely companion." He stepped closer, now only inches away.

I could smell his spicy, leather scent. Damn, I loved the way he stood there thumbs in belt loops, offering himself to me.

Was I going to take him? Damn, I wanted to, but I shouldn't for a thousand sensible reasons. I didn't date bikers. He was the worst kind of trouble. I'd have hell to pay when he left. And he would leave. They all left me.

But he wasn't pretending to be anything else. No, he only offered tonight. More orgasms tempted me. His sexy confidence turned me on. And unlike the other men who had complicated my life, he made it clear this was only about tonight.

Pride or pleasure? Damn him. He'd totally called it and wasn't even gentleman enough to pretend he hadn't. He'd stared at me with cocky assurance the entire time my internal debate raged.

"Why?" The word slipped from me. And I swore if he said something douchy I'd send him packing.

"Fuck if I know." He ran fingers through his short mess of blond hair. "I should run the other way, but I need just one more taste, Queen." The sexy rumble of his voice sent shivers through me.

Damn, his answer melted the little resistance I'd managed to dredge up. I needed to feel him tangled with me and discover if he'd be the dream lover I imagined.

I stepped forward into his arms and he held me. I lifted up on tiptoes and wrapped my arms around his neck as I leaned in for another kiss. He let me have my way for maybe thirty seconds before he claimed me with a kiss full of fierce passion I couldn't resist. His kisses consumed me.

He pulled away and I tried to reclaim those lips. "Where's your bedroom?"

I pointed to the second closed door off the living room.

With a nod, he scooped me up and carried me to my bedroom. The shut door didn't even slow him as he gracefully opened it and moved to my bed. With a gen-

tleness I hadn't expected, he laid me across the middle
of the bed with my legs dangling off the edge.

Wild yet controlled. For the first time I noticed his
Brotherhood tattoo on his chest and another on his side.
His chinos fell to the floor. Damn. He had a sculpted
body I wanted to run my hands over.

He prowled forward and clasped each leg below the
knee and pulled me forward until my ass almost hung
off the bed. Eyebrow cocked and that half smile on his
face, he stared down at me. "I'm going to make you
scream my name."

Words died in my throat. I wanted to challenge him,
to deny the claim, but I couldn't. He knelt between my
legs and scooted me toward him. He bent his head to
my mound, and I moaned as his tongue slid through my
folds. In seconds, he had me bucking, needing the release
he teased but didn't deliver.

"Now," I demanded.

He continued his assault. My fingers searched for him
and dug deep into his hair, but he didn't acknowledge
the pain, if he even felt it. I whimpered while he drove
me mindless with the pleasure assaulting my body. He
kept me perched on the precipice for an endless amount
of time. I struggled to come, needing the release to complete me, but it was just out of my reach. I rose higher
and higher with each stroke until I was sure I couldn't
stand another second, yet I did. The ecstasy transfixed
me, and I lived for the building need inside me.

"Fuck me," I chanted or maybe pleaded.

I needed his cock filling me up. I tugged on his hair
and bucked under him, but nothing stopped his campaign.
Then he slipped two fingers inside my enflamed sex and
I lost it. I came undone so fast and hard it ripped the

breath from my body, and a shattering orgasm crashed through me. My breath heaved and the world went gray. All I could do was ride this tidal wave of pleasure back to shore and hope I survived.

I took in a deep breath and opened my eyes but before I could focus on Delta, he'd kissed my sensitive flesh again.

"No," I whimpered. "I'm ready, please fuck me."

He glanced up. "I'll let you know when you're ready." And he dipped his head and started licking again. Hips pumping, my hands moved from Delta to my own breasts. I plucked my nipples but that wasn't enough. I sought some balance to the bliss threatening to pull me under. I pinched harder and the pain was perfect. The complement of pain and pleasure made my body sing a new song. A deeper kind of pleasure built inside me this time.

"Delta. Now!" I shouted the words as my body struggled to find the release it sought. He'd stolen my will and mastered my body. I hoped the defenses over my heart stood strong because I couldn't fall for this bad boy biker. And that thought gave me a moment of peace in the thrashing storm of pleasure.

A single finger slipped inside my pussy and I wanted to weep and scream. It wasn't enough to send me over, but more than enough to drive me insane.

"You need me?" Delta crooned. "Tell me what you need."

"I need fucked, please fuck me. Delta, fuck me!" I shouted the words. All control gone.

A feral smile settled on his face. He ripped a condom wrapper and slid the condom on before plunging deep inside me. I screamed and came around his hard cock.

"That's it Queenie, come all over my cock." He had

placed my feet on his shoulders and stood driving deep inside me, over and over again.

Slowly my climax receded and I focused on his huge cock filling me. A fierce lover, he rode me hard, pushing me for more and more. I didn't know there was this much inside me. Or how good it felt to let the wild side free.

We moved in synch, faster and faster, until I saw his face tighten. His finger massaged my clit and in seconds I panted, ready to fly apart a fourth time, or was it more. I'd lost count.

Delta met my gaze. "Come now."

I screamed his name as my body quaked with the most intense orgasm yet. My body was hot and cold, shaking with pleasure, exhausted but ready for more.

Delta bellowed his own release as his body shook. He didn't look away or close his eyes. He let me see deep in his soul as he came with me. The vulnerability excited and scared me. But the darkness I saw bothered me. I doubt he planned for me to see the loneliness and sadness that was hidden in him. I took in a deep breath and tried to erase the image from my mind. This was a onetime deal, and I didn't need to get caught up in his inner demons.

"Glad I stayed?" There was the cocky bastard I loved to hate.

"Get over yourself." I pushed at him. "It was pretty good."

"Oh Queenie, you can lie to me, but don't lie to yourself. I am the best you've ever had."

Damn him. He was right.

The petty bullshit was stacking up at work. The managers had been total bastards this week, but I was still dancing so that was all that really mattered. I applied my makeup in the dressing room, ready for the six o'clock show. I danced in three of the chorus lines and one special number tonight. It was the early show, but at least I was dancing more than I had before.

I slipped on my first costume, a star-spangled outfit, and stepped into my heels. Delta flashed through my memory and I shut that down. Over the past week, he kept slipping into the empty spots of my brain. I joined the other eleven chorus line members on stage and waited for the curtain to lift. Music blared out, and the curtain rose. I began the routine in perfect synch with the other dancers.

This dance was simple, as were most of the chorus line numbers, but I loved every minute. Bright lights, a cheering crowd, music, and me dancing my ass off—I was living my dream. When the special number was up, I changed costume for it. The singer—some person who'd won a contest on TV—sang a seven-minute medley from Elvis to Justin Timberlake and we danced with him. The choreography was tricky and fast. The routine would be nothing for a professional dance troupe, but it was challenging and rewarding to me. I loved the moves and that I was using so many styles of dance.

That was my last number of the night. Two of the show's bigger acts would finish off the rock variety show, and I wanted to make it to that dance crew.

Leo, the show manager, met me backstage, frowning. "You sucked tonight, sweetie." He shook his head. "Jerry needs a word."

Outrage filled me and my chest tightened as angry words filled my mind. But I clamped my mouth shut and stalked past the idiot. This was about Frankie. Tonight might be my last night at this casino if Jerry pushed me. But I hadn't made plans for a new job yet, so I really needed to try and salvage this situation until I found a new place to work.

I stopped outside Jerry's door to collect myself and squash my building temper. I could be cool and collected, just like Delta. Damn, he'd rocked my world in ways I hadn't ever experienced, but I was glad he was out of Vegas. I didn't need that kind of temptation.

I stood straight and opened the door to Jerry's main floor office. He also had an office up where the swanky card events were held. "You wanted to see me?"

"Glory, I hired you because of that spark I saw. But the last few nights, hell, a mannequin could dance with more feeling than you've been giving me."

The words stung and a retort sat on the tip of my tongue. I let it out. "Would fucking Frankie help my feeling?"

Jerry grinned at me but said nothing for a long moment. "You two patch things up? Hadn't heard that."

"Nope. Never going to."

"Too bad, that'd give you something to do with your free time now." Jerry's eyes turned cold. "You're down to the opening chorus line at six each night, no shows on the weekends."

"What the hell?" That was less than a part-time, pickup dancer worked. I could never pay my bills on that money. The Remington paid dancers by days and dances worked. The more complicated the dance routine, the better the pay. The more dances and more nights, the better the pay.

"We got plenty of special gigs for you to work to make

up that income. Someone of your talents might be better in the Reserve."

The prick was insulting me and trying to get me to quit, but I wasn't going to give up like that. I'd leave here on my own terms with another, better job waiting.

He slid over an envelope of cash. "Your payout from the date with Ren."

I felt dirty and wrong—a true whore. I wanted to throw the money in his face and walk out. I opened my mouth to do that and saw the call home asking Mama to bail me out. Dammit. I could handle this. I'd gotten into this situation and I would get out of it on my own.

"How can I convince you to let me dance the weekends?" That income would let me survive until I could move on.

"Be more of a team player. Do the special assignments."

"I do."

"Only a few of them. I got one tonight." He glanced at his watch. "If you change in a hurry. I mean, you're already dolled up."

I bit my tongue so I wouldn't undo all my efforts. "Where?"

"Suite 700. You'll need this key to get on the floor." He slid across a gold card—the ones they used for restricted access. "Be there in fifteen minutes."

That didn't give me much time. I sucked in a breath and nodded, not trusting myself to speak. Those were the parties Celeste had warned me to stay away from, but she also told me not to make enemies. I'd done that, and now I needed to make amends, apparently.

I clasped the card and smiled at Jerry. "I'll be there."

The creepy smile he gave me had the hair on the back

of my neck standing at attention. I rushed out of his office and to the dressing room to slip into a party dress.

All my life I'd been treated like an expensive trinket—something to show off and display but not something to value. I was a dancer—loved dancing on stage—but without this face I wouldn't have ever made it here. Or anywhere. And that sucked.

Sometimes I wondered how life would change if I were scarred. How would the world treat me then? Part of me craved to be treated like I mattered for more than my dimples and baby blues. And another part knew the opportunities I'd received because of those baby blues.

I smiled in the mirror and knew I was a hypocrite because these looks put me in Vegas. I was smart enough and a good dancer, but I was more a Vegas showgirl than a New York dance company type. Here I would live my dream to dance in front of hundreds or thousands. And I could make nice with a few creeps to follow my passion.

I hurried down the hall to the elevator and checked my watch. Five minutes until I needed to be there. I used the card in the elevator to access the executive floor—the same one where I'd met Delta at the poker game.

I moved down the hall to the room and used the same card to open the door to the suite and walked in to an empty living room. Where was everyone? Unease created gooseflesh on my arms. I glanced back at the door and tamped down my urge to run. The bedroom door opened, and four people strolled out. One was a dancer I barely knew. Mandy or Candy…something that rhymed with Andy for sure. She kissed the older guy and then blew me a kiss. "Have fun, doll! I did."

"Glory, I am Xander Lawson. Come in and I will tell

you about our party. It will be starting soon." He had a smooth, urbane voice that sounded like old money.

So I was here early. Some of my unease faded, but I didn't like the look of the goon standing beside him. He had mob written all over his thick brow. *I can do this.*

I followed them into the room and heard the lock snick behind me. An old guy, maybe sixty, sat in a high back director's chair and Frankie sat beside him. He met my gaze with a cold smile that spooked me and I started to back up, but Xander kept a firm grip and moved us forward. A handful of guys stood by a spread of food, but they were working-class types. Two other girls teetered in on crazy high heels and see-through dresses. Nothing like what I was wearing and that made me uncomfortable.

"Grab some food before it gets crazy." Xander still held me firmly. "A cocktail? Some wine?"

"I would love a water and a few bites." I batted eyelashes his direction. I never drank at these things.

The gray-haired man joined us at the table. "I don't believe you've been here before." He held out a hand. "I'm Angel DeLuca." The goon stood behind the mob boss. This was Frankie's uncle and head of the DeLuca organization. I should never have come here. He was probably pissed at the role I'd played in Frankie's banishment. Fuck, how could I get out of here fast?

I clasped his outstretched hand, which was very smooth despite its weathered appearance. "Glory. Nice to meet you." I didn't let my voice shake.

What had I gotten myself into?

"This was a mistake." I blurted out. "I need to—"

"Come with me." DeLuca snaked an arm around my middle and pulled me into him.

I struggled but couldn't escape his hold. He moved toward the closed door. "We need you." He spoke low in my ear. "Frankie needs you."

Shit. Shit. Shit. Ice shot through my veins and my heart beat so fast I was sure I'd have a heart attack at any moment. I glanced side to side but I was trapped between DeLuca and Xander, and the goon was just a step behind.

What could I do? *Think, Glory. Think.* I forced myself to stop panicking and focus. I needed to play along, to relax. I might have a chance to escape if I was smart. Escape what?

I had no idea. We walked into the other room, and bright lights made me squint. Cameras, lights, and the worker types milled around. "Excuse me, dear one, they are ready for me." Xander walked away.

I relaxed. "This is a nice setup. What do you do here?"

DeLuca assessed me. "Make movies and you're going to be a star. Don't you want to be a star?"

Movies? Porn. Holy shit, I had to get out of here. My mama would kill me if I made a porno. Hell, I could have done that without leaving home. The Jericho Brotherhood ran one of the best porn studios in the country right from my hometown. I sure as fuck wasn't coming all the way here to be trapped into making porn—bad porn, most likely. Good porn surely didn't trap the talent.

But I needed to fake it until I could escape.

"I always wanted to be a movie star." I gave him my best smile. "I thought you were doing something bad in here." I giggled. "This looks fun."

His grip loosened on my side. "And Frankie said you'd die first."

"Oh, he doesn't know me that well." I winked at him. "Can I watch?"

The idea of watching made me a little sick.

"Sure, honey. You'll be doing the same thing." De-Luca led me to a chair behind Xander.

I hopped up into the red canvas director's chair and DeLuca slid into the black chair next to me.

The goon had disappeared, and I considered that some good luck.

I spotted two doors. Which one led to the main room?

The door closest to me opened—the bathroom.

Great! The door out of here was in the filming zone, close to the bed. Maybe I should wait until they were ready to film me and then run. They wouldn't expect that.

On the bed, three girls surrounded one guy with the biggest cock I'd ever seen. One of the girls toppled over and giggled. "She's going to have to be on bottom." The guy stared at Xander. "You gave her too much."

Too much what?

Xander rearranged everyone then came back to his chair. "Okay, action."

The two girls started kissing and the guy shoved into the almost unconscious girl on the bed. She didn't even flinch as that huge ass cock was rammed into her. Ouch!

"Almost your turn." DeLuca glanced over at me.

"I want that cock." I hoped I sounded sincere. Because I had just lied completely. He might break my pussy with that beast, especially with no foreplay.

DeLuca nodded his approval. "Good girl."

I was not a good girl at all. Frankie headed our way. I didn't like the look he gave me.

"I need the ladies' room." I started to slide down from the high chair.

DeLuca squeezed my hand in a death grip. "Wait a minute."

Shit. Frankie was closing in on us and I couldn't break away from DeLuca. I scooted back in the chair. "Whatever you say, honey." I patted the hand throttling mine. He didn't lessen his hold.

There was a syringe in Frankie's meaty fist. Oh fuck me, I was in serious trouble. I couldn't escape if I was drugged.

I needed to run, now. But DeLuca held me firm.

I forced myself not to try and free my hand. That would only raise suspicion.

"That needle isn't for me, is it?" I gave my most pathetic look. "I hate needles."

I blinked quickly until tears formed and slid down my cheek. I never thought crying on demand would help me after I'd moved out of Mama's house.

"Please, no needles." I bit my lip and tried to look afraid. Meanwhile the cold tendrils of fear threatened to truly immobilize me. I couldn't run, couldn't escape, couldn't win. But I couldn't just give in because I was no coward or quitter.

"You will love the needle in just a few more seconds. You might even beg for it soon." He gave me a truly evil smile.

I shuddered and lost my cool, struggling to free myself from his grip. He kept on smiling and I did the only thing I could. I drew back my leg and aimed for his knee—kicking him as hard as I could.

DeLuca groaned and let go. I struggled to get up but Frankie was on me. He pushed me back down, grasping my shoulder. Pain shot out from my shoulder and down my arm.

However, this position put his crotch right in my sights. I kicked out hard and connected with his junk.

He dropped the syringe as he doubled over. I jumped out of the chair and kicked off my heels. I had to flee now. But I didn't make it three steps. My foot stopped mid-stride and I fell forward, smacking down on the hard floor. I glanced back to see Frankie grasping my ankle. He jerked me back toward him.

"You bitch." He loomed over me.

His fist cocked back and slammed into my cheek.

"Not the face" echoed in my ears.

Chapter 5: Delta

Pounding on the motel door woke me up. I stumbled out of bed and the room spun. Fucking hangovers. I'd drunk too much with the Renegades. I'd barely stumbled back to the motel room last night.

I threw open the door, and Thorn strode inside. The giant was six foot five and built solid—a badass by any definition. I'd worked with him many times back in the day when I worked for Brotherhood Securities, and I was glad to have his help on this bounty assignment.

"You look like shit." He sat at the desk in the black rolling chair.

I kicked the door closed and sat on the edge of the bed running hands through my hair. Head pounding, and mouth coated with scum, I just wanted to crawl back into bed. I squinted against the bright sun shining through the curtains. The room was clean and functional, but it had been designed sometime in the eighties, and the Ravens, who owned the motel, hadn't redecorated since then.

Instead, I leaned over and grabbed my phone from the nightstand and opened up my notes on the bounty. "I've got intel that says Chaos and Mayhem are staying over at the Golden Inn across town." I scrolled through my notes.

"One of the Ravens saw them two days ago, but I didn't want to chance them spotting me, so I stayed away."

Thorn nodded. "Any other Angels in town?"

"Not that I have found." I lifted a shoulder. "But that's not a sure thing."

He stretched his long legs out in front of him. "Tell me the plan."

"We take your Jeep, stake out the hotel—my source says they're in 113. We confirm and then take them down." These guys were bad news and I wanted to capture them at the motel where there was less chance for innocents getting in the middle of our operation. "Drive them straight to the Reno police station, and collect the cash."

"They're each worth a 100K?"

I nodded. "They put down the last hunter who tried to take them."

Thorn grunted.

"We're not making any mistakes today." I liked the cash—not that I needed the ten percent cut I'd receive, not after winning so much in Vegas—but I craved the thrill of the hunt. I loved taking down the dangerous ones, pitting my skills against theirs.

"When?"

"Give me twenty and then we roll." I grabbed my duffel before I stood. "You bring the toys I requested?"

Thorn smiled for the first time. "And some extra, like I always do."

The man must have been one hell of a Boy Scout back in the day. He believed in being prepared for every contingency. And that's one reason we'd never blown a mission.

I hurried through the shower, chewed up a few tablets of ibuprofen and shaved. I might need to do some undercover surveillance, and when I was clean shaven, I looked more business than bruiser. Thorn couldn't do undercover—he screamed biker even when he didn't wear his cut. The long hair, tats on his face, and general badass vibe were clear giveaways.

"Ready?" I asked as I stepped out of the bathroom.

On the bed were two automatics, four handguns, two grenades, and two C4 charges with detonators. And Thorn would have another gun and at least four knives on him—serious firepower.

"I see you are." I slapped his back. "Let's go earn our keep."

I holstered one of the nine millimeters in the shoulder harness I'd put on, then shrugged on the windbreaker that made me look more like a tourist than a bounty hunter. Thorn packed the other guns and goodies in a black nylon bag.

We loaded up and drove across town to the Golden Inn. The neighborhood was mostly boarded-up businesses and flophouses—just the kind of place the Angels liked. They thrived in neighborhoods where decent people refused to go and cops never patrolled. Those who lived the one-percent lifestyle were always rough and ruthless, but the Angels were the worst of our kind—lowlife scavengers who fed on corruption and violence. The two guys we hunted now had killed the entire family of a man who they said dissed them.

I'd be happy to put the animals behind bars—they gave us a bad name. Thorn glanced at me. "You'll stick out here."

"Good thing you fit right in."

He boomed out a laugh. "True that, bro. But you better hide the preppy, pretty boy face of yours."

"Fuck you." I gave him the bird.

"Their rides." He nodded to two choppers parked in front of room 113. He backed his Jeep into the far corner of the lot. We had a good line of sight but we'd be hauling ass to get to them if they saw us coming. We'd just have to be sure they didn't see us until it was too late.

"Rebel said you cleaned up in Vegas." Thorn glanced at me. "So why did I haul ass from Salt Lake then?"

"Because you're a sick motherfucker, just like me."

Thorn smiled again and I had half a mind to tell him to stop that shit. The dude was extra creepy when he smiled.

We didn't have to wait long before the door to 113 opened up and Chaos left, turning toward the front office.

"You take him, I'll get the other fucker." Thorn was out of the car and jogging toward 113.

Shit. Shit. Shit. I booked it across the lot to the motel office. I walked in a few steps behind Chaos and into the office with its gray painted cement floor, sagging desk and half-dead fern. The guy behind the desk assessed us and stepped back. Chaos sneered at me, dismissing me with a glance. I grabbed my plastic cuffs and moved forward with quick, crisp steps.

Chaos turned too late, I had my hand on his left wrist and flipped him to the ground with a judo move. He grunted as he hit the cement floor, and I followed him down, planting a knee in the middle of his back. Once the cuffs secured his hands, I pulled him to his feet. "Let's go, Chaos."

"You're a fucking dead man," he snarled at me.

"Not today."

He twisted in my arms and circled away. His leg was in motion, and I saw the blade on the tip of his boots too late. He sliced the arm I'd thrown up to block his kick. I took the blow and grabbed his foot, twisting off the fucking boot as he flew through the air and landed with a crunch on the floor.

"Hey, no blood in my office," the clerk yelled, holding a bat. "Read the sign."

Chaos was out cold, so I turned to the clerk. Above his head was a faded sign that read No Blood, No Urine, No Bodily Fluids. A classy place.

Ignoring my dripping wound, I hauled Chaos up on my shoulder in a fireman carry—he was a heavy bastard—and left with the clerk yelling after me.

Thorn sat in the Jeep just outside with his scary smile. Mayhem was unconscious in the back seat. I heaved Chaos into the back and slammed the door.

"He got you." Thorn already started in on me. "You're getting slow." I found a package of wipes and duct tape in Thorn's glove box, just what I needed to fix my cut.

"Could use stitches," Thorn suggested.

I kept wrapping the tape around my arm. I definitely didn't need stitches.

The ribbing continued all the way to Reno's main police station. When we pulled up in front of the station, Thorn stayed with the two bounties while I went in and wrangled cops to take the idiots off our hands. It took almost an hour to get the paperwork finished up, but two hundred large for a couple hours of work wasn't anything to complain about.

"We're going to lunch."

My stomach lurched at the mention of food, but Thorn was the club's sergeant at arms, so he outranked me in every way. I guess I was eating despite the hangover annoying me.

He pulled into a greasy spoon that looked like it hadn't been visited by the health department ever. Just what I didn't need—bad food on top of bad booze.

Thorn raised an eyebrow but I wasn't saying shit.

The inside smelled of old grease and peppermint—a terrible combination. We sat at a booth with a vinyl tabletop and faded orange plastic that pretended to be leather. The cook with a spattered apron lumbered from behind the counter and stopped in front of us. "What's your poison?"

"Give me that chili of yours." Thorn looked at me.

"Burger and fries."

The guy took the menus and left. At the counter he turned back. "Drinks?"

"Coffee—black," we both said at the same time.

He nodded and disappeared to the back.

"You coming home?"

I fiddled with a napkin from the metal dispenser on the table. "Think I'll head back to Vegas for a bit."

"Heard you had a thing for our Glory Ann." He winked at me. "You know she's Pixie's best friend, right?"

I did, now.

"And used to be Sharpie's girl?"

"I didn't say a fucking thing about her—you sayin' something to me?" I didn't like being warned off.

Thorn's deep laugh filled the empty diner. The cook came out with our coffee then. I just stared at the ass, waiting for him to get to the point.

"Fuck, bro, you got no sense of humor." He leaned back in the booth. "I ain't saying shit, the club ain't saying shit." He held his hands up, palms toward me. "Just making conversation."

I relaxed and made myself smile. No need to take my shitty mood out on a brother.

"So you heading back for another round?"

"I ain't in a hurry to get home. I may work a few more jumps out here."

"You ain't been home much since JoJo hooked up with his old lady." Thorn leaned his massive forearms on the table. "You doing okay?"

"I am fucking perfect." I ran fingers through my hair. "Just restless, and I don't want to catch whatever disease Rebel and JoJo caught—I am too much man for any one woman."

JoJo was my best friend, and we went all the way back to high school. We'd joined the army together, been kicked out together, and both ended up in the Jericho Brotherhood. It was a good life, but now that he had his old lady, he didn't need me as a third wheel.

"Shit." Thorn shook his head, then focused on me again. "You been a lone wolf lately—you're more of a loner than me."

Thorn had demons. Hell his demons had demons, and that had seriously fucked him up. He'd been a super soldier who'd been captured and held prisoner. When he got out, he'd lost some of what made him human. He'd gotten better over the past few years, but he was still way fucked up. What did it say that he was worried about me?

"Look, you can quit the mother hen shit. I'm good. Tell Elle I'm fine. Better than fine. Shit! I am surrounded by fucking women who want to take my balls."

Thorn smiled but I saw the worry in his eyes. Hell, I saw everything and that's why I stayed away. I didn't want to see JoJo's guilt, Rebel's worry, Elle's fucking pity. No, it wasn't what I needed right now. I needed space away from everyone trying to mother me.

"There's a new class of recruits to train. And that's your gig."

The guy dropped off our food, so I bit back the string of curses I'd been about to spew.

"Since fucking when?" I asked when the cook had left.

"Rebel said he told ya. You got maybe six weeks before you're considered AWOL."

Fuck. "I don't want any ducklings following me around. I can't be responsible for them. I just can't fucking do it." Panic pulsed through me, making the cut in my arm throb worse. No. No way. The last time I'd been responsible good men died, and that wouldn't be happening again.

"Time to get over the past." Thorn met my gaze with a brutal honesty I couldn't deny. "Jericho didn't cut me a single break when I played the crazy card. Nope, here I am in charge of keeping all the fucking club in line."

"You aren't fucking crazy."

He had a temper that could be fatal if you were on the wrong side of it, but he wasn't crazy.

"And you're leadership material." Thorn's index finger poked toward me. "You got to do your part—you have ten years in now. Time to step up."

"Yes, sir." I gave him a salute. "I'll report for duty in two weeks. One last taste of freedom?"

He nodded. "That works for me, soldier."

We finished eating in silence. I wanted to rail at Thorn and the club for forcing me to step up, but that's what it meant to be a brother. And Rebel had let me slide for a while, but it didn't make me happier. I'd been in charge of the investigation where two good MPs lost their lives. And when I wouldn't stop trying to figure out why, JoJo and I had been punted out of the army with a Bad Conduct Discharge as fast as they could get it done. We never solved the case and that pissed me off the most. There had been no justice for the private first class who'd been killed or for the two MPs, my two friends, under my command.

When we both finished, I tossed money on the table and we left.

In the Jeep, Thorn turned that hard stare of his on me. "We good?"

"We're golden, brother. I always do my duty." But, man, it was getting harder and harder. Part of me wanted to get on my bike and ride, leave everyone and everything far behind. The club was my family and I'd fight for them, die for them, but living the grind for them was harder by far. I wasn't sure I was cut out to move up the chain, but they were all I had.

"I did my duty to the club." Thorn sighed and shook his long hair away from his face. "This is just friend to friend." He held my stare until I nodded my head. "Good then. You know if this shit isn't for you—responsibility, leadership, all that shit—you could pass it up, and you can just be a soldier, not a commander. The army trained us to always step up, but the Brotherhood won't kick you out if you pass. Might limit your income—but that don't seem too big a deal for you."

I didn't need any scratch and wouldn't anytime soon. Maybe I should say no, be the lone wolf who did jobs when he wanted and let that life Rebel and JoJo lived— all for the club shit—let that go. I'd been lost since JoJo hooked up with Charlie. I mean I was happy as fuck for him, but we'd been stuck together for fifteen fucking years and I wasn't sure how the world worked now that it was just me against it. I stayed silent as we rode back to my motel room.

Once there, I asked the one question I had on my mind. "Not sure that sits right with me?"

"That's how I got my job. Damned if you do, fucked if you don't."

I exited the Jeep and looked over at my friend. "I'll think about it because I'm not sure about all of this... just not sure at all."

Thorn grunted, then put the Jeep in reverse. "You do you, brother. Fuck the rest of 'em."

With a nod, I shut the door and watched him drive away. If I only knew what I wanted then I'd be on top of it. I dropped my weapons in the room and headed out. I needed a drink to cure this hangover and quiet my mind.

Chapter 6: Glory

I licked dry lips, and pain burst in my head in a massive explosion. I squeezed my eyes tight and sucked in a breath. It was like I'd breathed in fire—my chest burned with a fierceness I didn't understand.

What happened? Where was I?

I struggled to fight up out of the darkness.

I needed to… What did I need to do?

The blackness sucked me down into its quiet depths.

Beeping woke me. My head pounded and the shuffling of feet registered in my slow-moving brain. I cracked one eye open, and the bright light made me squeeze both eyes shut tight.

"Ms. Atkins? Are you awake?" A soft female voice called my name. But I didn't recognize that voice. Why didn't I? Where was I?

I peeked out with one eye. My head throbbed but I ignored the pain and focused on my surroundings. The railing of a hospital bed was the first clue. I shifted my gaze up, opening my eyes wider, and made out the blurry shape of a woman in scrubs. A doctor? A nurse?

"You're awake. Good." The woman held a straw to my lips. "Take a sip, dear."

The cold water slipped over my thick tongue and trickled down my parched throat. I sipped the water and read her name tag Laura with RN under it. I swallowed the sweet water until the dry scratchy feeling abated.

"What happened?" My voice was creaky and sounded terrible. I searched my memory.

The brunette nurse patted my shoulder. "You want more water?"

I barely shook my head but a lightning strike of pain burst in my brain. What the fuck? I squeezed my eyes tight and focused on breathing. With each breath the pain lessened, or maybe I became a bit more used to it.

"Girl, you need to be still." She met my gaze. "You need more pain meds?"

I almost shook my head again. "No thank you." I needed some answers before I fell into a drug haze. The casino and the hotel suite flashed in my memory in slow-motion snippets. Frankie hit me and that was all I could remember.

"You remember what happened?" The nurse squeezed my hand with a kind smile, which reached her soft gray eyes.

"Not really. What happened?" I asked again.

"Maybe you should rest a bit more. The doc will be here in a couple hours."

Was the news that bad? Anxiety tightened my chest and made my ribs ache worse. I was afraid to catalog all the places that hurt on my body. "Please, tell me. I don't even know what day it is."

"Calm now, honey. We don't want you to hurt yourself." She let go of my hand to bring a chair over next to my bed. Older than me, but not yet forty, Laura had the kindest eyes I'd ever seen.

"Now, we don't know too much." She sighed and clasped my hand again. "Today is Monday and you're at University Medical Center, you were found out by the ER entrance about four Sunday morning. We don't know how you got here. Do you?"

I had no idea how I'd ended up at the city hospital. I would've expected DeLuca to dump me in the desert. "I don't know." My admission came out hopeless and helpless. I refused to be either.

Time to stiffen your spine.

"Don't worry about it. The police will figure it all out for you. They were here to see you today."

I doubted they could help. The police weren't a match for DeLuca. No one was. Fear backed up in my throat and I choked on it. I hated to be afraid, but I was in the fucking hospital. I wouldn't be here if I'd been less confident and more scared. Or at least more cautious.

"Anyway, your left zygomatic bone was fractured, dented in." She brushed the air above my left cheekbone. "The doc did reconstructive surgery—she's one of the best plastic surgeons in the city. That was the worst injury."

My cheekbone dented in. Well, there went my looks. What else had the monsters done? Had they raped me?

Laura kept talking before I could spit out my question. "...three cracked ribs on the right side and one on the left side—those can be painful as they heal. You're bruised head to toe and you have damage to your inner thighs and genitals—" She glanced away from me.

"Was I..." I cleared my throat and asked the question burning bright in my mind. "Was I raped?" It came out a hushed whisper. Shame filled me and that was total bullshit, but I felt what I fucking felt.

"Oh no, dear." She clasped both my hands. "You were *not* raped, that came back negative." She smiled at me. "I'm making a mess of this. That's why the doctors normally do this part." She gave a small laugh.

"Okay, then say it." I attempted a smile but my face screamed in pain. Clenching my eyes shut, I tried not to weep.

Fuck, that hurt.

I'd never experienced this kind of agony. Every small twitch of my body created a new kind of soreness that added to the swell of pain rising inside me. At some point, I'd just lose it and begin screaming. I wasn't proud or a martyr, I planned to drown the pain with all the meds the nurse could give me—just as soon as I figured out how much trouble I was in.

"Someone kicked you in the genitals, at least once but probably more. The doctor says you need at least a week in the hospital to recover and make sure there isn't any infection in that cheek." She smiled at me. "And you need me to pamper you. My name is Laura by the way."

"Laura, thanks for telling me." I squeezed her warm, soft hand that still held mine. "Two more favors, please."

"Anything, dear." She stood and looked relieved to focus on work.

"I need a mirror and then your best pain medication. I've never hurt so bad."

"Oh, let's skip that mirror for a day or two, and go straight to the good stuff."

Her offer tempted me but I had to know. All my life my beauty had defined me. Was it gone now? How bad was I? The uncertainty would eat at me worse than any reality.

"The mirror…please." I held out my hand. Even that simple motion irritated my battered body.

"Okay then." She moved over to a counter and brought me a small round mirror.

I stared at the woman in the reflection. That beaten and weary woman couldn't be me. I didn't even recognize the eyes staring back at me. The eyes were tiny, surrounded by swollen and bruised flesh. The left side of my face was a study in purples and green. The stitches were hard to see amidst all the swelling, but I brushed fingers across them. I gasped at the pain that shot hot through my cheek and down my neck, making every muscle tense, adding to the compounding agony. I wanted to scream, to pass out, to escape the pain and the reflection staring back at me.

I let my arm and the mirror fall to the bed. What had I done? I had no idea how I'd survive the healing process, let alone how I'd fix the mess my life had turned into. Each thought weighed me down, pushing me into a small, dark corner of my mind. I couldn't face this.

When Laura walked in with a syringe and a smile, I was sure she was an angel. Tomorrow, I'd figure out what to do. Tomorrow.

"You relax now." She inserted the drugs directly into my IV line. "This will help you sleep, now."

"Thank you." I think I said that aloud. Her hand held mine, and peace seeped into me. The medicine spread through me, obliterating the pain and pulling me down to the escape of sleep.

"Glory. Ms. Atkins." Laura's voice called me from sleep.

I didn't want to wake up. I was safe here. No pain. No bruises. No mob.

"Glory, the doctor is coming, and she needs to examine you." Laura kept talking and nudging me.

I blinked awake to see a blurry image of my angel. She saved me with the good meds. If I was awake, I probably needed more of those. Sleep. That's what I needed.

The door opened and a petite African-American woman strode to my bedside. She was a ball of energy, moving too fast. Or maybe my brain wasn't working right.

"How are you, Ms. Atkins?"

"Good." I think that's what I said. My mouth didn't work right.

The doctor studied the tablet in her hands. "Good progress. You're healing nicely." She handed my angel the tablet and flashed a light in my face.

"Hey." I protested at the bright light hitting my eye.

"The swelling is down and the contusions are progressing."

"Contuding?" I giggled.

"You're feeling pretty good right now?"

"Yeah, thanks to my angel." I closed my eyes. It was too much work to keep them open.

"Reduce the meds by ten percent each two hours and check her pain level. Let's try to get her to going-home levels."

"Ain't got a home." I blew out a breath. "Not now."

"We can call someone for you," the doctor said. "Who should we call?"

"Call Avery." I grinned wide. "She's my best friend."

"Do you have a number for her? You didn't have any contacts in your purse."

"In my phone." I wanted to sink back into sleep.

"You didn't come in with a phone."

I wanted to help her, but it was just too much effort.

"Let's get her up and moving today. Time for her to start recovering."

The door opened and tennis shoes padded across the floor. I didn't want to open my eyes, wasn't ready for what came next, but I couldn't stay here forever. How long had I been here? Time wasn't normal here. In this room, I couldn't tell if it was day or night. I wanted to beg Laura to let me go under again, to escape reality but I had to face my life, or the ruins of my life, sometime.

I cracked open my eyes but it wasn't Laura this time.

"Hi, I'm Shelly. Laura said to tell you it's her day off. She'll be back tomorrow." The young nurse straightened my covers. "We got to get you moving today. The doc says you can go home tomorrow or the day after."

Home. Where was that?

"We took the catheter out this morning, now you let me know if you need the ladies' room. We don't want you walking on your own just yet."

"Got it." My body was tender but the world-stopping pain wasn't there, yet. "Maybe we should try that bathroom thing now."

After Shelly helped me with that, I stood in front of the mirror. I looked more like me. No swelling anymore, just brown and green bruises. I tried a small smile and it hurt but not bad. "What day is it?" I asked the nurse standing beside me.

"Wednesday. They had you sedated for twenty-four hours to help the recovery process. Dr. Sheridan knows her business."

"I'm hungry." My stomach gurgled and backed me up.

"I bet. You have only had an IV since you came in."

She helped me back to bed. "I'll go get you some broth and Jell-O. You do good with that, we'll keep the food coming."

"Thanks." She left me sitting up in bed.

I reached over for the phone and called our apartment. The phone rang twice, three times and I was sure it'd go to voice mail.

"Hello," Celeste answered, a bit breathless.

"Celeste, it's Glory."

"Look girl, I'm gone, just packed my shit up and I'm out of here. You're in so much trouble here. Jerry's been asking about you. Where are you anyway?"

"What do you mean?"

"Word is you fucked over the big boss. Ain't no one wanting anything to do with you. Girl, be safe, but I gotta get gone." She hung up on me.

I stared at the dead phone and considered what to do next.

Chapter 7: Glory

I set the phone back in the cradle as Laura came into my room in jeans and a tee, carrying a hospital tray.

"Something's wrong with this picture." I gave her a small smile, not ready to try out a bigger one yet.

"I told Shelly I'd bring in your tray, she's swamped today." She set up the table over my bed and then removed the lid from the tray. "You have two kinds of Jell-O and chicken broth. Yum. Yum."

But it did smell like heaven. I was so freaking hungry.

"Why are you here?" I asked her between Jell-O cups.

"I'm worried about you. You haven't had a single visitor."

"Because no one knows I'm here." I sipped the broth and loved the warmth sliding down my throat.

"You need to call your people." She frowned at me.

"So I kinda remember Dr. Sheridan saying my phone wasn't with me."

"Nope, just a purse with a wallet in it with credit cards and a driver's license. But no phone."

I sipped my broth, already feeling full, which was just crazy. I could eat half a pizza easy. Yet a couple cups of Jell-O and some broth filled me up? Just another mystery in my life.

"You know, it's still real…even if you don't tell anyone. It happened."

I looked away from her, hating the way she figured me out so quickly. I could call my mama. She'd fly out, pamper me, and take me home. But I wasn't sure I'd ever make it back to Vegas if that happened. Honestly, after what Celeste said, returning might not even be an option for me.

For a long while I considered what I knew. Laura sat beside me and didn't say anything, but her presence made me feel safer. After several minutes ticked by, I'd come to some conclusions. One, DeLuca made porn that was likely illegal in many ways, not that I understood how. Two, they'd had no trouble beating the shit out of me. Three, if Celeste was to be believed, DeLuca didn't know I was in the hospital. Four, Mama wasn't equipped to handle this mess. Five, the police weren't going to help me.

"Will you hand me the phone?" I had to make a call to the only person I could trust and who had the resources to help me.

The door opened and two people walked inside the room. They both wore coats and ties, which meant cops. I'd already decided I couldn't tell them anything.

"Hello, Glory Atkins?" the tall one asked me.

"Yes, I am."

"I'm her friend Laura."

I gave her a quick smile and reached for her hand. "Will you stay?"

"Of course." She smiled at me.

"We really need to speak with just you," the shorter detective said. "I'm Detective Sanders and this is Detective Jones."

"Well, you can come back when I'm stronger, or we can talk with my friend here." I kept my voice frail. Even though I'd like to send them packing, it was better to be done with this.

Detective Jones stepped next to the bed. "Of course, it's fine to have your friend here. You've been through a bad time. Tell us what happened."

I glanced at Laura. She did give me courage.

"I work as a dancer at the Remington. My boss—"

"His name?" Detective Jones interrupted.

"Jerry Mancini. He asked me to serve as a hostess for one of our private parties. I entered the private floor and I remember walking down the hallway toward Suite 700, and then nothing."

"What floor?" Jones asked.

"Seventh floor. You need a special card to access that floor."

"And then?" Detective Sanders prompted.

"And I woke up here with a broken cheek, broken ribs and the shit beat out of me."

"You don't remember anything else?" Detective Jones frowned at me.

"Nothing, at all. Go ask Jerry. Don't those casinos have cameras everywhere? That's what he always told me." I bit my lip and let tears flow free. "I have no idea what happened, or why I ended up here."

The two detectives shuffled their feet and gave each other the look. No man liked dealing with tears. "Thank you, Ms. Atkins. We'll do that, but we may have more questions for you."

"I'll be here or at home." I wiped at the tears.

"Okay then. We'll be in touch." Detective Sanders dropped a card on my table and they left.

Once they left, Laura narrowed her gaze on me. "Did you just play those cops?"

"Obviously." I gave her a smile and it only hurt a little. "They can't help me."

"Not if you work at the Remington." She gave me a sad shake of her head. "Here's the phone. You're going to need a friend."

I punched in Avery's number—one of the few I had memorized. A recorded voice told me I couldn't make a long distance call. Now what did I do?

"My call, it didn't go through." I bit my lip and that smarted. "How do I call Oklahoma?"

Laura dug in her purse and pulled out a cell phone. "Use my phone—otherwise you gotta set up a collect call account—it's a pain in the ass."

This woman I'd only met a couple days ago just kept helping me, and this wasn't even her job. "You really are my angel."

She snorted. "Not even, you just needed a friend. And I have a soft spot for tough girls."

"Because you're one?" I asked even though it didn't sound a bit like her.

"No." She gave me a sad smile. "But my older sister was and I wish someone had helped her when she needed it. But no one helped, and she didn't make it out of one of those tough situations." She gave me a forced smile. "So I help everyone—you never know when it'll make the difference."

"You're too sweet, and your sister is proud of you." I squeezed her hand this time.

"I hope so." She wiped a tear from her cheek. "These aren't crocodile tears, either." She grinned at me. "That crying on demand must've gotten you out of all kinds of trouble."

I laughed and it was worth the quick burst of pain in my chest. "How'd you figure that out?"

"If you didn't cry when you looked in that mirror, then you ain't crying because of some detective poking around." She pointed to the phone. "Call your friend. I'll step outside and see how Shelly is doing."

I dialed the number. Avery picked up on the second ring.

"Hey, Avi, how are tricks?" I used my normal greeting even if this wasn't normal in any way.

"Hey you, you missed our Sunday call. Did you get a new phone?" Avery's bubbly voice greeted me and something inside me cracked open. I couldn't hold back the sob.

"Glory what's wrong?" Avery's high-pitched cry hurt my ears.

"I'm in the hospital." I spoke between the sobs. Why did I have to pick now to fall apart? "I need help."

"You know I got you, always." The certainty in her voice comforted me. "Rock, find me a flight to Vegas, now." Avery spoke fast to her man. Their quick exchange left me listening to snippets of conversation.

"Glory, tell me the details." Rock's deep voice replaced Avery's. The man got his name for a reason, nothing ruffled him.

"I was at work, and they started hassling me. I'd started working at a new place. They sent me up to a party—they were making porn—and I wasn't given a choice." I started crying again but forced myself to stop. Hysterics wouldn't help anything. "They were going to shoot me up with something, so I was out of choices.

I kicked the guy in the balls and ran for it, but I didn't make it."

"What happened? How hurt are you?" Avery spoke fast into the phone.

So they were both there.

"They broke my cheek, some ribs, and I'm bruised head to toe. But worse, it's the DeLuca family—the mob."

"Rock, we need to fly out there!" Avery shouted into the phone.

"Fuck!" Rock swore. "You're family. And we'll keep you safe."

Relief flooded through me and I realized how tense I'd been. Deep down, I had known when I called home, this would be the response. I should've called as soon as I woke up. But better late than never, I guess.

"Here's Avery, while I get someone headed your way."

"We're heading that way, Rock," Avery said. "Glory, I'm so sorry, tell me everything."

The whole sad story tumbled out of me along with the tears.

"Oh stop crying, you never cry." Avery blubbered along with me on the other end of the phone. "You should've called me when that bastard Frankie started bothering you. Once you're healed, I'm going to kick your ass all over again for holding out on me."

"So tough now that you're a biker bitch." I laughed through the tears running down my cheeks.

"I've always been scrappy. Now I'm just more dangerous."

And she was more dangerous since she'd learned how to use a whip and other tools to give her man the pain he craved. I didn't understand that level of kinky and would have run the other way if I'd been confronted with that kind of need. But Avery had always been braver than me.

"That's true." Hearing my best friend's voice made me feel better. "I miss you."

"Well, you'll be seeing me soon. And Rock says we got a few guys in the area, so he'll have someone there by morning."

"Thanks. I hate to bring my problems—"

"Don't even say stupid shit. We always got each other's back. Who beat up Joanie Sampson for me?"

"We were eight then, it's not the same thing."

"And who kicked Greg Landon in the nuts for saying that shit in high school."

I laughed. "We both did."

"Right, and we'll both take care of these people too." Avery was barely five foot, but she was full of grit and passion.

"Right. I'm going to get off here. Talk to ya soon." I pushed End on Laura's phone.

The door opened.

"You have good tim—" The words died when I saw two beefy guys walk in dressed in the mob uniform. Cotton short-sleeved shirts untucked with dress pants. They both smirked at me. "Glory, Angel DeLuca sends his best." The stepped toward me and the door opened again.

Laura walked in. "Hope you're done, girl." She stopped and stared at the two goons between her and me. "I don't believe I know you, and I know all Glory's friends."

"We work with her." The goon on the left gave her a fake smile. "Who are you?"

"A friend." She gave a fake smile right back. "And

the nurse said the doctor is on her way in. She should be here anytime."

"Great. You heard my friend, I need to talk with my doctor. If you'll excuse us." Fear made my skin clammy but I held my ground.

"Make sure that's the only person you talk to," the second goon muttered as they turned to go. "We'll be seeing you, Glory."

Once they'd left, I let out a breath. "Oh my God! That was not good."

"No, not at all." Laura agreed. "What did you get yourself into?"

"I really am out of my depth." My hands shook and I was so very scared. I just wanted to hide under the covers and hope this mess went away. But even I wasn't that stupid. Laura closed her hand over my still shaking one.

She gave me a nod and squeezed my hand. The simple gesture soothed me. I let the fear go and focused on my next chore. I needed to call Mama. My injuries would hit the Barden grapevine all too soon—it was just the nature of a small town—and I didn't want her to hear about my stupidity secondhand.

"I still need to call my mama, but please stay." I pleaded with my angel and now friend.

She nodded and sat in the blue vinyl chair by my bed.

I dialed in the number to the house phone my mama had owned as long as I could remember, and waited for her to pick up, while hoping I could put off this task.

"Hello." Mama's voice sounded chipper and full.

"Hello, Mama. How are you?"

"Did you get another phone number, Glory Ann?"

"I am using a friend's phone. I lost mine." I pushed

on before Mama could scold me. "I'm in the hospital in Las Vegas. I was attacked."

"Oh dear! Are you hurt you? Did you damage your beautiful face?"

I thought about the bruising and surgery on my face. "I am banged up and in the hospital, but it's not a big deal."

"You come right home and let me take care of you. That City of Sin is no good for an angel like you." Mama had asked me to come home a thousand times over the years. Even though she'd had a great time in her visits here, she wasn't a fan of my new home. Honestly, I wasn't so sure I was a fan any longer.

"Should I fly out and get you home?"

"No, Mama. Avery and her friends are coming out. I will come home with them if I need to."

"Oh that's perfect. Her husband is a peach, so very polite, and all those muscles." She gave a dramatic sigh. "Our Avery sure can pick the good ones."

I could remember a time not that long ago when Avery's choice of boyfriend had scandalized Mama. Now she'd married them off even though they weren't married.

"You sure you don't need me?"

"I always need you, Mama, but I'm fine for now. I'll come home if I need your TLC."

Mama chuckled. "I always could get you feeling and looking like a million bucks. Do you remember that competition in Austin when you were throwing up and I—"

"I gotta go, Mama. I will call you when I know what I'll be doing next." I hated that Austin story. I had only been six and with the worst stomach flu ever, but the show must go on, so Mama had doctored me until I could stand up and smile and do my tap dance. Hell, I'd even won second place.

"All right, my beauty. You rest up and let me know when you're coming home."

"Bye, Mama." I hung up and blew out a breath. My mama was a force of nature.

I handed Laura back her phone.

"That was light on details."

"Believe me, a Southern mama trying to rain hell on the mob would only get her in a bed beside me." I grimaced at the thought of her hurt. "So light on the details is best for her right now. I will tell her more when I think it's safe."

"When will that be?"

I closed my eyes and wondered the same thing. Would I ever be safe again?

A few minutes later the door opened and the doctor buzzed in again followed by an older man who was her exact opposite. Calm. Focused. In no hurry at all.

"Miss Atkins, this is my good friend Jason Langdon, a therapist on staff here." The doctor looked to me. "A licensed counselor is part of our treatment path for cases that involve violence and trauma. Please speak honestly with him. It will help us treat you best."

Laura and the doctor left, leaving me with this strange man.

"I am not telling you what happened. You'd be in danger."

He grinned at me. "You shouldn't tell me then. How does it make you feel being in danger like that?"

"Anxious. Worried. But my friends will help."

"Good friends to help you if the situation is so dangerous." He leaned back in the chair. "You are a lucky woman."

I was in the hospital with a dented cheek and bruises everywhere. I didn't feel lucky. But I could be dead. I could not have a way home. I could be in a lot worse shape.

With a slow nod, I agreed. "You're absolutely right."

"Are you threatened by my presence?"

"Nope. Should I be?" He was the nicest man ever. He kind of soothed me.

Again the soft chuckle of a laugh. "Not necessarily. Some victims of violence find men or anyone very threatening after an attack. Even if you don't feel that way now, it's a normal reaction."

"I fear people who need to be feared." Except I'd walked into that nightmare situation so confident. "Okay, so I might be a bit jumpy and I really don't trust my judgment at the moment. I made bad decisions that put me in the situation."

"Are you to blame for being here?"

"No that creep Fr...who did this to me is to blame, but I am more cautious, more nervous now." That was a good thing. I needed to learn some caution.

"What worries you most?"

"Nothing—well I did worry I was raped, but I wasn't. And I worried about how to get out of Vegas but my friends are helping me, so I'm not as worried now." I know the drugs were playing a role in my answers because I was never this chatty. Yet, it felt good to say it out loud.

"Does the idea of sexual intimacy again concern you?"

Well, my lady parts were seriously damaged, but beyond that, not so much. "I don't think so, but how would I know?"

"Think of the last person you were intimate with. Provided you were physically capable, would you wish to be sexually intimate with him again?"

"Yeah, totally." I giggled. "Okay so the meds are making me a bit too honest, but really, it doesn't make me panic or anything to imagine it."

He gave me a grin. "I'm sure he will be happy to hear that."

Jason stayed for about an hour talking, and I kept answering. Maybe because of the stranger thing—it's easier to talk to complete strangers—maybe because I was medicated or because I just needed to talk.

Chapter 8: Delta

My phone buzzed and I ignored it while I watched my target buy lunch at a truck. I hoped to find a less public place to grab Aaron Lloyd, a runner on an armed robbery charge in Houston. Lloyd walked down the street. I kept an eye on him, but I didn't start the SUV, yet. I wasn't sure why he was in the business district in Reno. What was his play?

The phone stopped ringing only to start again. "Fuck." I reached for my phone while keeping my eyes on the prize—it had taken me days to track the bastard down.

"I'm busy," I barked into the phone.

"Brother, I need a favor." Rock's Hispanic accent was heavy.

I focused on my phone—it was Lloyd's lucky day. He just got to breathe free air another few days.

"You got it. How can I help?" I started the SUV and backed out of the parking spot.

"My old lady said you met Glory in Vegas."

My blood ran cold. Based on Rock's tone, I was going to hate what he said next.

"Yeah," I grunted, holding back the questions that bombarded my brain.

"She's hurt pretty bad and in the hospital in Vegas."

"I will kill that motherfucker." Frankie was a dead man. I backed out of my parking spot and squealed my tires taking off. I needed to be in Vegas yesterday. "Tell me."

"She was beaten up when she refused to do porn for DeLuca." The anger in Rock's voice surprised me.

I'd never heard him angry before.

"Where is she?"

"University Medical in Vegas. We just talked to her about an hour ago." He blew out a breath. "My old lady is determined to get on a plane and kick ass. I may have to tie her down."

"I will take care of Glory and those who hurt her—you have my promise." I tamped down the need to punch something. I'd take out my rage on Frankie and those who helped him.

"I never doubted it, brother," Rock said. "I will be sending out Sharpie and Zero—they are already packing up and riding out. Glory is family for them."

"Thanks. I will get Thorn back down here, along with whoever he has close by." Plans already ran through my head. "Am I bringing her home?"

"That's what my old lady wants, but I'll leave that to you and her." Rock spoke to someone else.

"Delta." Pixie spoke into the phone. "You get my girl and you get the bastards who hurt her."

"I will make them pay in blood and pain."

"Finally someone who understands me." Pixie sighed. "Bring her home to me."

"If she'll let me." I already had my doubts that she'd want to come home, at least not to stay. "Talk to you soon." I hung up and hit the gas, heading toward Las Vegas. I considered stopping to switch from the rental to my bike, but my bike would be safe here, and the SUV would make more sense for now. As I hit US 95, I called Thorn. We needed to make plans.

I crossed into Las Vegas city limits in five hours, a personal record for me. Protecting Glory was a physical need pulling me toward the hospital. I wasn't used to feeling impotent, but that feeling had dogged me mile after mile until I wanted to scream or kill something.

Now that I was here, I had no idea what I should do. The proud woman who'd shared her body with me wasn't a victim. The need to crush those who'd hurt her surfaced, and I pushed it down again, but I didn't know how long that'd last. At least, she'd gone down fighting. It was the only halfway good thing Rock had told me. I grinned, thinking of her going on the attack—even against crazy odds—she hadn't backed down. I admired that kind of stupidity. She had my kind of moxie.

I pulled into University Medical in minutes. I didn't bother with information since I had all the vital details. Glory Atkins, room 317. I rode the elevator up to three and strode down the hallway. People stopped to look twice, even the nurses, but no one got in my way. I had that effect on people. They tended to steer clear of me.

I stopped outside the door and braced myself for what might come next. How was she handling the injuries? And I reminded myself that my rage wasn't an ally here. She needed comfort, support, and maybe even a shoulder to cry on. Fuck, there were lots of brothers better suited for this job.

I sucked at sympathy, and my primary emotion was rage, unless horny counted as an emotion. But those fuckers had hurt her in her most personal areas. Rock had told me every gory detail Glory had confessed in her call to them. Anger boiled out again. How dare they damage her like that? Someone or several idiots needed their junk cut off for that move. Surprisingly, the thought calmed me down. I catalogued the ways I'd make those bastards pay and I found the first bit of calm in hours.

I pulled open the door and slipped inside. Holy fucking shit—my Queenie was broken and bandaged. Bruises colored her face and arms. I'd fucking tear apart every one of them. When I found the bastards who'd marked her, then they were going to wish they were dead.

I ran a finger lightly down her jaw and she stirred. "Wake up, Queenie." I spoke low. My fucking chest clenched, but I remembered the cold she wore as armor. She wouldn't want my sympathy.

She blinked her eyes open, soft and out of focus. "Delta, how did you find me?" Her soft smile slid right past my defenses and lodged itself in my cold heart.

Then the sleep faded and her gaze hardened. "Of course it had to be you."

"You got a problem with me?" Shit I sounded like an asshole.

"I gave in for a night, and then I was never supposed to see you again." She squeezed her eyes tight and turned her head away. "I don't want anyone, let alone you, to see me like this. But my luck sucks, right now." Her words were slightly slurred. She must be on some great drugs.

The door opened and a young dark-haired nurse stepped inside and frowned at me. "She needs rest, so I'm going to have to ask you—"

"Don't bother, Laura." Glory gave an exaggerated wave of her hand. "He's the one who's going to save me." She rolled her eyes.

"Oh thank God! I was worried you were another threat

to my girl." The nurse gave me a huge smile, and it made her glow.

Threat caught my attention. "What kind of threat? Who's been here?"

"Guys from her work."

"They were DeLuca's muscle, trying to make sure I didn't say anything to the cops. As if they could help me." She flung her covers back and tried to sit up. "Double damn, that hurts." She held herself up with an unsteady hand.

Laura, the nurse, hurried over and helped her lay down.

"I gotta get out of here…not safe." Her eyes closed.

She was right, we needed to leave soon.

"When will she be released?"

"Two days." Laura looked from me to Glory. "You called a biker to rescue you from the mob." She stepped forward and her chin quivered just a bit. "Will she be safe with you?"

"What's it to you?" I didn't know why she cared, and the last thing I needed was an interfering nurse to hinder me or report back to the mob.

"I care about her, and I want her to be safe, not end up in more trouble." She fisted hands on hips and met my stare without blinking. She meant what she said.

"Stop, you two—you're on the same side." Glory frowned up at me from swollen eyes. "Be nice to her." She gave an exhausted sigh. "Thanks for coming."

"No one should be alone when they're hurt." I had been hurt and alone too many times and it sucked. "I'm glad you called for help—I'll make this all right for you."

She peered up at me as if reading the truth of my words, then gave a slight nod before wincing.

"Can you sit up?"

She started moving before I'd finished the question. I caught her upper arm and helped her. Muttering a curse, she pushed herself to standing and I think she'd have collapsed to the ground if I wasn't supporting her. "Easy there, one step at a time."

"This is the goal, right?" She studied me. "You want me to leave with you?"

"You need meds and stuff to leave—you can't just disappear." Laura gently pushed her back to the bed.

"We will have to leave as soon as she can." I had to get her safe, and if that meant tying up this busybody nurse to do it, then I would.

"Tomorrow." Laura glanced between us. "You can trust the doctor—she's top rate—and she can keep a secret. Trust her," the nurse implored Glory. The nurse believed what she said, but I wished I knew if she was a good judge of character.

"The doctor does rounds in the morning and if you wait until evening, I will be here to help you leave." Laura touched my shoulder. "You can wait until then?"

Glory could use the time to recover. We'd wait for the doctor, but I didn't plan to let Laura help. I was eighty percent sure she was on our side, but I wouldn't even take a one percent chance with Glory. My brothers were always reliable, so they could help us, but Laura's help was over.

"What can I bring you?" I glanced at my queen. The stitched cheek pissed me off most. They'd broken that bone and she'd had surgery to fix it. A cold settled deep inside me—every single one of them would pay.

"Uh, clothes, makeup, everything. My place isn't safe… I guess I have nothing, not even a freaking phone."

"Right. I'll see you in a bit and you'll have everything you need. Got me?"

She gave me a quick smile with her cut and swollen bottom lip. "Thanks."

I had shit to do. So I turned and left without another word. Her thanks was the last thing I needed. It was my fault she was in this mess. I'd stuck my nose in her business but hadn't fixed anything. Hell, I'd made it a thousand times worse. I had a whole lot to make up to my queen.

And I had to stop thinking of her that way—she wasn't mine, never had been and never would be.

I stopped at a strip mall in the regular part of Vegas. Tourist Vegas and real people Vegas were two different worlds, and I liked the real Vegas better than the glitz. I picked out a handful of outfits and grabbed a few underthings although I'd prefer she not wear any. After getting her clothes, I stopped to pick up girl shit—deodorant, toothbrush, shampoo, razors and a couple kinds of pain reliever. She'd be sore for days and we might not be able to pick up her pain meds. I spotted a cosmetics store and decided to chance it.

"Can I help you?" A overly made-up woman behind the counter gave me a what-the-fuck look.

That was exactly how I felt. "My girl needs new makeup and I wanted to surprise her with it."

"Surprise her by bringing her in—I can't show you makeup for a woman who isn't here." She crossed her arms.

Another guy walked up then. "What's the problem?" He looked from me to the out-of-sorts bitch giving me attitude.

"My girl was in a car wreck and we lost our luggage,

her makeup, everything really. She gets out of the hospital tomorrow and I know she'd feel better having it." I lied without a bit of guilt.

The woman harrumphed. "Wreck with your fist," she mumbled.

I stepped to the counter and the guy was there in an instant.

"Lady, I don't lay hands on women and be glad 'cause you're pushing me right now, making me wish you were a man."

The guy frowned at the woman before focusing on me. "I might be able to help you." He motioned for me to follow him.

I gave the now frightened woman another scowl and followed him down an aisle.

"Tell me the color of her skin." He looked at me and glanced away. "When she isn't beaten up, um, not that you beat her up or anything."

I knew what they both thought, and it pissed me off more. "Peaches and cream coloring with just a hint of a tan. She's got a layer of blue and green bruises and stitches over most of that now."

He nodded. "Is she a dash it on and go or more the perfectionist type."

"Perfectionist." I had no doubt she had to have everything perfect. "Make sure there's skin crap in there too—the full package."

He nodded and walked down another aisle. "What does she do?"

"Dances in a Vegas show."

He stopped and turned to me. "You might want to bring her in or get her brands."

"What do other dance professionals use?"

"If they don't use the stuff supplied by the show?"

I didn't know they even did that, but Queenie seemed like the do-it-herself type. "Exactly."

"MAC. And you can buy it here, but it ain't cheap." He walked over to a display. "Let me see a picture of her."

Well fuck, that was something I hadn't expected. I sent a quick text to Avery and she responded fast, but the guy gave me a strange look. I suppose most boyfriends had pictures of their girl on their phone—my barely held together lie fell apart.

I clicked the message and Glory's perfect face stared back at me. Damn, she was hot and that smile was so light and bright. She looked so much happier here than when I'd met her in Vegas, but I swore she'd smile like this for me.

"Here you go." I showed him the photo and he took my damn phone.

He picked up a small plastic bag and started with the moisturizers, plucking items and dropping them in the bag. In just a few minutes he was done and I trailed after him to the cash register. A thousand dollars later, I'd left the store with Glory's makeup, feeling good for the first time since I'd seen her in the hospital. I needed to pamper her, make her smile and forget, even for a minute, the terror of the past few days. I wanted to give her at least one bright moment.

And that was beyond fucked-up—I didn't do women, didn't do emotion, definitely didn't lay down a grand for a smile. Except I just had. I vowed I would not fall for her.

She was my responsibility, but I wouldn't fool her or myself into thinking we could be something more. I'd never even thought about wanting more with another woman, but I did with Glory. And that was the worst kind of stupid.

Purchases complete, I drove back to the hospital to do guard duty. I texted Thorn and got an ETA for the next day. He and Eagle would be here by afternoon, and with any luck I'd have Glory back to my place by then.

I walked in to find her talking with an older guy.

"Why are you here?"

"Someone's gotta look after you, Queenie."

"Is this the young man you said would be coming by tomorrow?" He stood and moved toward me. "I'm Jason, a therapist here." He held out a hand to shake.

I shook it.

"Yeah, he will be taking me home once I'm discharged," Queenie called from the bed.

"So glad to meet you. I was just going over the psychological healing process with Glory and you need to hear it too. It is important to understand the distress she may experience in stressful situations over the next couple months."

She glared at me. "He can just read the handout." She thrust it to me.

"Sit, sit, we're about halfway done." He smiled at my queen. "We won't start over, but he can hear what we have left to cover."

Glory sighed and I pulled up a chair and took the papers now lying on her belly again.

The doctor started talking, but I focused on the paper.

It was titled Psychological Symptoms of Trauma.

I'd seen these kind of handouts in the military all too frequently. I checked to see if the usual culprits were there. *Disoriented, withdrawn, anxious, depressed, panic attacks, emotional outbursts, fear, denial, anger, rage, grief, increased sexual appetite, increased recklessness, decreased sexual appetite*, and the list went on and on.

"There are so many ways trauma can manifest. Be most aware of sudden changes in mood, erratic decisions, fear, panic attacks or recklessness. They can be most common and create havoc in life." Jason turned to me. "Any questions?"

"Nah, I was an MP in the military. We were trained on trauma."

Jason looked to me. "Yes indeed." Then back to Glory. "Remember however you feel, it's okay. Your mind has to heal as well as your body." He stood up and nodded to each of us. "I'm sure Glory feels safer with you here." He walked out, leaving me with too much information and not sure what to do to help her.

"She does not." Glory glared at me. "What did you bring?"

"Look and see." I retrieved the bags and dropped them on the bed.

She rooted through them and came out with a new iPhone.

"Yay."

"It's a new number."

"Good. I don't need anyone following me from here."

She looked in the second bag. "Son of a bitch. You got me makeup?"

I glanced up to see a grin that reached her eyes.

"Who the hell picked this out? 'Cause I know it wasn't you." She laid out each tube of makeup beside her. "This beats the coffee."

"Some guy looked at your picture and picked it out."

"You have a pic of me? Stalker-like." She laughed.

"Settle down, Queen. You need to sleep and so do I."

"You're staying here?" she squeaked.

"All night."

A different nurse came in and gave her meds and she conked out soon after, but sleep wasn't easy for me.

The next morning I left her asleep to go grab breakfast and coffee to bring back.

As I walked toward her room, I wondered if she'd still be sleeping. I opened the door to find her taking wobbling steps across her room.

"You'll fall." I dropped the breakfast bag and rushed to her with coffee in hand.

She gave an irritated snort. "And then I get back up." But she leaned into me and gave me a lopsided smile. "That smells like heaven." She nodded her chin to the coffee cups I carried in a cardboard contraption.

"Let's get you back to the bed before you drink that stuff. And I brought food."

With small, unsteady steps, I helped her to the bed.

"Now give it." She held out a hand in demand.

We both had a thing for java.

She took her first sip and sighed. "God, this is real coffee, finally. The stuff in here, ugh."

She stayed quiet while she downed the coffee and scarfed down her breakfast sandwich.

The door opened and a small woman in a white coat walked in. She had a sophisticated beauty that made me look twice.

"Hey, doc. You gonna let me out of here?" Glory greeted the doctor.

"You could use more recovery time." She scrolled through her tablet. "Your pain level seems to be decreasing. How do you feel?"

"Better." Glory glanced at me and back to the doctor. "The thing is that the guys who put me in here are watching me, so I might need to slip away."

"Call the police."

"Um, they aren't the solution."

"I can't recommend early release, but if you insist, I will print out your prescriptions." The doctor reached in her coat pocket. "I was giving you this today anyway." She placed two tubes of cream on the bedside table. "This is my special formula—it will help with the bruising and especially the scar."

"Right, it's best to be prepared in case I have to check out early. You can't stop me, right?"

"No, I can't keep you here, but you'll regress, slow the healing, if you try to do too much." She frowned at me. "You were seriously injured and it will be weeks before you're approaching normal physical conditions. And sexual relations should wait—"

"That's not an—" Glory tried to interrupt.

"At least three weeks, maybe four." The doctor stared at me as she spoke.

I wasn't going anywhere near her again—that was more trouble than I could handle. If I went back, then I'd want more and more. No. It was best to get her back home and this situation resolved. I had nothing inside me to give another. Hell, I'd let down everyone who ever relied on me.

Chapter 9: Glory

When Dr. Sheridan said "sexual relations," I blew my cool. "That's not an—" I tried to interrupt as the doctor glared at Delta.

"At least three weeks, maybe four." The doctor spoke anyway.

I needed to disappear into a hole—right now. "Thanks for that." I growled up at the doctor who still stared at Delta. "I don't think you need to worry about that. I am capable of running my own sex life."

She turned to me and laughed. Actually laughed. If it didn't hurt to move, I'd strangle the woman. "Right. I will bring back in your prescriptions in case I'm not here when you need to leave." Her dark eyes bore right into me. "Although I urge you not to. I want you to fully recover."

"I understand." But I valued my life too much to lie around here waiting for DeLuca to surface.

She sighed and left. Finally.

I gave Delta my frostiest look. If I didn't confront the sex thing now, I might never be able to do it. "One night. And I'm still not interested in more."

He cocked an eyebrow in that smart-ass way of his. "An amazing night."

That was true enough, but I wasn't admitting it to him. "But I totally agree—one night."

A pang of something made my chest ache. Was I disappointed? Hurt? That was so damn ridiculous. I didn't want him, yet a big part of me apparently wanted him to want me.

Stop this, I ordered myself. *Be grateful for small blessings.*

"Great." I sounded put out. Dammit, I had meant to sound easy and unconcerned. That failed. "Now go away. I need privacy to get ready." I motioned him toward the door.

He just cocked that irritating eyebrow again and gave a single shake of his head. "Not a chance, Queenie."

There was that name again. I was getting to the bottom of this. "Why do you insist on calling me that?"

He bent forward as he laughed.

I huffed as he just kept laughing. "Stop that."

He wiped the corner of his eye and leaned back in his chair. "You are totally superior from the way you hold your head to the way you expect others to do whatever you say. A fucking queen."

That didn't sound so great. I wasn't like that, was I?

Fuck him. And his nickname. "I know what I like and what I don't—I'm not apologizing for that."

"Exactly." He tilted his head to the side. "It's what I like best about you. You get what you want."

A warmth spread through me at his praise, and that pissed me off even more. I didn't want his opinion to matter. I couldn't let it matter to me because I'd never be enough for him. Never be first for a man like him. He was married to that damn club, and I didn't come second, ever.

Maybe that made me a queen, and if it did, then fine, I deserved to be the most important person in someone's life. When I gave away my heart, I would be first, last and only for him and him for me.

I was done talking with him. I took a fortifying breath and swung my legs over the side of the bed. Dizziness flooded me and I closed my eyes, trying to fight the disorienting swirl. I pushed myself to my feet and let the pain wash over me. Embraced every throb and stab until it was a part of me. It did no use to fight against it—instead I used it to fuel me and make me stronger. I would survive this.

I opened my eyes and focused on my feet, one step. Pain exploded in my center and shot down over my sex and then struck each leg. My knees tried to buckle but Delta stepped up and steadied me. I wanted to castrate whoever had bruised me so bad.

"Together." He stepped forward and I followed.

Each step created a new strike of pain that stole my breath, but I pushed on. They would not defeat me. The bathroom loomed so far away. In reality it was less than twenty feet away. Eventually we made it. Once I rested on the closed toilet seat, he loped back to the bed, gathered my bags and was back in a flash. Would I ever move that easy again?

He set the two bags in the sink. "Should I stay?" He gave me that wicked smirk that made me think of how he'd made me come during our one night together.

I pointed to the door. "Out."

"Fine." He strolled out and closed the door behind him.

I wanted to play in the makeup but I knew better than to start there. Priorities. And clothing was a higher priority than makeup. I reached for the clothes and decided to skip underwear for now. My poor bruised flesh needed any break I could give it.

I slipped on the yoga pants. Each inch was torture as my body protested the tight fit of the knit against my skin. I suddenly wished for a dress that fit like the hospital gown. But I kept working them up my legs. I used the sink to pull myself up and knew there was nothing to help this last part so I jerked up the pants.

"Son of a bitch!" I hissed and held tight to the porcelain sink. My body shook and I breathed in and out, trying to settle myself. My private parts throbbed and sent pain up my torso. I clenched my teeth and rode out wave after wave, waiting for it to lessen.

Eventually I pried my eyes open and looked at the shirt and bra that waited for me. No way I'd get that sports bra on today, so I left it and picked up the shirt. Even this hell would eventually end, and oddly, the thought comforted me.

After the clothing ordeal, I didn't have much energy for makeup. I did the skin care regimen and added a bit of lip gloss and mascara. I didn't have the tenacity to try and cover up all these bruises today—maybe tomorrow or the next day.

When I opened the door, a wheelchair sat there with flip-flops on the floor in front of it.

"Ready?"

I wanted to protest the wheelchair, but it was necessary. I bit back my angry retort.

Damn it and this weakness. With a sigh, I settled down in the chair.

"The doc brought those prescriptions, and I'll get the rest of your stuff. Then we're out of here." He gave me a two finger salute and went around the chair to the bathroom. We were out of the room in minutes, and he wheeled me to an SUV. He stashed my meager belongings in the back. Before I could even consider how to get in the ride, he picked me up and placed me on the passenger seat.

With narrowed eyes, I frowned at him. "You're too high-handed."

He shut the door and jogged to the driver side. He sped out of the lot into the hot Vegas night.

"Stay away from the strip," I warned.

"Figured that one out already." He arched a brow. "We need to talk about what happened that night."

"It's a long story." My voice quavered.

He lay his hand atop mine. "We'll start early in the day and go through step by step."

"Okay." My voice was stronger now. "I want those bastards to pay."

"I give you my word they will pay—pay dearly."

I stared at the hard line of his jaw and believed him. The bastards would pay—Delta would make sure it happened. Maybe I should be the passive kind of girl who wished her attackers peace, but that was bullshit. I believed in an eye for an eye. Or ten punches for one. There was no excuse for someone stronger to ever hurt a weaker person—those assholes hurt me for the fun of it. No, cowards like that deserved anything Delta handed out.

We drove through the tourist part of town with flashing signs and offers for every type of fun imaginable and things I thought sounded horrible—like the three wedding chapels we passed. Vegas was tacky and the tourists loved it. We passed the invisible barrier into the real Vegas where the workers who fueled Vegas lived. Delta ran fingers through his golden-blond hair and I understood why it was always messy—he made it that way. Then he pierced me with stormy eyes.

He had sculpted muscles, a hard jaw and a rugged handsomeness that made me think of a Viking. He was the sexiest man I'd ever met. Too damn bad he was one of them.

I just needed to focus on how much he pissed me off. He was sexy, but when he opened his mouth, he drove me crazy with his arrogant, high-handed nature.

We turned down a residential street and into an apartment complex. It was nicer than the one where I lived. Who did he know in Vegas?

"Why are we here?" I hated the way he'd just taken over. Sure, I needed his help but that didn't mean he could decide everything without me.

Although he probably thought so. The Brotherhood bikers weren't big communicators—their talents lay elsewhere. Primarily between the sheets, at least that had been my experience.

"I have keys for a place here—a friend of a friend." He startled me when he spoke. I hadn't expected him to answer. "I use the apartment when I'm here for long stays or when I'm tracking a bounty."

I glanced down at the fingertip-sized bruises that mottled my arms. A fresh wave of anger washed over me and built to an impotent rage that made me want to scream forever.

I knew Rebel had started a bounty hunting business but that's all Avery had said. "Were you the one who caught Avery's bastard of a father?"

He lifted an eyebrow in question. "I was there."

"Good." A vicious sense of satisfaction tore through

me. That bastard had put my best friend, his own daughter, in the hospital, and he deserved to rot in jail.

"Dammit." It hit me that the three of us—Avery, Lila and now me had all been physically violated.

He parked in a numbered spot in a carport. "Stay there." Then he was out the door and coming around to my side.

I didn't protest because getting out of this thing would hurt my bruised ribs. He opened the passenger side door and scooped me out, but he didn't put me down on the ground.

He loped up an outdoor staircase. And gracefully managed to hold me, unlock the door and carry me inside. If we were married, then this moment would mean something. We hadn't done the Vegas drunk-married deal, but walking over that threshold still sent a cold prickle of awareness shooting through me.

With a gentleness I hadn't expected, he set me on the living room sofa. Then strode back through the door, leaving me alone in the apartment. The living area was clean but sterile with its planned neutrality, as if whoever decorated was afraid of offending someone. I liked color and boldness—this place had none of that. But it wasn't the fleabag motel I'd expected, so he received points for that.

The door opened and he packed in a few bags and compact duffel. He didn't dump the stuff inside the door but kept going toward the back where I assumed the bedroom, or bedrooms, were located. Thumps and the crinkle of sacks carried from the back, but I was too sore to investigate. He intrigued me with his aura of badass mixed with the sexiness I still craved. He was everything I wanted and despised rolled into one.

I closed my eyes and tried to center myself, preparing for what came next. I'd rather pluck out my eyeball with a spoon than tell my story. He returned, scooting me over on the couch before he sat gently beside me.

He caressed my ankle, then peered at me with that all-seeing stare—it was as if he dissected me. "We have to talk about that night." Calm and distant, he continued to hold my gaze.

Panic skittered through my middle but I dismissed it. We Atkinses were made of sterner stuff.

His grip tightened, comforting me. "Start from the beginning. This is the job Bear arranged?"

Oh shit, I didn't want to admit the magnitude of my mistake. But I would in order to get retribution—fuck justice.

"I changed jobs from the Starlord to the Remington recently."

"Why?" He scowled at me.

"I wasn't getting promoted, and Frankie was there all the time. He made a real pest of himself after I ended it with him."

"So you went to his place?" The scorn was clear.

"I didn't know it was his place. My roommate convinced me to go there to 'get away' from the prick. She had to be working with him."

He texted something.

"What the hell are you doing?" I tried to lean forward but my ribs protested.

"Texting Bear—he thought you were hurt because of the Starlord."

"Damn, is he pissed?"

"He was planning on coming out in a couple days." Delta kept typing on his phone.

Shit. That was scary—the idea of Bear pissed off. Delta had to be lethal but no one carried the menace of Bear, a tall, lean black man who was in charge of the Brotherhood's porn business. He'd helped me find the job in Vegas, and now I knew why he hadn't sent me to the Remington.

"Keep going." His fingers rested on my calf, then began moving in slow, comforting circles.

I focused on the beige wall and let the story flow out. "At the Remington, you not only dance but have to hostess—it's where we met." I'd hated that duty. "And I was choosy in the jobs I took." Not that it had mattered in the end. "Anyway, I was like fifty shades of stupid when I chose the Remington. I dated Frankie, not realizing he was part of the mob or however you say that. I was warned but I believed the crap Frankie fed me." I'd never learn how to pick a good man. "Anyway, eventually it was clear that he wasn't exactly right in the head. Possessive, bad temper and just plain mean sometimes. So I broke up with him, and the trouble started."

"What kind of trouble? Be specific."

"Notes in my dressing room, dead roses on my car and on my doorstep. That's how it started." I remembered thinking it was a crazy admirer at first. I had dismissed it. "Then he caught me alone after a show one night and made my choices clear. I could go back to him or quit working in Vegas. So I took my roommate's advice and went to the Remington."

A tick in his jaw became more pronounced as he clenched his jaw tight.

"I'm stupid. I guess you can't take the country out of the girl." I shrugged. "I thought DeLuca owned the Starlord and that's why Frankie had such good access."

I rolled my eyes. "He was there all the time and could go anywhere, so I went to a new casino, thinking I was leaving my trouble behind me."

"It's not something a lot of people know."

"Well, there I was working for DeLuca—signed and sealed—before I knew any better." Frankie had been so damn superior when he'd told me about it. "And he wasn't the pest he'd been at the Starlord, but he made it clear my future was in his hands, but I refused to take him back."

"So no more flowers and notes?"

"No." I gave a dry laugh. "He had me where he wanted me." With a sigh, I met Delta's gaze. "We were playing cat and mouse the past month or so. He'd show up when I was working with another girl or by himself. He'd ask me to go out with them both sometimes, but I always said no. And that's where we were when he came to that poker game—another first."

"And I made it all worse." Delta erupted from couch and knocked a lamp off the end table.

The explosion of violence startled me and I curled up tighter, making my bruised ribs ache more. "I think he'd planned it for a showdown of sorts—I was going to be his that weekend. So you didn't make it worse, at all."

"Not how I see it." He paced in front of the couch. "What happened after I left?"

"Nothing the first day or two, then I started getting shit from managers, and that night—" I couldn't get the words past the tightness in my chest. "The night they beat me." Shivers shook me and tears welled in my eyes. "Jerry, the same guy at the poker game, he called me to his office, and took all my dances, which meant income, away. I should have just quit and walked out."

"He wouldn't have let you—not if Frankie wanted his pound of flesh."

"Instead I tried to salvage my job until I could find a new one. He said he'd let me dance if I showed him I was a team player and directed me to go up to Suite 700. Celeste had warned me away from those parties. Not that she turned out to be much of a friend.

"I walked into the suite and it was all nightmare stuff from there. They led me to a room where they were making porn, and the girls, who were other dancers, were hopped up on something." The feeling of panic raced through me.

"Angel DeLuca was in there with Frankie and the director and all these drugged women. I started planning my escape." I'd hated those moments feeling so trapped. My breathing became fast and shallow and I closed my eyes, trying to calm myself. I could feel the anxiety Jason had talked about building. If I didn't control it, I'd end up in a full panic attack.

"Anyway, that failed! They came at me with a needle and it was try and escape or end up like the other girls. I wasn't going down like that, so I kicked Frankie in the balls and he smashed his fist into my cheek." I held my finger up to the line of stitches on my face. "I don't remember anything else—I woke up in the hospital." I had never felt so helpless in my life. Alone and in pain in that hospital had been horrible. Thank God for Laura.

His pulse beat a fast tick in his clenched jaw and his fists clenched and unclenched. "I will make them regret every single bruise."

Chapter 10: Delta

The anguish in her voice drove me fucking crazy and I crashed my fist into the wall, denting the drywall. She flinched and a scream escaped. Immediately she looked away embarrassed.

Fuck me. I had to control myself. Trauma. She had suffered serious trauma, and my indulgence in anger wasn't helping anyone. A tear streaked down her face.

I knelt on the carpet before her. "Sorry, Queen, I lost my cool. You don't need to see that, and I won't make the mistake again."

She sniffed and met my gaze with a cold glare. "You're a prick."

"Yeah, but I'm your prick, the one who's going to get you revenge."

A hint of a smile showed on her face. "I hope so. And I want to help." She trembled, then breathed in and stilled herself.

I smirked up at her and resisted the urge to claim her bowed lips. "Not happening, Queenie." I traced my finger down her unbruised chin.

"I need to—"

"You asked for help?"

She frowned down at me. "Well, help isn't—"

"You want revenge." I knew her that well.

"Of course I do, look at me. Those bastards didn't need to—"

"You want to go home or stay here after this is over?" She was used to ruling over men, but that wasn't happening with me. I yearned for her fire but I wasn't ever handing her my fucking balls.

Her highness turned frosty. "Stay, but that—"

"Then you do what I say and quit being a brat," I teased, although I meant every word.

"I am not a brat," she groused.

"You are too, and I bet you always have been."

She sighed. "I hate this. I am not a victim."

"No, you're not. You are a badass queen."

Her breasts heaved as she sucked in quick breaths. She had a damn fine rack. I stretched up and kissed her with a gentleness I didn't feel, gingerly wrapping my arms around her. I wanted to squeeze her tight to me but I wouldn't damage her more.

And she pulled me under just like before. I was a drowning man and I surrendered to her, letting her control our kiss. She tangled fists in my shirt and held me close. So fierce and passionate.

Fuck, I am in trouble.

Her tongue flicked and caressed then she bit my lower lip and I moaned.

Her moan wasn't from pleasure this time. I moved back with a curse. Fuck, I kept forgetting myself. "Shit! I'm so sorry."

She jutted her chin with extra attitude but I saw the pain in her baby blue eyes. "I'm fine."

I needed distance before I screwed this up worse. "You should rest," I threw over my shoulder as I hurried to the back bedroom. I had to get myself under control and that meant no more kisses. Hell, I didn't even like her so why did I want to taste her again so damn bad?

I lay in the bed and fumed over my stupidity, over the unfairness of Glory's injury, and all the ways I would exact vengeance for her. I tried to sleep but it wouldn't come. Instead Glory's expressions flitted through my head over and again. Fear. Loathing. Pride. Those had been her go-to emotions as she'd told me her story. She'd been naïve and she'd paid for it. I would be repaying those bastards tenfold.

My phone pinged. Thorn texted he was here.

Come on in. I texted back.

I sat up and moved down the hall.

"You?" I heard Glory yelp.

Thorn dominated the room, staring down at Glory, who sat shaking on the couch.

"Why…why are *you* here?" She pressed back into the corner of the couch.

I glanced from her to Thorn, not knowing they'd met before. Eagle stepped in behind Thorn.

"You know Thorn?" I scowled.

Thorn stepped forward. "You're Mama and Pixie's friend."

That's right. She would've hung out with her friends at the club.

"You stay away from me." She pointed at Thorn with a shaky finger.

"I won't hurt you."

"Like you didn't hurt Lila." She glared at me. "Why is he here?"

Shame made Thorn look away. I'd totally forgotten about his incident with Mama, Dare's old lady and Glory's friend. Thorn had lost his shit and hit Mama when she'd turned him down for some fun. The brother had been in a dark place then and that mistake had made him get some help. He was much more stable now, but that was by no means normal. After the torture he'd been exposed to when he'd been in the black op world, I doubted he'd ever approach even the club's definition of normal.

"I don't need another fist to the face." Anger had replaced the fear. "If I don't fuck him will he beat me up too? I think I've had enough of that shit for now." Tears threatened to spill and she covered her face.

"Thorn isn't a threat." I made my voice calm as possible. I felt for Thorn. I knew what it was like for a mistake to keep shadowing you.

"Leave her be," Thorn rumbled.

I joined her on the couch and moved her stiff body from the corner of the couch, out and onto my lap. She trembled and came willingly. I hated to see her afraid. "Thorn is here to help me get revenge. So is Eagle, the one beside Thorn. We're all on your side."

Her body sagged into me and she buried her face in my neck. "I understand, it's just—"

"I didn't think about you even knowing Thorn. I should have." I soothed her. "He and Dare's old lady are good. You good?"

She gave a small nod and then sat up and met Thorn's gaze. "I'm sorry." She gave him a weak smile. "It's been—"

"We're good." Thorn cut her off. "You have a right to be jumpy given the shit you been through."

Thorn turned to Eagle, who lounged against a wall by the front door. "This is Eagle." Thorn nodded at the guy. "He's in our security detail, been guarding people for years, so he'll be here with you."

Glory nodded, relief clear on her face.

"Delta and I will be tracking down Frankie. He needs a few lessons in manners."

Glory grinned. "He does, give him an extra lesson from me."

Thorn nodded and he and Eagle headed to the back bedrooms.

I understood she was under stress. Trauma fucked with your mind in many ways, but even before she ended up in the hospital, she had a thing against the Brotherhood. I needed to understand her issue because I couldn't have her going off every time one of us showed up. Hell, she'd asked for our help, after all.

I touched her chin. "What's your problem with the club?"

She turned her head away from me. "I don't have a problem."

"Bullshit. From the moment you knew I was from Barden, you gave me and my club serious shade."

"You guys are all rah-rah-live-and-die-by-the-club. I don't get it, and your club has caused my family and the town lots of grief over the years." Her cheeks reddened with temper and she stood, wobbly, and then hobbled away from me. "I don't understand why you need a cult—a boy's only cult—to feel like men."

Anger flared in my chest and I stood and stalked toward her. "Don't dis me or my club like that again."

"Or what? You'll walk away? Just as well walk because you and I both know I'll do it again. You can't make me drink the Kool-Aid. I see it straight." She glared at me with all the ferocity of a cornered wolf.

I grinned, couldn't help myself when she went all defiant like that. "No, your highness, I will bend you over my knee and spank you like the damn brat you are. So watch the temper, yeah?"

"You will not," she commanded with the affronted dignity worthy of any royal.

"Try me, Queenie." I smirked, knowing it would piss her off more. I heard Thorn's footsteps in the hall. "This is done. I expect a little more respect—you called us in to *help* you."

She fisted hands on hips and opened her mouth, then snapped it shut.

"We gotta jet," Thorn said. "We have a location on Ricci."

Glory turned to him. "Already?"

"You'll have your justice today," I said over my shoulder as I walked out the front door.

Why the hell did I let her provoke me? Now I'd have to spank her bare ass because there was no way she'd ever mind me. And for my efforts, all I'd end up with was a raging hard-on and a sore hand.

"You got a problem, brother." Thorn smacked my back. "That one is fiercer than a badger and she's not shy."

"She's just a favor—same reason you're here." I headed to my ride.

"That's bullshit—she's picked you."

I belted out a laugh. "I thought you were the quiet one."

The bastard climbed into the SUV beside me. I backed out and turned toward the strip. We needed answers.

"So how we doing this?" I asked.

"We're going to take pound for pound out on Frank

Ricci. He'll be lucky to be alive when I'm done with him," Thorn growled.

"We'd be committing the club to retribution if we hurt him that way." I wanted to rip his nuts off, but I wasn't sure the club was down for that.

"This is what I know." Thorn tapped his thumb on his thigh—he was nervous. "Mama and Pixie call her their best friend. She and Sharpie were a thing before he joined, and Zero and he are riding like the Devil is chasing them to get here. Bear is ready to throw down for her too."

"I met up with her when I was in Vegas last, so I want this right for her, but—"

"Jericho never mentions it, but that spitfire is his cousin on his mama's side. So you should put a cut on her back—she's one of us even if she doesn't want to be." Thorn stared at me. "You understand me?"

"We make it right for her. And that's complicated 'cause she wants to be dancing here again."

"Then we make that happen." He smirked. "Are you part of what she wants?"

"Fuck that, I'm here because a brother called."

"Good plan. I'd steer clear."

Thorn was in charge of this mission and my senior in every way. "Is that an order?" The club could tell me to stay away.

Thorn's booming laugh filled the vehicle. "Fuck no— just free advice."

A smart man would take that advice.

Thorn glanced at his phone. "Turn up here. He's about five minutes away."

"I wish we had better intel on Frank Ricci. We know he's a nephew to DeLuca, but what's his role in the organization?" I hated not having all the details, but Thorn had made a good point. We needed to retaliate fast and send a message. This wasn't about business, and we wanted to keep it a personal situation.

We pulled into the apartment complex right off the strip, entirely too close for most natives, but this guy probably got off on the thrills the strip offered. First we both pulled on tight leather gloves—we didn't want to leave fingerprints. I tucked my phone into my back jeans pocket as I got out of the Escalade. Thorn and I headed up the outside staircase to the third floor where Frankie's apartment was located. As we headed down the outside corridor to apartment 327, we spotted someone coming out of the apartment.

It was Ricci. Thorn and I closed the distance to him and each of us grabbed an arm and dragged him back to his door. Thorn snatched the keys from Frankie's hand and we were inside in seconds. He'd decorated in all modern shit done in black and white—a player's pad.

Frankie licked his lips and opened his mouth, then shut it again. "I left just like you said. Why you fucking with me? You know who I am?"

"The man who hurt Glory. The fucker who will wish he were dead soon. I told you she was under my protection and that means you took on the Jericho Brotherhood when you beat her up."

No one fucked with us or what was ours. And Queenie was mine, or ours anyway. I shook the notion of mine out of my head as I stared at the prick. Sweat beaded on his brow.

"That was Angel. She went against him." He smirked at me. "You really going to push that door?"

"It wouldn't be the first time we'd evened the score

with the mob—you heard of Lucky. He fucked with us once."

Frankie lost color. Thorn shoved him onto the white couch while I snapped a before picture.

"What the fuck?" he belted out when my flash blinded him.

"I want Glory to see the before because no one will recognize you after I'm done here." I thrust the phone back in my pocket and focused on the bastard who'd caused this whole mess. "I warned you, but you didn't fucking listen to me."

"The whore asked for that shit," he spat.

I shot my right out and broke his nose. He howled with pain.

"Fuck, man." He spoke with a nasal tone now as he tried to stop the bleeding.

Thorn squeezed his throat until Ricci couldn't speak. "Never call her a whore. She's our sister, get me?"

He nodded and blood splattered the white couch. The red splotches already improved his décor.

"Why didn't you just let her go?"

"I break up with the wh—" He shot a nervous look to Thorn. "I mean she doesn't leave me." He gave us a cocky grin. "You don't want to fuck with me." Somewhere in the past two minutes he'd found some courage.

Good. It'd be fun to strip him of it and then watch him beg me to stop hurting him.

"DeLuca going to get revenge? For a piece of shit like you… I don't think so," I taunted him.

"I'm his—" He stopped speaking and gulped when Thorn growled. "I'm not someone to fuck with."

I gave him my three shot combo, right, left and jab. His head snapped back before he slouched forward, unconscious. I picked him up, slung him over my shoulder, and hauled him toward the back. With a kick, the bedroom door splintered and hung on a hinge. Thorn raised an eyebrow and went in ahead of me. I dropped the prick to the bed and looked around for what I needed. I found an extension cord that was sturdy enough to use as rope.

"In here," Thorn called.

The bastard had a huge walk-in shower with large sliding glass doors. A solid glass ledge housed the sliding-door mechanism. Thorn grasped the ledge and hung there. If it held his muscle-bound bulk, it'd hold Frank. I threw him the extension cord and he grinned. We had the same plan in mind, which came from working together too many damn times.

I rifled through Frankie's room and found a sap, a bat and a butterfly knife. There was something unnerving about being tortured with your own weapons. It sent a message almost more powerful than the beating.

It took your shit and beat you senseless.

Yeah, it induced a whole other level of fear.

Staring down at the idiot, I pulled off his shoes and socks before slicing off his shorts, underwear and T-shirt. I hauled him to the bathroom and held him up while Thorn tied him up so he could barely stand. I wanted him vulnerable in every conceivable way. Thorn and I had done this maneuver before on assignment. I had the precision to mete out pain without going too far too fast. A subtlety Thorn didn't possess. He tended to do too much damage, but we'd agreed to trade blows. And he'd promised to use control—at least enough to leave him alive.

I opened cabinets and doors in the kitchen until I found a deep pot—it'd hold a good amount of water. I filled it in the sink and carried it to the bathroom where

Frankie hung unconscious. I threw the cold water on him, aiming for the mouth and nose. The best way I knew to wake someone up.

Thorn stood back to avoid the water.

Frankie sputtered and coughed awake. He stared at me with hatred in his eyes. "You're going to die."

"We all are—some sooner than others." I flicked open the butterfly knife. "You first."

"No, man, my old man will pay big to keep me alive." Sweat ran down his temple.

"I won't be ending your miserable life, although you might wish I had."

His eyes tracked as I tossed the knife from hand to hand, then sliced across his cheek.

"Fuck, not my face."

I sliced the other cheek, likely not deep enough to scar. But enough to get his attention.

"How much pain can you take?" Thorn stepped forward and rang his bell with an openhanded slap.

He shook his head. "Uh…no, man, don't…" He kept talking but I tuned him out.

My first punch hit him in the gut, then another.

Thorn connected once in the gut and Frankie puked. I jumped back to avoid the splatter.

"You recognize this?" I grabbed the bat I'd found in his bedroom.

"Don't break anything," he pleaded as I connected with his knee. The sick crack of broken bone was as clear as his scream.

I worked him over with the bat with a slow precision. This work sickened me, but I remembered Glory's face, her bruised body, and I shut down the recrimination.

I dropped the bat and noticed the fucker was out again.

"Thorn." I nodded to the unconscious Ricci. He left to go get another wake-up call.

In a couple minutes Thorn was there with the same pot full of water. "Salt water." He tossed it on Frankie, who woke up screaming.

Picking up the sap, Thorn moved forward and landed the first smack on his junk. Ricci only thought he knew pain. On the second blow he threw up again, but nothing came up.

Ricci passed out again. Probably for the best because this next part would sting the worst. I took his knife and sliced across the top of his cock. He'd never think about fucking the same way again. That would definitely leave a scar. Every time he tried to fuck after this, he'd remember the lesson I'd taught him. I took the knife and sliced near his balls, wanting the suffering to last for weeks.

I glanced at Thorn, who nodded and untied the prick. He dropped to the tile floor. The cream tiles were smeared with blood and vomit.

"We gotta move him." I didn't want him accidently dying by choking on his own puke. I lifted under his arms and dragged him into his bedroom. Thorn kicked him as he walked by. I moved him, leaving him on his side on the white carpet. Ricci was still breathing, and he should count his blessings.

As we left his condo, I left the door wide open and hurried to the Escalade.

"Should I call the police?" Thorn pulled out a burner phone that all the security guys carried.

"Probably. We don't want him choking out."

Thorn made a call and we sped across town to the dealer and turned in the Escalade for a Mercedes SUV.

In a more compact vehicle, Thorn barely fit in the passenger seat.

"We need to send the message."

Thorn nodded and called home. Jericho had agreed to have a middle man reach out to DeLuca and explain we were square—to gauge what, if any, blowback we might expect.

My knuckles were bloody, but I'd avoided blood on my clothes. I'd never been the kind to get off on violence, but I'd had no trouble seeking retribution for my queen. I wondered what Queenie had been doing while I'd repaid the bastard who hurt her.

Chapter 11: Glory

"So what's your deal?" I frowned at my keeper. I'd shake him to demand answers but I hadn't recovered that much, yet. My body ached and that was after I'd taken the powerful pain pills the doc had prescribed.

The stoic Eagle just sat at the kitchen table playing solitaire. But the smallest sound had his eyes moving—he was a total predator. Yet I didn't feel safe.

I'd wanted Delta far away from me. But as soon as he left, the unease crept in and I hated it. The damnable truth was I felt safe with him, apparently only him.

Eagle didn't even glance my way.

"You could talk to me."

He didn't even show a sign he'd heard me. And that pissed me off on top of all my other churning emotions. I didn't need him. I didn't need Delta. I didn't need anyone.

Liar, my snarky inner critic shot back.

I needed to talk to someone. "Give me your phone," I demanded from my seat on the couch. He ignored me.

With effort, I pushed up from the couch and accepted the stabbing pain that greeted me. Once the pain had settled, I stomp-limped back to the kitchen and held out my hand. "Give me your phone."

The stout, bearded biker raised a single shaggy eyebrow at me, then turned back to his game.

"I need to talk to…" I almost said Avery but that wouldn't cut it with Mr. Silent. "With Rock."

He gave me a hint of a smirk and kept playing solitaire. I wanted to sweep those cards to the floor but I restrained myself. It wouldn't do me any good, and I refused to let this man provoke me into a full blown fit.

His phone pinged and he pulled it out of the front pocket of his blue flannel shirt, read the message and dropped it back inside.

"What?" I shouted in the empty kitchen.

He threw his head back and laughed, and not a quick laugh, but a long, good laugh. I had no doubt it was at my freaking expense.

The door banged open and Eagle stood up. "Fucking glad to see you." The first words he'd spoken since Delta left. He shot me a glance still full of laughter before he hurried out the door.

"You harass Eagle? He doesn't like people, you know." Delta smiled down at me.

"Me harass him? He wouldn't talk to me! And he laughed at me." I fisted hands on my hips and gave him a fierce scowl. "Tell me shit about what you two were doing, or give me a phone to call Avery."

Thorn shook his head. "I'm leaving this shit to you." He turned to walk past me. There was lots of room between me and the living room coffee table, but that biker was gigantic and dwarfed me and the living room.

I tapped my foot and tried to stay mad, but I couldn't, not with that idiot grinning at me.

"You should've been nicer to Eagle." Delta stepped forward and pulled me close to him, then swooped me up and carried me to the couch, placing me on his lap, yet again.

God, he smelled perfect with a mix of leather and cologne. I could've gobbled him up. But I didn't want him. If I kept repeating that then maybe I could remember I didn't want the blond Adonis. The arrogant jerk wasn't my type. I liked a more refined man. Hell, I had tried to like more refined men, but the rough-around-the-edges type always drew me in. Mark, Zero, Delta.

"What happened?"

He moved forward, kissing me with a gentleness I didn't expect. I fell into the kiss like a pathetic girl who'd spent the day craving it. Which I had, but I didn't have to act like it, did I?

Nope! You have some pride.

But my body was imitating a horny teenager who finally landed the quarterback. His kiss was dangerous, igniting a burn deep inside me that swept through me like a wildfire, the gnawing hunger of lust drove me forward. Maybe he wasn't what I wanted but he was everything I needed right now. I wrapped my arms around his neck and kissed back for all I was worth. I couldn't deny the tangible thrum of need flowing between us, and I needed some good, no, I needed some great!

My body melted into his until it felt as if we were one—merged together—the same pulse, heartbeat and breath. I'd never been so completely lost in another, and I didn't want to find my way out. No, I just needed to burrow deeper until he'd consumed me. Safe. Cherished. Possessed.

His arms tightened around me.

"Ow," I yelped in pain.

"Goddammit," he cursed, dropping his arms to his

side. "You make me forget everything." His finger traced the stitches on my cheek. "Like this and this." He stroked my bruised face.

He leaned away from me and I wished he were closer. "We took care of Frankie." He smiled at me. He slipped his phone from his pocket. "Want to see photos?"

I didn't. I thought I was bloodthirsty, but I wasn't. I mean I was glad he'd paid, but I was equally glad it wasn't me who'd done it. "Not really." I felt like a coward for saying that.

"Better that way." He nodded. "I didn't want to show you but it's your choice."

"Okay. What's next?"

"We gather intelligence on DeLuca and his protection. I'll want to shut down that porn business and make sure Angel gets the message that you're off-limits."

"How will you convince him?" I couldn't see how that would work. DeLuca was powerful, more powerful than the Jericho Brotherhood.

"I'm very persuasive." He traced my jaw. "I promised you I'd make this right, and I will." Without another word he stood and picked me up. "You need to rest."

"Put me down." I smacked his shoulder.

He opened the door to the room that held all the bags. "This is your room." He gently placed me on the soft bed. "TV remote there. And full bath in there. You need to rest and recover." He pointed to one of the bags. "That one has the cream from the doctor."

"Thanks." I smiled at him. "You can be nice when you try."

"Back at ya." He gave me a two finger salute and left.

I decided to relax with a hot bath. Lord knows my aching body craved it.

Over the next three days all I did was rest. Eagle never came back, and Thorn left for hours at a time, but Delta stayed with me. I wasn't sure if that was because he wanted to or because I'd irritated the silent Eagle. Either way, by day three I was feeling almost human again. The swelling was nearly gone in my face and the bruising much lighter. My sex and inner thighs still ached, but they no longer sent horrible random strikes of pain through me whenever I moved. I was on the mend. Today I hadn't even had to take the pain pills the doctor prescribed. Although I still took the ibuprofen to help with pain and the swelling. And I used that cream religiously because it really helped.

"Here's a suitcase." Delta stopped in my room. "Can you pack up your stuff?"

"Are we going somewhere?"

"Soon, maybe tomorrow, and I like to be ready."

I wished he had told me where or what was going on but I was happy to have something productive to do. I packed up the clothes he'd bought me along with the makeup. I still couldn't believe he'd done that. He'd been the best lover I'd ever had and he'd swooped in and rescued me without a single complaint, but the makeup had changed something between us. That was the action of a caring man, and it had touched me down deep where it counted.

I started down the hall toward the kitchen for a snack.

Delta came out of his room. "Thorn." His low voice was barely above a whisper.

I turned to see the giant in the doorway of a third bedroom.

Delta pointed to my room and mouthed. "Stay there."

What was going on? I had no idea why they were freaking out.

Then I heard it. A step, then two outside the door on the landing. Shit. Were we about to be attacked? I moved quickly to my bedroom and Thorn followed.

"Stay here until one of us comes for you." He thrust a gun in my hand. "Anyone but Delta or me comes through that door, just point and shoot." He winked. "Try not to shoot us."

I waited a minute, then peeked around the corner of my doorway so I could see the entrance to the apartment. I had to know what was going on.

Delta was on one side of the door and Thorn stood on the other, right where the door would swing to, but I didn't think even a door slamming into Thorn would slow him down.

Both of their gazes had homed in on the knob that was twitching.

"Fuck this." I heard the muffled expletive moments before a large crash of the door being knocked in deafened me.

Thorn stopped the door's momentum and shoved it back into the first guy through the door.

Delta whipped around and kicked the guy in the throat, I think. Anyway he dropped and Delta did something to the second guy and then I couldn't see, but I heard the crunch of broken bone and the wet smack of skin hitting skin. Thorn stepped over the fallen guy, peered outside, then turned back to me.

He picked up the bag in my room and grabbed two in Delta's but nothing from his, which I found strange. But this was no time for questions. I followed after him, staying a few steps back for good measure. He held up a hand to stop me, then turned the corner. Delta popped up and scared me because I was expecting Thorn to round the corner.

Delta gave me a quick grin and motioned me forward, clasping his hand in mine. I was freaking crazy because I smiled too. Why wasn't I freaking out? I stepped over another guy laid out flat. All in all, they had taken care of the men in seconds, really.

We made it to the parking lot and climbed into Delta's SUV. Thorn was smooshed up in the back although I'd offered to ride there. He muttered something about a clown car and folded himself into the back.

"You should have kept one awake," Thorn said.

"Bring one with us," Delta ground out. "I wasn't taking chances with Glory there."

"Fuck," Thorn grunted and pried himself out of the truck.

"Is he bringing one of the mob guys?" I frowned. "That's not a good idea."

Delta grinned with a scary smile that sent a chill down my arms. "We need intel, and between the two of us we'll extract all he knows."

"That's downright wrong."

The smile vanished. "This is your life, and I don't fuck around when it comes to people close to me. Get me, Queenie?"

I swallowed. "I didn't mean to criticize." But I had. "Sorry, this is just all scary."

Thorn opened the back hatch and threw in a bound man. This night was surreal.

Chapter 12: Delta

I drove north determined to put distance between us and the mob. Once I left the Vegas city limits behind I breathed easier. I took the exit for highway 95, and while it was busy, I could still spot a tail. And the mob wasn't known to leave Vegas without thinking twice. I hoped by leaving the city, it'd buy us some time to figure out how they'd found us and what I needed to do next.

The woman beside me was one hundred percent trouble. And I wasn't talking about the people chasing her. She was the dangerous kind of woman. It was easy to fuck and forget a simple woman, but a complicated queen with a bit of sweet underneath was a different matter entirely. She could snare any of us, and I didn't want it to be me, for a ton of reasons, not least of which was that she hated me as much as she wanted me. That love-hate vibe was really doing it for me and that was so fucking wrong.

To distract myself, I made a to-do list in my mind.

New wheels topped my list. I had a place in mind to question our guy and take stock of the situation. Then I needed to ship Queenie away from me before I did something totally stupid. Or maybe right after I did something totally stupid. I was me after all.

My ringing phone stopped me from further dangerous thoughts. "Go, Eagle."

"You need to evac, now." Eagle's voice echoed through the Bluetooth in the radio.

"Warning's too late, brother," Thorn boomed from the back.

"So you heard about Ricci?"

"What?" the three of us said at once.

"What are you talking about?"

"A team attacked the apartment a half hour ago."

"Fuck," Eagle grumbled. "Ricci is dead—just heard it. They'd been keeping it hush-hush the last couple hours."

"How? We left him alive?"

"Spleen damage—he died in surgery."

Fuck, that was bad news. An unease spread through me—we hadn't meant for this to turn lethal. I hadn't wanted to kill anyone. This shit just got a hundred times more complicated.

"You guys whole?"

"We're good. We left several of DeLuca's guys down at the apartment," I said, while trying to figure out how the fuck they found us.

"How'd they track us?" Thorn asked the question I'd been thinking.

"I don't fucking know, and I'm already heading out of town. We'll have to figure it out, though," Eagle said.

"See ya at the rendezvous." I punched End.

Glory looked at me. "We're fucked."

"We're fine," I said, although she was right. We were fucked.

Five hours later, I drove into Reno and headed straight to the Crow's Nest—a place owned by the Ravens. The Nest was a bar, casino and restaurant with a row of rooms out behind the main building. A bastard clubhouse and business in one, but it was as safe as anywhere could be. I could purchase additional firepower here before I headed back to Vegas. I had a lot of questions, but I knew one thing—I'd be back in Vegas fixing this mess. Ricci was dead. And that took this to a war—a war where we were way outnumbered.

I pulled up front. "Wait here, hide your face if someone comes looking."

"What the hell—"

I was gone and didn't hear the rest of her lip—she was too damn sassy, sexy and sweet. I hurried inside and grabbed a key from Mouse, the kid who worked the front desk for the club. After a quick exchange, I told him to have their prez find me when he had a few minutes.

Back in the car, I drove around back to the last one in the line—it was my preferred spot. I'd spent quite a stretch of time here three years ago, and I stopped in at least every other trip to Vegas to stay a night or two.

"Let's go." I opened the door to the room and Glory strolled inside. Maybe I should have gotten two since we'd be questioning this guy to figure out how much he knew. But I didn't like the vulnerability of having us in two locations, not until I had more reinforcements and intel.

Thorn carried the restrained guy inside and dropped him on the floor between the wall and first bed. "Going for a run." He turned and ghosted out the door. He didn't do enclosed spaces well, so for him the back of the SUV had been a prison.

Glory whipped her head between me and where Thorn had been. "I don't understand."

"You don't need to, Queenie." I chucked her chin,

then went to retrieve the desk chair. "Go get the bags from the car."

She opened her mouth to sass me.

"Or stay here with the bad guy."

She snapped her jaw shut and walked out the door with only a slight limp and returned a few seconds later with our bags.

"Good girl."

"Don't do that Dom stuff with me." She fisted hands on her hips.

"Do you want me to be your Daddy?"

She turned pink, then darker red before settling on crimson. "Don't even think..." she spluttered and stomped her foot. "Men." She threw her hands in the air.

I threw my head back and laughed.

"Are you like the others?"

"A biker?"

"Duh." She rolled her eyes. "I meant trained at the sex club—into all that kinky shit."

"You have to be more specific." I loved revving her up. "Which kinky shit?"

"Domination, submission, pain—kinky shit!" Totally pissed off now, she almost vibrated with anger.

"Well, I am not into any of the kinky shit you named, but that wasn't a thorough list."

Confusion battled with pissed-off on her face. Queenie was an innocent in all the ways that mattered. That should make me want to stay far away, but instead I had a hankering to educate her in my kind of pleasure. She bit her lip, so damn sexy, and wrinkled her brow. "What else is there?"

I swallowed the laugh because Queenie wasn't the kind of girl to laugh at, and she'd likely hand me my balls if I cracked a smile. "If you're brave enough, I'll show you."

She crossed her legs with a huff, but I wasn't sure that was a no.

I hated to change the subject but we needed to talk about the coming interrogation. "The guy there." I pointed to where the man lay struggling. "We're going to question him, hurt him most likely, until we know everything he knows."

She glanced down at the man, then away. "Why?"

"They shouldn't have been able to find us."

"Then this is because of me, and I'd be the worst kind of stupid to say don't hurt him. Do what you need to." She stared at the wall, not making eye contact with any of us. She was damn adorable. "Would it be a bad thing if I were to shower while it was going on?"

"I'd prefer it that way."

She didn't need to see either of us like that.

Thorn walked in and ended our discussion. Glory grabbed her bag of clothing and hurried into the bathroom. The snick of the lock was the only sound in the room.

"You going to wake him up?" I rolled the desk chair over and picked him up. Thorn scooted past me to the sink next to the bathroom and filled the small plastic ice bucket with water. I grabbed the duct tape from my go bag and secured the guy's arms to the chair supports.

Thorn threw the water in his face and he woke up. "This will be painful."

I crossed my arms and stared down at him. "We already know a lot, and pain will be dished out for false answers."

"Who do you work for?" Thorn bellowed.

The man turned his head but Thorn slapped him when he didn't answer fast enough. A slap from Thorn was like my punch, and the guy's head whipped from side to side.

"We need the knives." I rummaged through my go bag and pulled out a set of three razor-sharp knives. I could create pain with them. "Grab his shoes," I told Thorn as I unrolled the plastic sheathing. Three thin stainless-steel blades in increasing lengths lay in their protective case.

Despite what others advocated, I preferred working over the feet with knives. Thorn liked the stomach, but it was easy to go too far there.

I turned with my shortest of the three knives, pricking the tip of my finger with the point.

"DeLuca family, so don't fuck with me." He tried to sound tough but his eyes were so wide I could see lots of the white orbs. He was so scared right now.

"We're going to do worse than fuck with you." I let the threat hang there. "What's your name again?"

"Jimmy. Jimmy Ricci—Angel DeLuca is my uncle." He puffed out his chest as if this knowledge would save him. It wouldn't.

"Was Frankie related to you?"

The guy gulped and sat up straighter. "You know nothing! You killed Angel's son. You boys are dead even if you don't kill me." Satisfaction gleamed in the kid's wideset eyes. He wanted us to be scared of what was coming, but he should be more scared of us.

I drove the knife tip through the fleshy part of his shoulder under the shoulder blade. The idiot screamed loud and then louder still when I pulled it out.

"Explain that."

His head dropped but Thorn jerked him up by the hair. "You killed his son."

"Frank Ricci is Angel's nephew?"

"Nah, I am a nephew. Frankie is the bastard son—Angel's favorite."

Fuck me. We'd screwed the pooch bad. I'd sensed something off with the intel, but I'd gone ahead. Now the club was in deep. And unless we got creative fast, we'd be in a bloody war that lasted years.

Thorn punched him and the prick was out cold.

"Goddammit Thorn, he was just starting to talk. We still don't know how the fuckers found us."

Glory sauntered out just then in shorts and a T-shirt all fresh smelling with damp hair. I wanted to push her against the wall and fuck her right then. I managed to restrain myself. She stared at the guy duct-taped to the chair. "He spill it all?"

"Only about half of it before Thorn knocked him out." I pulled her to me, inhaling the scent of her shampoo. Not as great as the peach. I sat on the bed and pulled her onto my lap.

"What did you find out?" she asked again.

"That you need to be out of Nevada." Thorn had his phone in his hand. "Zero will be here in two hours and he's taking you back to Barden."

"What the fuck?" Glory shot up from my lap.

I just stared at Thorn.

He gave me that intense scowl he wore most of the time. "You can go back and protect her or take care of shit here."

He was giving me a choice? I always rode into danger. Protecting assets was someone else's job. And it would be this time. "You sending Eagle with them?"

"Nah, he'll stick with us. I have him on recon now."

Thorn nodded at Glory. "You need clear of this until we make peace here. Frankie was DeLuca's son."

"Fuck me." She stumbled. "I ain't ever coming back here."

"Yeah, Queenie, you will reign in Vegas if that's what you want." I stepped in and tilted her chin up until she met my gaze. "I promised you that."

"That was before you…before we knew—"

"I keep my promises. The club keeps their promises. Get me?" I spoke too harsh but the woman was under my skin.

"I get it." She rolled her eyes. "So you guys do manly stuff while I stay safe."

"Let's get food."

Thorn glared at the guy in the chair.

"I think we can let him sleep it off until after Zero gets Glory."

Thorn gave a nod and headed out the door. I waited for Glory to put on shoes and then we walked across the parking lot to the restaurant.

"The chicken fried steak is damn good." I expected some shit about her figure because she had a tiny waist.

"Sounds good." She sashayed that heart-shaped ass right past me and into the restaurant.

Before we'd ordered, we'd attracted half the Renegades to our table. They said it was to see me and Thorn but it was Glory who brought them over.

I might end up breaking heads before this meal was done. I had never been jealous, wasn't jealous now, but the way the Renegades eyed her just rubbed me wrong. She wasn't theirs—she belonged to the Brotherhood, whether she wanted to or not.

Chapter 13: Glory

The guys in the Renegades were sweet enough, but I
was done with them before I even finished the delicious
chicken fried steak.

"I got some business, you hang here." Delta nodded
to one of the bikers and they left together. Thorn had already disappeared.

I was sick of being left behind—the guys had left
me with the other bikers while they did secret club shit.
God, I hated the Brotherhood and the way everyone kept
picking it over me. Petty much? Hell yeah, I was. Mark,
Avery, Delta and MJ all those years ago. She'd started
the war with the Brotherhood when she'd torn our family apart. My mama had told me nightmare stories of the
drama back in the late seventies when Oliver Jericho had
ridden into town and swooped up my aunt, MJ, stealing her from Avery's dad, creating a scandal that still
rocked Barden. MJ had been engaged to marry Avery's
dad, and had left him days before the wedding to shack
up with Oliver Jericho. The two of them had formed the
Jericho Brotherhood. And MJ's betrayal had turned the
town against the club. Forty-five years later, there were
still ripples from those decisions. When Rebel joined
the club, his family abandoned him. Avery's dad had put

her in the hospital for marrying a biker, and the dissension continued to grow. My mama had made me swear to never join them, and I had, but that wasn't what really stopped me from falling for a biker. Bikers loved the club most, and I wasn't ever going to be second.

"Baby doll, you should come on over to my lap."

"I'm so thirsty." I cleared my throat. "If it isn't any trouble." Two bikers scurried away, and I was off the hook for sitting on a lap. I wasn't the approachable girl next door like my friend Lila. No, I was Cleopatra or Marilyn Monroe. Lonely women who ended up killing themselves. Overdramatic? Yeah. But I was ready for someone who saw deeper than the package I came in.

The guys brought me a beer and set a pitcher on the table. "Thank you, sweetie." I patted the one guy's face before I took a sip.

"You know, we'd love to have you stay with us until you can make it back to Vegas." Crow, the Renegades' leader, winked at me.

"I'll think about it, handsome, but I do miss home." A blatant lie. I never wanted to return to Barden, but I didn't want to be claimed by these guys either. Bikers were worse than cavemen.

Delta strode through the door, and my body went on point like a hound that had treed its prey. He glanced at me and then away, moving away from me to the bar.

He ignored me so I flirted with Crow. He had a thing for me, and if I liked hairy overweight guys, he'd be my man. These guys didn't follow the Brotherhood's muscle-bound example—most of them were kind of flabby and all around worse for wear. The Brotherhood bikers had always been muscle and gristle instead of fat, so I guess I thought that's how they all were.

"You're too damn cute for words. You should come on to the back with me." Crow smirked.

A cold chill raced through me as I glanced into his dead eyes. He might be a friend to Delta, but I got the impression that if I were alone, it wouldn't be a request. Just like with the Remington, I understood these guys were not my friends.

Glancing over at Delta, I said a small prayer of thanks. He could have been like Crow and his ilk, but he wasn't. I'd pushed him hard, yet he still protected me. Damn it. I hated to admit the Brotherhood bikers were damn decent.

And now they were going to what? I wasn't sure but I knew it'd be illegal. Delta and the others were risking their freedom and their lives because of me. Sure, they'd say it was about honor or some shit, but in the end, I'd called and they were here. My fucking white knight rode a Harley. I'd always dreamed of a white knight swooping in to save me, but he'd never ridden a Fat Boy and wore leather.

The door jingled, and I turned to the side to see the best damn sight I'd seen in two years. Zero strode in with that ruffled ebony hair and trademark smirk. Behind him a step was the redhead I'd lost my virginity to. I jumped off the tabletop where I'd been sitting and flung myself into Mark's arms.

He stumbled back with a laugh. "Hey, G, I missed you too." His voice had deepened some and he was a different man, or maybe a man, period. Another guy followed them—I didn't know that kid.

"Mark, you're sexy with those muscles." I gave him a smacking kiss on the lips. "Tell me what's happening at home. What's A doing?"

Mark chuckled and guided me to an empty table.

Kicking a chair back with his foot, he sat down and pulled me onto his lap. I happily sat there. He was as familiar as my room at home yet completely different. "You've changed." I narrowed my gaze and tugged his goatee.

Zero and the other biker walked over to where Delta held court.

"And you haven't." He flicked my chin. "Still getting in trouble and calling me to bail you out."

I frowned. "I think I called Avi, and Delta answered."

Now Mark frowned. "Are you two together?" Everything in him tensed.

Were we together? I sort of wished we were, but that would be a fantasy. He'd all but run away from me every time we'd been close. Besides one night wasn't a relationship, not that I was telling him that. "Please, he's got too much ego and too little respect for me."

Mark stared at me with those eyes that knew all my secrets. I wanted to hide away but I couldn't ever hide from him. "You slept with Zero, why not Delta?"

"Fuck you!" I tried to pull away but he held me tight.

"Stop throwing a fit."

I froze and stared at him.

"I ain't the boy you used to boss around, G, get that straight, yeah?"

"Did you just biker yeah me?" My temperature was close to boiling.

"I did. You better get me now because I ain't chasing you like a whipped pup."

"I didn't ask you to." A pain pressed into my chest, making it hard to get a decent breath. "I didn't…" I turned away from him.

"You did and I let ya. But that's over." He squeezed

me in a comforting way. "We got heat and passion—just no goddam sense between us." He whispered the words into my hair.

I just sat there trying to sort the way Mark had turned my world sideways. This man was the guy I'd known and he wasn't. I needed space and time to figure things out. "I want to get one thing clear with you."

"Get over here." Thorn's booming voice cut me off.

I looked up and saw the Raven Renegades were gone. I sashayed over to Zero and gave him a big hug. He was the same anyway—all he ever wanted was a good fuck. I frowned at Delta for making me face Mark and putting me in this goddam situation. Well, I had put myself here, but I didn't like being square between two alpha bikers bent on telling me how to live my life.

"Okay, you three take off—the less time here the better." Thorn made eye contact with Zero, then Mark.

That didn't make sense. We could wait here. "I want to wait—"

Thorn's quiet gaze scared me silent. He was one alpha biker I wasn't arguing with.

"Right, I just need to get some things."

Thorn used his boot to slide my bag across to me. "You need to go." He must have collected my stuff for me.

Mark nodded like a perfect soldier and hauled me out to a slick-looking Charger. At least it wasn't motorcycles because I didn't think my thighs were up to the challenge.

Chapter 14: Delta

I needed some fucking fresh air. Seeing Glory with Sharpie and Zero was far worse than watching her flirt with the Renegades. Sharpie had a claim on her and that pissed me off even more. I didn't want her, couldn't want her, but I did anyway.

A black sedan pulled up in front of my room. No one should be down there since Thorn and I had the two rooms at the end. As I got closer, I noted the dark jackets and wide shoulders. It had to be more of DeLuca's men. How the fuck had they found us so quickly? Had they marked me? Tagged the guy we'd captured? Too many questions and not enough answers.

I pulled my knife from my back pocket—never left home without at least one knife. I walked past the car, acting completely oblivious and let myself into the room. I heard the car doors open and the shoes hit the pavement. They rushed the door and I let them run in with no resistance. The first guy stumbled as the second guy plowed into him. I kicked the first one in the head and brought my heel down on his head to make sure he was out. Never leave an opponent to come back after you.

I shoved back and kicked the other guy in the chest, then came down on him, holding the knife to his throat.

He immediately stilled. With my free hand, I patted him down and discarded the gun I found in his waistband, fucking unprofessional.

"Get up, go to the chair."

He swung wide, trying to clock me, but I grabbed that arm and twisted until I heard the snap of bone. I pushed him forward and he went. In a few quick moves I had him secured to the last chair in the room. I bound the guy on the floor with the handcuff zip ties I always carried.

"We will just keep coming."

"Tell me how you found me." This was twice they'd found us when they shouldn't have.

"I found him." He bent his head toward the still unconscious guy.

The statement might be true, but I didn't think it was the whole truth. A good bluff is how I ended up with a million bucks, so I decided to bluff again. "That's not what he told me."

The guy looked from me to my cut. Why was he looking at my cut?

"Just because I lured you in doesn't mean I didn't know."

He spat blood onto the motel carpet. "Then keep on wearing it because when we don't come back, he'll send others after you."

"You should know better than to fuck with my colors." They'd pay for tarnishing what was mine.

He sneered and I knocked him the fuck out. I knew enough for now. I beat ass over to the Nest and tracked down Crow, the Raven Renegades prez.

"I need shit that will locate trackers, wires—that kind of high-tech shit."

"Wish that sweet piece had stuck around."

I wanted to fuck up his face for talking about Glory that way. I didn't like the look in his eyes, but I had enough enemies right now. "She's going home."

He pointed to another biker. "Take him shopping."

I followed the tall, thin biker down a hallway and outside to room one. Inside the furniture had been removed and shelving lined the walls and stood in rows in the center of the room.

"Back here." He weaved through the shelving units to the very back of the room. "This is the surveillance shit, likely this one will help you." He pulled down a device from the top shelf. "It fell off a federal truck, latest technology out there." He flicked two switches on the device and then started at my boots. "Lift your boot, sometimes you can walk on one."

Now I hadn't considered that, but it'd be a useful way to track bounties. "You have those?"

"Yeah, expensive though. They're the new bio kind… We have 12 hour, 2 day, or 3 day bio trackers—only onetime use."

"I rarely can retrieve the normal kind so that's not a factor for me." It was good that I'd won so much in Vegas because I was going to splurge here. I loved tech toys. JoJo would be so damn jealous. And Elle would try to steal them. "The app's easy to download?"

The guy nodded. "Yup, as long as you can download off market apps." He laughed as if anyone who came to this room wouldn't have already done a jailbreak on their phone.

It was standard in our club, and we had two prospects who were great at all the phone tech shit.

"So what do you want?" He wanded up my jeans and the front of me. He made it to the top and twirled his finger for me to turn. The device beeped three times and went silent then three beeps again.

"Fuck, you have one of the bio ones on you. There's no way to know how long it will last."

A burning anger consumed me. They had sullied my cut and insulted me. I would make them pay. "You got something that will block the signal?"

"Nah man, I don't. I haven't even researched how to block them. I'd fuck that prick up." The guy shook his head. "So whatcha want?"

"Give me four of the two-day bio trackers, that wand, a sharp knife, three throwing knives, and two Glocks." I turned and looked at the semi-automatics. "Give me one of those too." I pointed to an MP 5.

He whistled low. "I may need a damn calculator, that's over ten G, you need approval?"

I shook my head. The club wouldn't be paying for these toys.

"And extra ammo. And a handful of the normal trackers and two grenades."

"You going to war?" The man eyed me in a new way. Most did once they saw the bloodthirsty side.

"They fucked up my girl and now my colors. What would you do?" Why did I say stupid shit? She wasn't mine, and likely she'd be another brother's woman before this situation was finished. No way my brothers would let her slip away again. Women like her were coveted in the club. She had the hardness needed to thrive and the sweet we all craved.

I craved her but I wouldn't give in, so I'd push her out of my system.

"I'd take all my brothers and decimate those bastards, but you're talking mob, and that's serious shit."

"So I need serious weapons."

"I'm Cash by the way." He stuck out a hand. "Don't think we really met before. I just took over the armory."

"Nice gig." It was a big job and that said a lot about the guy in front of me. "I'm Delta. I'm a Vegas kind of guy, so I see you boys fairly often."

"You should plant out here—we could use another good club to have our back." Independent clubs like the Renegades and Brotherhood were different from the national ones. A chapter in every major city gave a different flavor to a club, so the independents tended to stick together.

"Not really our goal, but it'd be sweet to be close to Vegas."

"If we had another strong independent at our back, we'd move back to Vegas in a minute. The damn mobsters are too fucking bold."

I spied the black leather cuts they used for members on a back shelf. "Add one of those to the pile." I nodded my chin to the cuts.

"We don't sell them, but you can have one. You burning that one?"

"Nah, I'll put it to good use." I didn't believe in wasting opportunities. "Do the bio trackers work on skin?"

"What they were made for, although they work on any surface, and water doesn't matter. They just quit working when the electrical charge wears down."

I nodded. "The damage?"

"Twenty large and that's the price I give people I like." He assessed me with the cool savvy of a business man.

"Ten in cash and wire transfer the rest?" With a nod and handshake the deal was done. I wired the money and told him I'd bring over the cash. "I need a bit to fix my cut. Can I do that here?"

"Yeah, need a leather needle too?"

He moved to the small desk back by the bathroom, leaving me to slice off all my patches. Each one stoked my rage. My name, my one percent patch, our location, the small logo patch, the bounty hunting insignia Rebel had created.

The hardest to slice off was the image and club name on the back. I planned revenge as I popped each stitch. I'd sewn each of these stitches and they were part of my identity. I might be questioning my place in our organization, but that didn't change my loyalty in my club and what we'd achieved. Once the cut was just a vest again, I scanned the vest with the tool I'd purchased. The wand beeped, showing the tag had been placed. But I wasn't assuming there was only one tag, so I wanded each of my patches and they were clean. And those boys in my room got to stay alive. If they'd tarnished the patches, I'd have skinned them and left their corpses in the middle of Vegas.

I spent the next hour sewing each one back in place, then slid the new cut over my shoulders, but it felt foreign. I'd lived in my old cut for ten damn years and this one wasn't it. Cash headed over with three duffels loaded with my purchases.

"Man, you have skill, took me twice as long to do that." He nodded to my cut.

"I got all kinds of skills, most are deadly though."

Cash laughed and smacked my back. "That I believe." We separated and I headed on to my SUV, and he moved toward the Crow's Nest. I stowed the weapons in the back of the SUV and thought about going to the room to check on my prisoners but they didn't need my attention yet.

I strode inside the bar but the place was deserted. Thorn and Eagle sat at a back table and a couple of the older club members nursed beers at the bar. Apparently, Glory had been the draw.

Thorn turned his attention to me. "Well, what did you find out?"

"They bio-tagged my cut."

Thorn growled low in his throat.

"I agree." Fucking with a biker's cut was stupid, because it was the worst insult you could hand one of us. "This is a new one, but I kept the stripped vest in case we need to send a message."

Thorn grinned and turned all kinds of scary—I wasn't a man easily intimidated, but I was glad I hadn't pissed him off. "Let's load the garbage up. We don't need to bring trouble to the Renegades."

True enough. We crossed the parking lot, I laid down the back seat to make room for our cargo before I joined Thorn inside. With a shove, I rolled the one guy out of the room, pushed the chair down the steps. Hefting up the chair and the guy, I heaved it in the back of the SUV. The asshole's lip and nose bled, but he'd see worse tonight. Thorn carried the second guy bound to another chair out and tossed him in next to the guy in the chair. Both guys were wide-eyed, lying on their backs staring up at the roof. The whirl of spinning wheels made it all kind of comical, but those guys weren't laughing. Hurrying back into the room, I dropped three hundred on the bed for the chairs we'd taken, then grabbed the last guy taped to a chair we'd borrowed from another room. Thorn was behind the wheel, so I tossed the last fucker in the back. He smacked against the wheels of the chair and groaned. I shut the back gate and hatch before climbing into the passenger seat.

Eagle stood at the driver-side window talking to Thorn. "You sure you don't need me?"

"I need you to figure out more about DeLuca, and you can't do that in the desert. We'll take out the garbage." Thorn and Eagle clasped hands before Eagle took off in a rented truck.

"We need to teach a lesson and I have a place in mind." Thorn turned the SUV back toward Vegas. "You sure sending her away without you was the right play?"

Who was this dude and what had he done with the badass I knew. "You going soft?"

He gave a single shake of his head. "You two had something, I could almost taste it." He gave me that steady stare of his that had made lots of enemies crack.

"And I don't want it, so I did the right thing—the only thing."

Thorn nodded. "May not be that easy."

I ignored that comment and focused on the mission. "What do we need to know? You know what it'll take to make this right." I didn't phrase it as a question.

"DeLuca gone, and his organization wrecked." Thorn squeezed the wheel tighter. "Leave a void in Vegas, and that'll be on us to make right too."

"The Renegades—"

"Short-term fix at best." Thorn cut me off. "But we can't let DeLuca keep chasing after us, sending fuckers after us at his leisure."

"That will be two families we've crossed," I reminded him.

"You may be out here for a long while keeping an eye

on the situation." Thorn didn't look my way but I saw the vein pulsing in his temple. That meant shit was as real as it got. Most of the time, he didn't give off any tells. The man had been through such serious shit that nothing really registered anymore.

"Me? I'm nobody." I didn't want to take the lead.

"You're a soldier. Are you questioning the orders?" Thorn glanced over with those dead eyes.

"Never, brother. It's no hardship for me to be out here." In fact I liked the sound of it. Queenie's face flashed in my mind, but that was foolishness because she'd end up an old lady in Barden. And if she did, then that was the last place I wanted to be.

Thorn nodded. "We need to scorch the earth. But in a careful way. DeLuca has to vanish, his organization dismantled, but not even a whisper can attach itself to our club. You get me? We will do this, and no one can know we ever did it."

"Black op, all the way." I nodded. While I had investigated some covert shit, I had never really been part of the hidden world of black operations while in the army. Thorn as a Marine and then some kind of unmentionable secret soldier had lived the life for years.

"We get caught, it's on us alone."

I understood what that meant. "This is one woman, do we need to really go there for her?"

Thorn raised a single eyebrow. "This is about what we did to the heir—it's us or them. You know DeLuca has put a hit on both of us."

I whipped my head around. "What the fuck?"

"Eagle called me earlier, so I got the go-ahead from Jericho for this plan. He'll send us more brothers if we need them but I said less was more. Although apparently

Bear has an issue with DeLuca from years ago, but so far he's staying home."

The world we lived in—the edge of evil—was small and so many of us were connected to those who lived fully in the dark. The Brotherhood as a club walked a thin line of legality—we stayed on the upright side of that line, but we weren't afraid to descend to the dark. Like now. We'd take care of business and be done. However we'd found ourselves immersed in the murky depths of illegal too often lately. But each choice had been the right one and this one might not be right but it was the only one left to us now.

I had fucked up yet again. Now the club was in peril if I didn't fix my mess.

"I got no issue with fixing shit here and keeping watch after." There were brothers who would have a problem with what needed done, but Thorn and I weren't among them.

Chapter 15: Delta

Thorn gave a grunt, and silence descended as we took an exit off the highway and onto a blacktop road in the middle of the scrubby land that made up most of Nevada. Thorn didn't have his phone out but the man had a scary accurate memory for locations. We turned off on a dirt road and ended up in some low hills with no sign of civilization around.

"We bring them all out, let them watch. Leave the guy who attacked the apartment to last," Thorn said as we got out of the SUV.

"Got it." I opened up the back and dragged out the first one, and rolled him out into the desert scrub. Thorn grabbed the chair with the guy who'd been sent to get us today and basically threw it out of the truck, and the guy landed with a thud and muffled yell.

Thorn lifted up the original guy we'd captured and carried him over next to the other guy, then dropped the fucker and the chair flipped over. Blood oozed from a cut on his temple.

I set up the two who were on their backs. We had three prisoners lined up in a row, bound to chairs, trying to appear tough. It wasn't working.

"So this is the way this works." Thorn waited until

all three looked up at him. "We will know all you know, and it's just a matter of how much pain you want to endure in that process. There is a bare minimum required for fucking with us, but there can be a whole nightmare world you could avoid by telling us what you know."

Thorn stripped off his cut and handed it to me before stripping off his black tee. His torso was a maze of scars from his service. Whip marks, knife scars, burns and things I couldn't identify crisscrossed his chest, stomach and back.

I had almost nothing in comparison—a knife cut and a single gunshot wound scarred my body. I grabbed Thorn's duffel because it had the tools he would want in it. I'd worked with him enough to know he'd come prepared.

"We'll start with you." He rustled in his bag and brought out a Glock. He shot one of the guys in the knee.

The man howled. "What did I do?" He whimpered and moaned. "I'll tell you anything."

And he did. He told us about DeLuca's organization, his second in command, his compound and all he knew—low-level stuff. However my job was to watch the other two, especially the original guy, to see what he didn't want shared. My ability to read people was something I used with ruthless precision.

When the kid mentioned the number two man, the other guy looked at the man we'd captured the first night. The exchange had been quick but it told me something truly amazing—DeLuca's second in charge was taped to a chair. Apparently, he'd led the assault at the apartment and Thorn had chosen him as the one to take. Bad luck for him and great luck for us.

But the kid didn't realize it because he never looked

over to the second in charge, so number two couldn't even warn the kid off.

"They'll come for us." Number two spat the words. "We're all tagged."

I held up my old cut. "Yeah, I suspect they will."

Confusion lit up the other two guys' faces since they couldn't figure out why I'd bring it with me knowing it was compromised.

"Your turn." Thorn turned to the guy who'd arrived with the kid.

I thought of him as Stooge. Stooge was sweating and glancing at the kid, who was writhing in pain.

"He needs a doctor." Stooge frowned up at us. "You know we'll kill you, wipe you the fuck out."

Thorn didn't even look, just fired and hit the kid in the thigh. "What else you wanna say?"

"Shit, man, you're fucking crazy."

"Yes, I am, but Delta is crazier." Thorn stepped back and I took center stage. Everyone expected crazy from Thorn—the dude had it tattooed in his features—but I appeared so very normal in comparison. So my brutality shook them even more.

I cracked my knuckles. "You *will* tell me everything you know." I looked at the second in charge. "But I don't want you to know what I know." A single right cross to his jaw and number two was out before his chair back hit the dirt. "Check him." I nodded Thorn his way. While I was almost certain any guy would go down, I'd rather Thorn be sure.

"Tell me who he is." I asked Stooge once Thorn confirmed the other guy was out.

"Just a guy who works for DeLuca." Sweat beaded

on Stooge's brow and his gaze flicked between the guys on either side.

The sun was low on the horizon and soon it'd be dark and cold out here. The scavengers would be looking for a meal. And we'd provide them a feast.

I stepped forward and whipped out one of my throwing knives, letting it loose in a blur of motion. The knife came to rest in the fleshy part of Stooge's left biceps.

He howled. "Dammit, that hurts." He was hurting but not nearly as bad as he let on. The pain hadn't made it to his eyes yet. I yanked the knife out and drove it through the back of his hand down into the armrest of the wheeled chair.

Genuine pain drove his yell way up the intensity scale. The stooge's eyes were dilated and tight—finally had his attention.

"Try one more time." I pulled out a new knife and flipped it in the air.

"Jimmy Ricci—he's a nephew to DeLuca." The guy's voice was high and thready.

I pulled the knife from his hand. "And he is what number in the DeLuca organization."

He flicked his eyes to both sides and considered lying to me. I held up the knife with his blood on the tip so he could see it clearly.

"Alright already, he's number two." The guy looked at Jimmy, who was still out cold. "You guys are digging your own graves—our guys will be here soon."

I hoped so. Thorn had left me to question while he worked on something in the back of the truck. I hadn't asked questions but I knew the way his mind worked. Whatever surprise he was working on would be nasty and lethal. We were operating in the black now.

"Tell me, how do I get into DeLuca's compound."

He shook his head and kept shaking it even after I quit talking. With a flick of my wrist, a knife dug into his thigh, inches from his manhood. He screamed, but that was nothing. I grabbed hold of the knife and pulled it toward me, slicing open the top of his thigh. I purposely missed the artery, but that didn't do shit to stop the pain.

His eyes fluttered and I grabbed a handful of hair. "You don't want to pass out."

His head bent forward and he was out. I moved to my bag and grabbed the container of salt I always carried. It wouldn't take much. I smacked his face lightly enough to annoy and rouse but not enough to put him under worse. When he began to come around, I sprinkled salt in the fresh slice on his thigh.

"Fuck." He panted and shivered as the agony of salt in the wound spread through him.

He was almost done for—shock was setting in, so in quick order I sent questions his way.

"The access to DeLuca's."

"A code. It changes all the time—my code won't work by the time you get there."

"How many guys on guard?"

"What's the day?" His eyes rolled but he didn't go out again.

"Friday."

"Four on the weekends. Six on the weeknights. He likes—" Stooge licked his lips "—privacy on the weekends, but that could change after this shit."

"What scares him most?"

"Dying, having nothing to pass on—it's why that shit with his son is so bad. You killed his heir—the future he had planned on."

"Good." I spat the word.

"Man, he'll keep coming until you're in a desert grave." He tried to look tough but it was too hard.

"I know."

I spent the next ten minutes quizzing him on DeLuca's schedule and the details he might know. He sang with no more need for pain. He wasn't ever going to be a holdout. Number two thought he could hold out but he wouldn't. We'd barely scratched the surface of the pain we could give.

Our old boss had matched Thorn and me on several of this type of information-gathering missions because of Thorn's knowledge of pain and my ability to read people. The truth was that most people were just not equipped to deal with pain. And the random application of gruesome kinds of damage unnerved event the baddest of badasses. These guys stood no chance.

Thorn strode over with a bag and my former cut. He draped the bare vest over the guy, then knocked him the fuck out. The kid had passed out from the pain of his two gunshots, so no one was awake to witness Thorn bring out an IED he'd fashioned from some plastique explosive, a simple timer and bolts. He attached the device to the back of his chair, then turned the guy to face number two—that way Jimmy couldn't see the device either. By the time the sun set in another hour, no one would notice until it was too late.

"You take number two, I mean Jimmy?" I glanced down, wondering what else was in his backpack.

Thorn gave a single nod. "You don't need to stay."

"But I want to." I slapped him on the back. "We're in the black together."

Thorn searched in his bag and brought out wood

toothpicks. I took the left and he took the right. We began wedging them under his nails. He woke with a start as I finished the third finger.

"Fuck you doing?" he screeched.

"Morning, sunshine." Thorn grinned at Jimmy.

I shoved in the next toothpick and he jerked back, tipping the chair over, and I let it fall to the ground. Eyes wild, he looked around taking in the state of his two compatriots. "You're fucking dead." He spit the words out and Thorn slowly brought his huge boot down on Jimmy's chest and pressed until the man coughed.

Thorn eased the pressure until the man sucked in a rough breath. "Answer the questions."

"You'll just kill me—" The guy coughed as Thorn reapplied the crushing pressure.

"Worse things than death." Thorn's cold, detached tone spooked me.

"Yeah, okay, okay." Jimmy looked at the other guy. "Charlie, hey, Charlie." When his friend didn't answer, he glared at me. "You kill him?"

"Nope, not for me to do. But I suppose it's up to you if he lives." A lie that served me well.

"How's that?" Jimmy was calculating odds as he spoke. I could see his wheels turning as he tried to figure out the winning move in this no-win situation.

"I need you to answer me straight. Charlie already gave it all up, but I need confirmation, and every lie you tell me is longer these two have to bleed out, longer you will suffer in pain."

"What you going to do to me?" He gave solid attitude despite the pain that coursed through him.

"Nothing." I smiled. "My job is answers, but his

job—" I pointed to Thorn "—is to mete out the pain, and he loves his job."

"Keep fucking around, please." Thorn's menace carried through the words.

The guy gulped and his eyes met mine.

"How do I get into DeLuca's compound?"

"Fuck you." He tried to spit at me but lying back on the ground, that didn't work out for him.

Thorn grinned wide and knelt down to yank off his left boot. "The feet have so many nerves in them and so many tiny bones that a surgeon can never properly repair."

The man tried to pull his foot away but that wasn't happening.

I waited for the pop of the first dislocated toe and the scream to subside. That hurt like a bitch. "Compound code." I went right for the good information.

He gave it up without any attitude and the next three questions.

"Who else besides DeLuca, the bastard son, and you are in position to take over if DeLuca falls."

"No one, we're all he trusts."

That was a partial lie. I nodded to Thorn who dislocated, then broke each of the toes on his left foot. Jimmy's screams echoed in the night. Coyotes howled back. "Jimmy, maybe the scavengers will come for you before your friends arrive."

"Fuck, just kill me—I told you everything."

"Not even close." I walked past him, brushing those broken toes. "Still have a foot and two hands left."

"And his junk, we can break that too," Thorn added.

Jimmy pissed himself. "Okay, there are four other guys who could step in." He licked his lips. "Two are my sons but let me send a message and they will walk away." Tears streamed down his cheeks.

I nodded. "We can do that."

"The other two are Lucky Barnes and Jerry Mancini from the Remington."

Well, Jerry was much better connected than I had thought. It made me unreasonably excited to know I could visit serious hell on that particular pissant. He was the one who put Queenie in the situation to begin with.

We spent another twenty minutes with Jimmy double-checking and digging deeper, but he didn't offer any resistance—we'd broken him.

Thorn pulled out his phone to record the message. "Say what you got to say."

"Boys—two bikers, one too pretty and one a giant will be coming your way—"

"Thorn and Delta," I interjected.

"They mean business and I want you to go to your uncle in Jersey, stay there. No retribution, no power plays in Vegas—that's my final wish. Nothing but a clean start. You obey me, boys. I love you two."

Thorn turned it off with a nod. "They'll see it. For what it's worth, I hope they listen to you."

"They will, they're good boys." Jimmy licked his lips. "Finish it."

"Oh, how did you find me that first night?" I'd almost forgotten about that. I needed to know who to pay back for the loss of my cut.

"Frankie tagged you—only smart thing he did." The guy gave a hacking laugh. "Or maybe the fucking dumbest."

It was the dumbest, maybe second dumbest. His worst mistake was touching Glory. I met Thorn's gaze and we both cursed. We'd totally missed it. "Did he tag my friend?"

"Nah." He coughed again. "Only had the one."

As soon as we were back to the SUV, I'd wand Thorn—no way we were leaving here with any trackers. The next forty-eight hours were critical and the plans only worked if they didn't know what was coming or where we were. I grabbed the wand and flicked it on before running it over Thorn from top to bottom in a slow, steady sweep. No lights or beeps—he was clean.

"We wouldn't have needed that explosive if that bastard had marked me." Thorn's low rumble was almost inaudible, but I'd heard him.

"So we're good with this outcome?" Leaving these guys to draw in the others was a ballsy play because it required us to stay right here until we saw headlights closing in. Then we'd set the timer and drive out through the brush.

"Yeah, even if we only take out a couple of them, it will set the tone." Thorn grinned at me. "Scare the fuck out of them."

And frightened enemies were weak ones, so I couldn't argue with his logic, although I wanted to. I wasn't into blowing shit up or torturing my prey—a clear victory and clean kill when absolutely necessary—it was just how I had been trained.

We shot the shit as night descended. The scrabble and yips of scavengers grew closer, and the guys outside became more restive, hollering for us to help them and maybe crying.

I considered getting out and knocking the pussies out again just so I wouldn't have to listen to their bullshit.

"I see the lights." Thorn jumped out of the vehicle and

ran over to the three men. He knocked each out with a tap before he did something to the back of the one chair, then jogged back to the SUV. He started the vehicle and moved away, navigating without any lights and without running into any of the stubby bushes or small boulders. He had to have cat eyes to see without any light.

We were about ten minutes away when the explosion lit up the sky and shook the ground. Not earthquake big, but noticeable in the quiet no-man's-land. Thorn flipped on the lights and drove on. We'd started the war now, and I hoped we could get out of this whole.

Chapter 16: Glory

After a long day on the road, we stopped somewhere off the highway at a motel. It had seen better days and that was how I felt. My body hurt from sitting too long. I was beyond stiff, and I didn't look forward to moving. I'd thought I was more recovered, but eight hours in a car without the ability to stretch had done a number on my battered body.

Zero ran into the office and was back in a couple of minutes. "We're in 116 and 117, around back." He hopped in the passenger seat and Mark drove to the rear of the place.

Mark helped me out from the back seat of the vehicle, and I would've protested but I'd have fallen without his help. He frowned and guided me into room 117, and the inside was far seedier than the outside. The room sported two beds and an avocado color scheme that even the seventies couldn't have loved. The owner must have bought it all at an ugly décor sale because while outdated they didn't look forty years old.

The door I'd assumed was a closet opened and Zero walked inside. "Where you all sleeping?" He wiggled his brows. "You two down for the horizontal kind of catchup?"

Shit. I didn't know what Mark was thinking, but that wasn't even possible. However, I didn't feel like telling them about my bruised and swollen sex.

"Fuck off back to the other room," Mark growled.

Zero held up hands and backed up. "I'll order pizza while you sort shit out."

"Close the door," Mark barked.

The door swung closed with a snick of finality.

Before that confrontation would have flustered Mark, now he stared at me with those steady nutmeg eyes. "Want a shower before we talk?"

I swallowed and shook my head. We needed to figure out this crap as soon as possible. Delta's icy eyes flashed in my mind, and I felt like the worst kind of traitor. To Mark? To Delta?

It should be to neither because I didn't want anything to do with the Jericho Brotherhood.

"So?" I stuffed hands in the band of my yoga pants.

"So." He patted the bed next to him.

"Um, okay." I sat beside him. When had he become the take-charge kind of guy? The four years we'd been apart was like a decade, a lifetime.

"So, Glory." He met my gaze. "I spent the ride here thinking about us—about this minute."

I hadn't given him much thought at all. Who was a jerk? Me. "And I haven't."

"You've had a few things going on." He grinned at me. "And part of me wants to scoop you up, comfort you, and keep you close—but that depends on you."

"What do you want? If it's me in Barden, well, I ain't staying there."

"Then you aren't for me."

That stung. Not that I'd expected any different—it

was why we'd fizzled out before. It was the reason we weren't meant to be. That and his devotion to his club.

"Haven't we had this conversation…like a thousand times?"

He sighed. "Yeah. But this time we have it before we fall into bed together and you twist me up inside."

"Are you trying to be an asshole?"

He smirked. "Not really, but I am protecting myself, this time."

Ouch. How bad had I hurt him? "I never meant—"

He put a finger to my lips. "Neither of us ever meant to hurt the other, we just inflicted the pain without trying. But that's done."

"I didn't…you chose them," I sputtered trying to find the words I needed.

"I did." He didn't even have a glimmer of guilt. "And I would again. But we also get tangled faster than my earbuds, so I want us to be straight with each other."

Shit, he had grown up. Maybe more than I had. "Okay."

He gave me a sad smile. "Then we stay friends 'cause I'm done riding the Glory-go-round."

"Friends it is then." I struggled to keep my voice clear.

I'd lost him five years ago. There was a time I'd been sure he was my white knight. Maybe some girls just didn't get one.

"Ah, baby don't cry." There was the old Mark, the one who'd taken my virginity in the bed of his truck on an air mattress he'd bought just for the occasion.

I wasn't crying because of Mark—that had been inevitable. I was crying because I was still alone, and I was tired of being the strong woman alone. Tomorrow I'd be strong again, but tonight the world weighed me down.

"Stay there." I held out a hand. "You chose and I chose." I sucked in a steadying breath and tried to reassemble my armor.

"Bullshit." He strode over and folded me into his arms. "You're still my best friend," he whispered in my ear.

I fell apart. Being brave was too hard. I cried and it wasn't delicate or ladylike. Huge wails and heaving hiccups sounded in the room as I let out all the pain I'd held in. My bruises pulsed in pain, my body ached, and my soul was torn. No one tells you how much a hole in your psyche hurts—it was so much worse than all the physical pain combined. But I cried most because I'd lost the confidence I'd had before they'd hurt me. Now I was broken, wounded, and might always jump at shadows. Frankie and DeLuca bore most of the responsibility, but my willfulness and confidence had landed me in the situation. A situation others had tried to protect me from, but I was spoiled, protected, and hadn't expected life to treat me badly. A fool at best and a willing partner in my own downfall at worst.

"I did this." That's what I was repeating.

Mark soothed my hair. "Nah, girl you didn't do this."

"Fucking idiot." I sobbed and couldn't stop the tears or the freight train of memories of how I'd ended up in that room trapped.

I shuddered in Mark's arms. Then another person held me from behind.

"We got you, girl." Zero's deeper voice sounded from behind me.

What had I done to deserve men like this? Nothing. Truth was that I didn't deserve it.

I eventually cried myself out and opened my eyes to find myself sitting sandwiched between Mark and Zero, each holding on to me. What should have been hella awkward was only comforting.

I wiped my nose on my sleeve and sniffed, trying to get my shit together again. "Thanks." I cleared my throat. "I don't deserve this kindness."

"Yeah, ya do." Zero's certainty was deep and something in his voice dared me to question him.

"I changed jobs, right into that den of shit—thinking I knew everything, I didn't check them out with anyone or even consider life was like this for people like me."

Zero grinned. "I like that about you. You expect the world to bend to you."

"Well, I ended up laid out flat—so forgive me if I don't agree." Tears escaped and I wiped them away. "I am such a brat. Why do you even care?"

"You're our brat, Glory. And we protect what's ours." Mark rubbed my back in slow circles.

"You know what Delta calls you?" Zero gave me that playful half smile that probably got him laid every single night.

"Who knows? He and I bump egos on a minute by minute basis." As much as I appreciated his protection, that man irritated the hell out of me. "I can't be in the same room for two minutes without fighting with him."

"Well, just unzip his jeans—" Zero stopped speaking when I leveled my death glare at him.

Mark smacked the back of his head. "He calls you Queen."

Oh yeah. "I hate the name."

"It fits you." Zero grinned. "And queens rule—just like you do, babe."

Mark lifted and turned my chin until I met his gaze.

"This wasn't your fault. You have every right to expect people to be decent, or at least not be evil."

I laughed but it was hollow and cold. "Is that what life has taught you two?"

They both turned away, looking everywhere but at me. I didn't know Zero's story, but I'd bet he'd had more than a few hard knocks along the way.

"So we agree I fucked up." Guilt gnawed at me. All the feminists of the world could tell me I wasn't to blame but I was, and I hated stupidity, especially my own.

"We'll pay them back a hundredfold." Mark's dark anger surprised me.

"What? Why do you care?"

"I love you, G."

"Shit, am I interrupting—" Zero scooted back.

"We might not be the ones for each other, but I love you just as much as Avery or any of my brothers—you get me?"

Tears fell again.

Zero smacked Mark. "Way to turn on the waterworks again." He pulled me into his arms. "It's all right, Queenie, you got us even if you don't always want us." He held me. "Hell, I'd cry too if that idiot told me he loved me."

I let out a warbly, watery snort.

"Go shower and fix that makeup." Mark patted my shoulder.

I needed to regroup, and a shower sounded like heaven.

"We'll head out early tomorrow."

"Can we stop more tomorrow?" My body hurt. Only pride kept me from limping and moaning about the shooting bolts of pain that dogged each step.

"Sweets, I'll tell you in the morning. It depends on the news from Vegas." Zero sent a dark look to Mark.

Worry for Delta pierced me. "Will he be okay?" I bit my thumb. "What will they do?"

"Can't talk about it, but Delta is as badass as they come—he'll be fine." Zero grinned. "You're looking mighty raccoon-like with all those dark mascara marks."

They wanted me gone, so I did what I was told. I went into the bathroom and turned on the shower, but then I leaned against the door with one of the glass cups they had in there. I wanted to know more than they were prepared to tell me.

"You didn't claim her?" Zero's baritone was distinct.

"I told you my deal, and she wants Vegas." Mark's voice was muffled.

His choice—my choice—both still bothered me. I wanted to be the most important thing in someone's world, and I had been once in Mark's world, but I'd been too young—we'd been too young and now that was over.

"Fuck—this shit will get complicated." Zero kicked something. "Delta is sniffing around but that won't save her—she has old lady written all over her—someone's going to want to claim that."

"And that's not even the trouble that might come from Vegas." Mark's boots made scuffing noises on the carpet. He was pacing—a sign he was worrying. "How can we send her back there alone? Someone could claim retribution even if Delta wipes out the DeLuca organization."

I couldn't breathe. Delta was doing what? I slid down the door to the floor. What the hell had my stupidity caused? Guilt pressed me down, but I couldn't get much lower. A good man would have blood on his hands because of me. Why hadn't I just stayed at the Starlord like a sensible woman?

I didn't even know how to pay back this kind of debt. I took in a big breath, then another and another until finally I forced myself to stand up. I stripped off my clothes and stood under the scalding shower. One word was burned on my brain—*retribution*. As the water washed away some of the shock of what I'd heard, another question surfaced.

Was I selfish enough to go back to Las Vegas where I might not be safe?

I could have a good life with someone. Mark was the past—we both realized that now. But according to Zero, I was in demand. Did Delta want me? A shimmer of liquid pleasure washed through me and suddenly I wished he did. However, that wasn't reality. He'd shipped me away as quick as he could. No, Delta wasn't an answer to my problems—he'd already sacrificed too much for my mistakes.

I stayed in the shower until it ran cold, trying to delay the reality facing me. I dried off and each pat on one of the bruised areas reminded me of the beating I'd received. I needed a do-over, but just how far back would I have to go to make my life right? All the way to the beginning most likely, so there was no point in wishing away what couldn't be changed. Instead I needed to own my mistakes and not compound my trouble with more.

I slipped into the shorts and tank that Delta had bought me. They fit perfectly and that made me question just how many women he'd shopped for. Jealousy reared its ugly head, so I stuck a tongue out at myself in the mirror. "Stop being a brat," I told my reflection.

The bruises looked worse in the fluorescent light of

the bathroom. Of course it could also be because I was
paper pale—the day had drained me and all my color.
The marks on my face and arms were dark contrasts to
the rest of me. While I didn't ache as bad, my ribs protested every time I moved, and on my inner thighs a net-
work of bruises ached from the ride. With the makeup
gone, I looked like someone had used me as a punching
bag. And the deep purple and green bruises on my thighs
peeked out of my shorts. Maybe I should put the yoga
pants back on. I couldn't hide—not my stupidity, my injuries, or anything else. It was better to face it head-on.

I opened the bathroom door to the smell of pizza. My
stomach grumbled. The guys were sitting on the bed with
their back to me, phones in hand. I hurried toward the
food and grabbed a big slice with the works on it—just
how I loved it. The guys turned and stared at me.

"What?" I said around a mouthful of pizza. Mark
dropped his slice on top of the box and prowled around
the bed toward me—his gaze never left me.

"Why aren't you still in the hospital?" Zero growled,
his own pizza left on the bed.

"I'd be out now anyway," I protested. Wouldn't I?
"And it wasn't safe." How had my life changed so much
in so short a time?

"Did you even get any meds?" Mark demanded.

"Yeah, but I don't need them anymore." Although
maybe I'd take one tonight to help me sleep.

"Lift your shirt." Zero's dark gaze wasn't something
I was used to. He always had a smile on his face and a
funny quip. But that guy was gone and in his place was
a biker every bit as dangerous-looking as Delta.

"I am not—"

Zero tugged it up so quick I didn't have a chance of preventing him.

"Fuck, Glory!" Mark shouted. "Those bastards." He whirled around and hit the motel wall. His fist went through the cheap wall, leaving a hole behind.

I jumped back at the violence.

Mark spun to face me with anger creating hard lines on his face. "We drove eight straight hours here with you in this condition. Why didn't you say anything?" He dragged fingers through his strawberry blond hair. His gaze zeroed in on my shorts. "What the fuck happened to you?"

I stepped back and back until I stood with the wall to my back. I couldn't get my breath, and the harder I tried the more faint I felt. Flashes of Frankie's fist coming to my face repeated over and over. Spots floated in my vision.

"Shit." Zero hurried toward me. "Come on, hon, sit down, bend down and breathe in slowly." He rubbed my back. "Breathe in, one two three, now hold it for three. Now breathe out for three."

I made myself do what he said although it felt like I'd pass out from the lack of oxygen. Heart pounding loud, I fought to control each breath until finally I started to recover. Eyes pressed shut, I calmed and forced the image of the fist from my mind.

I glanced up to see Mark, head bowed, standing where he'd been when I freaked out. My first full panic attack—another first I didn't want.

"I'm better now."

Mark didn't look up.

"I said I am better, but the doc said I could have these

weird reactions for a while." I forced a smile. "No way for you to know."

Zero shook his head and shot a hard look at Mark. "We knew because Delta told us and sent a link and everything. Sharpie just lost his shit."

Delta had sent a link and told them? "But not that I was bruised?"

"Seeing it is a lot different than knowing it. We shouldn't have pushed you so hard today." Zero looked away.

"I am fine."

Neither looked at me.

So I shouted it. "I. Am. Fine!"

Both whipped their heads toward me.

"Stop with all this guilt. You didn't beat me up. I am a lot better and will be totally fine real soon."

Mark and I stared each other down—neither wanting to give in.

Zero strode forward and put a light hand on my shoulder and another on Mark's shoulder. "You heard the lady—let it go."

I clamped my mouth shut to keep from screaming.

"No wonder Delta is on the warpath." Zero shook his head. "None of us like women being marked, but he takes that shit personal."

"Why?" I desperately wanted to know more about him.

Zero's face went blank. "Ask him."

Stupid men and their codes—it wasn't like I'd asked for his darkest secret, or maybe I had. I was tired and sore and ready to rest. "Get out of my room." I made shooing motions. "I want to sleep."

"No, we need—" Mark still had that pity in his eyes.

"Leave the door open and get out." I couldn't stand another minute of their hangdog looks and grim anger. I knew I'd screwed up, and seeing it reflected on their faces didn't help a damn bit. At least Delta hadn't pitied me. He'd given me revenge and respect.

Mark booked it out, but Zero grabbed one of the pizza boxes before following Mark back to the other room. I lay down on the board-hard bed and stared up at the dirty white ceiling that had seen better days. We were both tattered, but a fresh coat of paint wasn't fixing me. I'd put on a brave face for the guys but their reaction had laid open the wound created by those thugs.

Maybe I wasn't cut out for Vegas and the hard edges there. I was a small-town girl who'd walked into one of the oldest schemes around. I should've known if it appeared too good to be true, it was. Otherwise everyone would be vying for a spot there. What was so clear to me now hadn't even occurred to me before.

I was spoiled rotten, used to getting everything handed to me, and that had been my downfall. I wasn't a horrible person, was I? Just one used to getting my way, and even in Vegas where beauty stood on every street corner, I'd assumed different rules applied to me.

That ended tonight. I would never be selfless like my friend Lila or sweet and funny like Avery, but I could get real and accept responsibility for my life. Delta's piercing blue eyes flashed in my mind, replacing the heavy thoughts. I wanted him and I didn't. He was everything that could devastate me, and I didn't think I could take another blow.

I'd become good at protecting my heart, and maybe that should change too. But not where Delta was concerned because I wanted love and a family, but he didn't.

I was almost thirty, and it was time to move to the next stage in my life. With that thought, I drifted off to sleep.

The guys' voices comforted me when I woke in too much pain the next morning. I focused on getting out of bed and in the shower before they descended on me. The car ride yesterday had been a slow kind of torture, and my body told me how much it had hated the ride. I snagged my bag by the bed and hobbled into the bathroom, locking the door behind me. I stood panting and willing the pain to recede. With effort I dug out the pain meds and took one. I'd need it if we were traveling as far as we did yesterday.

When I turned, a piercing pain shot through my left eye socket and through my brain. I braced myself on the sink and waited for it to pass. With ginger movements, I eased under the spray of water. The water hitting the bruises stung, then the heat eased into me. My muscles relaxed and my breathing slowed. I made myself leave the shower and spent another twenty minutes applying makeup and blow-drying my hair.

I straightened my shoulders and swore I'd punch the first idiot who pitied me today. I strode out, ignoring the twinges of pain with my head held high.

Zero glanced my way then back again. "Someone woke up sassy."

I flipped him the bird. "Let's get a move on." I threw my bag over my shoulder and suppressed the wince that came from the impact of bag on bruise.

We stopped at a small café and the guys ate a huge breakfast, though I didn't have much appetite. While the guys stuffed themselves with food, I pushed mine around on the plate.

We left Albuquerque about ten thirty in the morning

and by noon we'd stopped again. The guys were taking it a lot easier today.

"Got a message from Delta." Zero checked his phone. "We can take our time." He glanced at me. "I have no idea when they'll be back, but he says the threat to you is minimal."

I nodded and wished I knew more, but secrets were another annoying biker quality. "Let's go—we're wasting daylight."

We spent another night on the road, then rode into the club compound around ten in the morning on the third day.

The front door of the clubhouse banged against the cement side of the building and Avery barreled through. I'd barely gotten out of the truck when she rammed into me, squeezing me tight.

"Ow!" I yelped when a wave of pain tore through me.

I stepped back and Mark steadied me. "She's injured."

"Yikes." Avery jumped back and her eyes widened. "Your beautiful face…" She reached out a hand. "It's so bruised." Her face screwed up into a tight scowl. "Those bastards—they better pay."

"They will." Mark gave Avery a one-armed hug.

Rock, Avery's man, strolled out with his stacked muscles and badass frown. "You okay?" He scanned me up and down.

"I could use a shower and a rest." I needed a bit of time to myself. In the past, it had always been Avery, Mark and me, but that had changed. They all wore Brotherhood cuts, they were a family, and I was alone. I was an outsider, and had been for years, probably why I hadn't come home for the past four years—I hadn't wanted to face the truth.

"Come on. You okay with one of the club's rooms? They are tacky but clean with a bed and shower." Avery kept up a nervous stream of chatter as we walked through the club's main room. It was less cluttered and cleaner than before. About twenty bikers sat at tables with the remnants of breakfast on their plates. Eyes appraised me as I strode through trying to look stronger than I felt. I didn't need this kind of attention. It was as if every one of my bruises was a flashing neon sign drawing attention to my stupidity.

We finally made it to the room and Avery shut the door. She gave me her goofy grin and a much gentler hug. "Tell me everything." She plopped onto the bed.

I opened my mouth but nothing came out. Exhaustion stole my words. I had nothing to say, and worse, I felt like a stranger sitting here with Avery. Our lives had diverged and the distance between us felt immense.

"I'm so tired. Can we talk after I shower and nap— my body aches so bad." That was the truth. But I had no idea how to close the chasm separating us.

"Sure." Avery patted my leg. "You rest. I'll be here for you." She jumped up. "Now that you're back home, we'll have tons of time to catch up."

Did she think I was staying? "I am going back to Vegas as soon as Delta says it's all clear."

My best friend crossed her arms and gave me that stubborn look of hers. She didn't agree with me. "Shower and rest. We'll talk after."

She ducked out the door before I had a chance to say anything else. I sat there staring at the closed door. Why was coming home so hard?

Chapter 17: Delta

The alarm on my phone blared and woke me up with a pounding head. It's a fool's task to try and outdrink Thorn, and I'd been the fool last night. My mouth was hairy and my memory full of holes. I trudged into the bathroom and flipped the shower to scalding before stepping inside. The hot water peeled away the fuzz clouding my brain. We'd spent the past day gathering information, and now it was time to plan. In fact that's how I'd ended up with a headache, by trying to plan when Thorn had been in a drinking mood. All we'd ended up doing was rehashing what might have been if we hadn't fucked up DeLuca's heir.

And that's when the night grew fuzzy. Thorn had pounced on me, trying to get to me admit feeling for Glory. I refused to buckle and had ended up with this hangover as we emptied bottles while we argued. Queenie had attitude and could make even Thorn dance to her tune if she tried. A woman like that was trouble, and if you were a lucky bastard, she'd be your personal trouble for your life. She wasn't for me.

But one question haunted me. If I had the ability to do it over, would I do it differently? Nope, not really. Glory Atkins was worth a hundred entitled gangster royalty.

After I got a text from Thorn to get ready for breakfast, I finished dressing and hurried to the SUV. He was already behind the wheel.

"Took you long enough." The man didn't show a single sign of a hangover. He put the vehicle in gear and drove a few blocks to the dive diner where we'd been eating since we'd returned to Vegas.

The door beeped as I swung it open and strode inside. The furniture and décor had been outdated twenty years ago, and the smell of grease and cigarette smoke hung in the air. The waitress stopped by with coffee and grabbed our orders. Thankfully the food came damn quick.

"Why don't you get hangovers?" I grumbled and dug into the steak and eggs she'd set in front of me. I loved a bloody steak with sunny-side up eggs.

"Who says I don't. Just don't let it bother me. Not worth my time." He ate his ham steak then gave me a smug grin. "How we doing this?"

"We need to make it appear that another gang took DeLuca out."

Thorn nodded. "I have Eagle checking into the tension between DeLuca and others. We need the right misdirection, maybe even need to set up some noise between DeLuca and a rival."

"I hate this covert shit."

Thorn just smirked and focused on his plate. We ate quickly without small talk.

"You should have gone back." Thorn mopped up the last of the egg with his toast.

"Fuck you." I'd already finished and sipped my fourth cup of coffee. "She's not mine. You didn't see the way she lit up when Sharpie walked in."

Thorn shook his head. "You're wrong there, but whatever."

I wasn't wrong.

"You know it'll happen. She's coming back here, and you'll be here…just saying."

"Maybe she'll stay in Barden." I didn't think she would.

"Nah, and Sharpie won't leave there, so that's not happening. Zero isn't falling for one chick, so she's going to be here with you. All that sexy so close—no way to resist that shit." Thorn gave me a shit-eating grin. "I'd fuck her in a minute if she wasn't scared of me." His gaze went distant.

"That waitress doesn't have that problem."

Thorn grinned wide. "I know that shit is right, and I'm gonna tap that, soon. Want me to see if she has a friend?"

I hadn't been laid in days, and normally my answer would be hell yeah, but I wasn't feeling it. Not that I'd be admitting that aloud. I scraped back the chair on the worn tile floor and stood. Dropping a twenty on the table I strolled out. I walked back to the hotel, and in my room I changed into running clothes. A run would clear my head and get those endorphins pumping. Before I'd made it a half mile, sweat soaked my shirt. It was 94 now and would only get hotter but still nothing like the Iraqi desert. With headphones blaring some hard-core metal I picked up my pace, needing the burn.

I cataloged the facts I knew, which should have reassured me, yet I was unsettled. I juggled and shuffled the facts but I couldn't get them to balance—something was still missing. How did a group like DeLuca's have any power in Vegas? What was their business line? And what did Jerry do that put him so far up the food chain?

Jerry could provide answers. With a plan of investigation, I felt better. Seek and destroy was Thorn's thing—I'd been trained to find answers, and I needed a lot more of them.

I sprinted the last mile back to the hotel. I ran up the steps to my second-floor room. The waitress was leaving Thorn's room. "Hey, cutie, you fuck like your friend?"

I threw my head back and laughed. "He's one of a kind." And I slipped in my room, turning down the offer she clearly made.

I showered and came out to pounding on my door.

"Where the fuck you go?" Thorn plopped down on my bed.

"Run to clear my head."

"I found the cure for all that bothers you." He grinned and lay back on my bed. "That old girl had some tricks."

I didn't mention the offer she'd thrown my way because I didn't need any more shit on my lack of sex—hell, I didn't even understand why I wasn't interested.

"I'm going to go see Jerry and get some answers."

"Eagle is on his way over with intel."

Thorn's phone buzzed then a few minutes later a single knock sounded on my door. I opened it for Eagle. He looked at us both and shook his head. "Why do I always get the shit jobs?"

"Your mama cursed you with a forgettable face." I grabbed the bottle of whiskey from beside the bed. "Drink?"

Eagle took my bottle of Pendleton and drank it down. "That's smooth." He set the bottle on the TV stand. He strode over to the desk and rolled the chair away before he settled in. "Why do you guys pick rattraps?" He lifted an eyebrow.

"Where are you?" He was known as a bit of a hotel snob. But in the security business, you spent lots of time in a hotel or motel. In fact some of the guys didn't even have a house, just moved from job to job.

"Off the strip in this great boutique place—nicer by far." He pulled a small notebook from his front T-shirt pocket. "What I know is pretty simple. DeLuca has three new bodyguards since last night. You guys killed all three of the ones we captured and got two of the others who came to the rescue. Three made it back to report." He looked up with a wolfish grin. "Good job with the IED." Eagle had never told me what branch of service he came from but I knew he'd been in black ops and it had ended badly for him.

Thorn nodded. "Had to send a message."

"And they listened. Let's see. Jerry is at the Remington hosting some high-roller deal today." He glanced at me. "You invited?"

"Yup, planning on getting more info from Jerry as soon as we're done here."

"What I can tell from the compound confirms what you found out about the layout and security. DeLuca cancelled his plan to go to Jerry's party and is holed up at the compound. Right where we want him. His sedan is armored and he travels with all his guards now, so the compound is our best bet—the protection is spread thin there."

"What are their business lines?"

"Hard to say, and I have tried to find out. People say they have a hand in porn and prostitution, a bit of loan sharking, but that doesn't add up to a seat at the mob table in Vegas. They have to have another line, but no one is talking about that." Eagle flipped the page in his notebook. "My gut is saying money laundering—it makes some sense, but I can't confirm it."

"Whose money?"

"I'd say other mob money but I have no fucking clue, hopefully Jerry does." He glanced up again and frowned. "As far as I can tell, Jerry is the only one on your list from the targets who isn't at the compound—oh, except that guy's kids—they are out of town and arriving at the airport about five tonight." He blew out a breath. "What will we do with those kids?"

"Do what we told Jimmy we'd do." Thorn sat up. "I'll meet them at the airport and send them to Jersey on a plane." He didn't say anything about option two, but hopefully the boys were as smart as their old man.

"Tug on them about the money laundering. Could be Jimmy is sending them away to preserve the business." Eagle frowned. "That actually makes a lot of sense— better shake them down."

Thorn sighed. "Does having kids make you a prick? The fucking father is always about protecting the empire, not the children."

"They're in their twenties." Eagle shrugged. "What's next?"

"You find out about enemies?" I needed this op done and over with.

"Not much there. Maybe some tension with the Chinese mob—but that's with the Italians in general. The 14K Triad is building a presence in Vegas."

"Okay, follow up on that, Eagle. I like that idea." Thorn grinned at me. "Take him with you to see Jerry. Let's meet later and see if a plan develops."

We all left my room, and I followed Eagle to his truck.

"Thorn is a spooky brother." Eagle buckled up beside me.

I hadn't worked with Eagle often. Over the years, bikers in the security business created their own small squads. Thorn, JoJo, Mole and I had made up a squad many times in the old days. "Who do you normally work with?"

"Levi, Nitro and Bravo. I worked with Ringer back in the day." He grinned. "Now he's getting fat at home."

"Don't know about fat, but definitely lazy." I laughed. Ringer was good people but more uptight about shit than either Thorn or me. "You good with the plan—it's scorched earth."

He licked his lips, his biggest nervous tick. "Yeah, I'd be lying to say I'm not worried but I'm good. I've missed the last couple hot encounters, so I'm in."

"Those are the magic words."

"You really come here and fleece these pro players?" Eagle grinned at me. "You don't seem the type."

"You're not the only chameleon, brother."

Eagle had a way of fitting in everywhere, and while I wasn't as good at it as he was, I could change up my look and demeanor when it served me.

We pulled in at the Remington and Eagle let the valet park his truck.

I strode through the door and two men with hulking muscles and bad-fitting suits headed straight for us. I picked up my pace and kept going for the one on the left. I pulled back and clocked him on the jaw, he stumbled back, and I kicked his knee. I heard the squish of cartilage and tendons—he was down and out. I moved to the staircase with Eagle on my heels. His guy was down but I hadn't watched how he'd done it.

"What floor?" Eagle asked from behind me.

"Seven."

He swore low but didn't say anything else. We ran double time up the flights of stairs—something we'd both trained to do in the military. Sweat ran down my temple by six—I needed to do more stair laps in my training. I glanced over at Eagle—the motherfucker wasn't even breathing hard. Worse, he had a shit-eating grin plastered across his face.

"Need some PT?"

I rolled my eyes with a snort—cocky bastard—then went through the door. It was quiet here. We were about three steps from Jerry's suite when the door swung open and two more gorillas rushed out. Eagle dashed past and into the suite, leaving me to face the ape twins.

They turned, surprised Eagle had raced past them. I used the moment of confusion against them by rushing the one closest to me. I kicked out to connect with his knee—big guys often had weak knees. The familiar crunch sounded as he dropped to the ground. I connected elbow to jaw as he fell, knocking him out. Idiot two had cocked his arm back but I slid low and punched him in the family jewels. He dropped and I ran past, giving a quick double knock. Eagle opened the door and I walked in to find Jerry staring at me, already duct-taped to a chair. I wasn't the only one who worked fast.

"Jerry, you little bastard. I'm going to enjoy making you squirm." I cracked my knuckles and Jerry swallowed hard.

"I'll tell you anything, Ren…just name it."

"The name is Delta, and I'm sure you will."

* * *

Two hours later, we left the hotel suite with all Jerry knew. I'd bet my last dollar on it. We'd had one tight moment when more of Jerry's bodyguards tried to break up our party, but I handled them. He deflated when we'd taken those guards down but had held out until Eagle pulled off his thumbnail. That was serious fucking pain. At that point a blubbering Jerry told us everything. We had access codes, guard counts, security measures, everything we could think to ask, including the secret— DeLuca laundered money for two other mob families, which made the Chinese angle look better. Taking out DeLuca would cripple three organizations and hurt the entire system.

When I'd gotten everything I could from him, I gave Eagle the nod. He went to stand by the door. I knocked Jerry out and Eagle and I carried him out to the elevator. Using Jerry's badge we took the elevator straight to the underground parking where we stuffed him in his own trunk. Eagle drove his car back to the motel where Thorn and I stayed.

We knocked and Thorn let us in. Guns, ammo, explosives, gizmos and knives were carefully arranged on one bed. We could capture a small island, hell a large island, with this kind of hardware.

"What the fuck?" Eagle's jaw dropped.

"I like being prepared."

Gaping at me and back to Thorn, Eagle just shook his head and didn't say another word.

"You get what we needed from Jerry?" Thorn lay on the other bed in the room.

"Oh yeah, more than we need." I started laying out all the juicy bits Jerry had told us. Eagle jumped in from time to time. "What's the tension like with the Triad now? Will a hit be believable? And how would they hit them? We need more intel, brothers."

Thorn sat up and grinned. "I'll research the 14K war style—I know a guy."

"And I know a couple guys who can tell me about the Triad and mob tensions on the ground." Eagle gave a nod and left.

"That leaves me watching DeLuca, I guess."

Thorn nodded. "And Jerry needs to be gone." He made a motion across his neck. "Be best if no one could find a body."

"I will take care of that." He'd been just as guilty as Ricci in my book. "And watch DeLuca."

With a bit of luck, I could totally start real tensions between the two organizations with Jerry's death. I couldn't think of a man who deserved it more.

I'd investigated a Triad case as an MP, and I remembered three things: they liked knives and fire, each clan had a lot of independence, and they hated the Italian mob. I planned to use all that to my advantage.

I started Jerry's car and drove across town to the small Asian district in Vegas where the 14K clan of the Triad had set up shop. I would use Jerry's death as a play in our black op. I called Eagle to see if he had better intel on where to dump the body within the Triad territory. We wanted this to look like a professional hit that would withstand at least a little examination by the cops or the mob.

Eagle didn't pick up, so I texted the question. In a moment my phone pinged with an address—just outside the heart of their district. He left me one other set of instructions. Burn everything.

I put in the address on my GPS and ended up under an interstate overpass—there was no one in sight. I knew what I needed to do but it soured my stomach. Murdering Jerry, because that's what it was, was hard, and to put two to his head while he was out—that wasn't how I operated. I pulled out my Glock and went to work. Two to the forehead and then I slit his throat—Triad style—before I torched the car. I started the fire in the driver's seat because I sure as fuck didn't want any of my DNA or fingerprints making it to the Vegas police.

I walked down the access road and across a couple other streets to a biker bar I'd been to a few times. I ordered a double of Johnny Walker before I texted Eagle to pick me up. I'd ended Jerry and that fucker deserved it, but any man deserved to go out with a chance to fight back. I'd killed for Uncle Sam, so killing for the Brotherhood wasn't an issue, and I refused to let this particular kill bother me. Thorn wouldn't have even given it a second thought, too bad I wasn't him.

Eagle walked in before I'd finished my drink. "You okay, brother?" He slapped my back and ordered a round of whiskey.

"I'm good. What's next?" I wanted this over because there was a blonde in Barden who I needed at least one more taste of before I brought her home to Vegas. We would never be the forever kind of thing, but right now I craved that peaches and cream scent. Buried inside her, I could forget the crap that ate at me, and pretend I were a different kind of man—the staying kind.

Chapter 18: Glory

I shouldn't have come home. Only a day had passed, and I wanted to run away and never come back. Home reminded me of what I'd lost, and what I might never get back. What if I had to stay here?

Part of me wanted to look as good as Avery did on the arm of her biker, and that scared me. I couldn't settle. I wouldn't settle. But the longer I was around these women and their strong bikers, the less it felt like settling.

So I kept my distance, even put up barrier between me and my bestie, trying to rein in my jealousy. I didn't want these bikers, but I couldn't argue that the love I saw in my friends' lives made me envious.

I'd talked myself into joining Avery and Mark for breakfast the second day—it was as public as you could get and that way I didn't have to tell them my sad stupid tale, yet. I left my room in the clubhouse and walked out into the main room. More than forty bikers sat eating but I didn't spot Avery. Mark waved and I headed toward his table by the door. He, Zero and Rock sat there along with a couple others I didn't know. I had just sat next to Mark when I heard her squeal. She barreled over to me and gave me a huge hug, and in that moment, everything was right in my world.

"I'm not letting you leave my side," Avery whispered in my ear.

Another reminder we needed to get my living arrangements settled. I wasn't staying in Barden.

I glanced at Mark, who shrugged and dug into his food. "Better get some grub." He motioned with his fork to the line.

As I came back with biscuits and gravy, Avery leaned over and kissed Rock. She was so damn beautiful. Then I noticed him pat her belly. Damn, she was expecting. Tears welled in my eyes and slid down. She'd always wanted to be a mother—she wanted to and could do it right, better than her fucked-up parents.

"Why didn't you tell me?"

She flipped to me and said, "Shh, we haven't said anything."

But I could see the love there and I fell apart crying. And of course she joined me.

Once I got the waterworks under control, I dug into the food, embarrassed by my outburst. I never cried and now all I did was cry.

Conversation flowed around me, and it hit me, this was a family. Avery's family. And I wasn't a part of it. She hadn't called me when she found out, or told me when we talked. Mark didn't call me anymore, either. They'd found family together, and I was intruding.

Mark told this story about a new recruit and Avery touched my arm. "You haven't met Van yet, but he's a great artist, and he'll be a great biker in a year or two." She assessed me. "He's our age and might be perfect for you."

"I'm not staying." The words were louder than I intended. "I'm going home as soon as I can."

Avery frowned and grabbed my hand. "This is home. You can't go back to Vegas, it won't be safe for you. Rock said that—"

"My heart, calm down." Rock frowned at me as he patted Avery's hand. "Of course she is staying here, especially now." He glanced pointedly at Avery's stomach.

How easy would it be to just say yes, and then back out later, but I didn't do that. Nope. "This isn't my home and I'm not staying. I have to go back and that's that." I stood up, hands on hips.

"Stop saying that!" Avery stood, tears running down her face. "When did this stop being home?"

I backed up, glancing at all the bikers frowning at me. They didn't like me upsetting Avery. "I don't know, but it's not home for me." I turned and almost ran out the door, stumbling into the bright sun. I began walking down the driveway, heading somewhere, although I didn't know where. It was too much—I'd panicked and run away. I always ran away from what I couldn't face. Breath heaving and heart pounding, anxiety beat in time with my frantic pulse. Was this another panic attack? It didn't feel the same as my first one, but I wasn't okay. Would I ever be okay again?

"Glory, wait," Mark yelled.

I stared at the man I barely knew anymore.

"Come back here, you can take my truck." He motioned for me and then jingled his truck keys.

Feeling stupid, I hiked back to him, not sure what to say.

"You really needed to do that?" He frowned at me. "You know she's pregnant? Not even six weeks yet."

I hadn't known, and that was the point. She'd called Mark, not me, to share the news. This life wasn't mine and was never going to be mine. "I panicked. It's all too much—I feel too much—I am a fucking mess." I sobbed the last words.

Mark pulled me close and held me while I wept. "I'm so screwed up. My brain, my feelings, all of it's too much." I had to stop breaking down like this. I sucked in a breath and pulled away, wiping my eyes with my sleeve. "When will he be back?"

"Delta?" He shrugged. "A few days."

I didn't want to think about what Delta was doing because of me. I didn't want to think about him, at all. "I'm so messed up in the head. And the club and all the stuff here—it overwhelms me."

"Is this more of the trauma stuff?" Mark stuffed hands in his pockets.

"Maybe. All I know is I can't do this right now—not even for Avery."

He held out the keys to his truck. "Keep it while you're here."

I bit my lip. I didn't deserve friends like him. "Thanks."

I held back the tears and drove away from him and the scene I'd just created. The truth was they were too good for me. I'd known that for a long time now, and what's more, I'd proved it, yet again. God, I was a complete bitch.

I drove to Mama's house. She took one look at me and broke down crying herself. Mama pampered me and treated me just like she always did when I was sick as a child. She made me her homemade chicken and dumplings, covered me up in soft blankets, and told me everything would be all right. And that felt absolutely wonderful.

Three days later, I sat in my bedroom feeling sorry for

myself, staring at the beauty pageant trophies that still held their place of honor on the top shelf of a bookcase Mama had bought to display them. Of course, my Miss Teen Oklahoma trophy sat in its place of honor on the mantel. I doubted Mama would ever move it, although I hated looking at it. It reminded me of my biggest failure—I'd been second runner up for Miss Teen USA. And I'd broken Mama's heart and lost out on the best scholarship I could've ever hoped to receive. No one cared about the second runner-up going to their school, so I hadn't gone to college. I hadn't been a very good student, and solid Bs in a small town school didn't impress anyone.

I made myself get out of bed and sit down at the vanity where Mama had taught me how to do makeup before I'd learned to read. Looking in the mirror, I saw the bruises were almost gone, so I started applying the makeup to make them disappear. My cheek had a red incision line that was beginning to fade. My thighs and other naughty bits were far from healed and made their dissatisfaction apparent every time I walked. I truly prayed a couple times for those magic kinda thighs that don't touch when I walked, but each step and swish of thigh against thigh stung. I couldn't sit with my legs crossed, either—I was spreading my legs wider than any guy I knew.

"Glory Ann, you have a visitor." Mama peeked in my room. "I'll tell her you're freshening up and will be down soon."

"Who is it?" I'd been hiding out here because I didn't think any of the bikers would come here. And if they did, Mama would send them packing.

"Why it's Avery, of course! She stops in to see me from time to time, you know." Mama blushed. "Such a sweet girl."

"But she's in the club." I wasn't sure if Mama was going senile. She hated the Jericho Brotherhood.

"Well, you know, they sponsored Founder's Day last year and that one they call Mama, she's even joined our ladies' club." Mama grinned. "I hate to speak ill of family, but I think my sister thrived on strife. Since she's been gone, everyone gets along."

"So you aren't in the Brotherhood-hating club anymore?"

Mama had the grace to blush. "Goodness, no. After all that trouble Gerald caused, and it was that club who set things right! No, it'd be wrong to hold a grudge."

"So I can go and marry a biker and bring you biker babies?" I laughed, knowing some things would never change.

Mama rolled her eyes. "You're made for better things, Glory Ann."

Teasing Mama had made me forget for a few moments that Avery was downstairs waiting on me. God, I didn't want to see her, but at the same time I needed to see her. I'd missed her more because I knew she was right down the street from me.

I finished putting on my face before I ventured downstairs. Mama might be letting her standards change when it came to the club, but she'd never accept less than perfect from me. She'd insisted on it since I could remember, and it'd become one of the bonds that held us together. Silly that something I had no control over—my looks—mattered so much to her. But it did, and I would always do my best to make her proud. It was how she'd raised me.

In the living room, Avery was staring at all our family photos standing like soldiers waiting for inspection on the piano top.

"Mama says you two made peace." I tapped my fingers on my thighs. I stood only a few feet from her but I didn't know how to close the physical distance, let alone the emotional distance that had grown between us.

She didn't move either, maybe she was as uncertain as me. "Yeah, the divide isn't really there anymore, and that's a good thing." Avery gave me a tentative smile. "Mark's parents and my brother Chet have both come to club get-togethers. Things change all the time…" She trailed off, looking from the piano to me. A tear slipped down her cheek. "When did we become strangers?"

Of course, she went right to it. Tears slipped down my cheeks faster and faster. "I guess it happened slowly, and now, how do I get you back?" My voice broke.

Avery closed the distance and her arms were around me in a second. "Like this." Her words were barely a whisper.

I embraced her and held on tight. "I'm sorry." I repeated the words over and over. I'd driven the distance between us by not coming home. Had it been pride or fear that had kept me away? Probably both.

At home, I had to admit my life in Vegas was far from the glamourous one I'd bragged about. And in Barden, I had to admit my friends had found a happiness more fulfilling than mine. And worst of all, I still wouldn't trade my life for theirs because I knew that was my place. This wasn't my home, even if these were my people.

"Shh," Avery consoled me. "You have nothing to be sorry for." She stroked my hair and soothed me the way only she could. "I didn't come to you either." She stepped back from me and looked me in the eye. "I have a confession."

"I know about the baby." I winked at her, trying to lighten the mood.

Her eyes lit up before she waved my words away. "No, silly, about not coming to see you. I did that on purpose, so you'd miss me so much you'd come home." She looked at the floor. "But you didn't come back, and I stayed away to punish you, maybe, for leaving me." She sniffed. "We could've come, Rock suggested it, but I always had a reason to not go."

"Look, you didn't need—"

"Yes, I did, dammit!" She fisted hands on her hips. "I'm your best friend, and I stayed away to hurt you. Then I felt bad, and then I called less, and then we were apart—for real this time."

"I did that too. I only came home once." I hugged her.

"I was wrong. I'm sorry! I was so wrong." Avery held me so tight my ribs protested, but I didn't say a word. It felt too good to have my best friend back after all those lonely years.

"I was afraid you didn't need me anymore. Afraid you'd try and make me stay. I was just so damn afraid." I whispered the words. I'd always been the brave one— at least that's what all our friends said, but honestly, Avery was the bravest because she'd always lived by her own rules. I hated that our dreams lived in separate cities hundreds of miles apart, but I loved that we both lived our dream.

"I was wrong. Forgive me." She sniffed again and wiped her nose with her sleeve.

"If you forgive me." I gave her a watery smile. "I

didn't know how to make it all right again. You and Mark have this whole other world that just isn't mine."

Avery nodded. "I know." Her acknowledgement held this sad finality to it. "Rock made me see that after you left. He's so damn smart—if I didn't love him so much, it'd irritate me to hell and back again."

I laughed. "I'm glad you have him. Have this…everything you dreamed of."

She gave me a proud smile. "I do have it. And so I get a little smug and forget that we aren't the same no matter how much I want you here with me. Tell me about how your dream was going before the douchebags put a crimp in it." Avery sat on Mama's green couch and crossed her legs crisscross applesauce like she used to do when we were little.

I sat but couldn't that way, so I angled toward her but had to keep my feet on the floor and legs spread wide, and even then my thighs throbbed. "Dancing is hard work, and everyone is as pretty, or even prettier than me." That sounded kinda like a whine.

Avery laughed. "Good! You always had it easy here."

I agreed but wasn't about to admit it. "Anyway, I loved it. I had to work for every dance and every spot in the line. It's hard, demanding, rewarding, and perfect for me." I threw my head back and laughed, remembering all the fun I had there. "But it's lonely, and the other dancers aren't that friendly, not like real friends." I remembered how Celeste had sold me out and wanted to punch her. Not that I'd punched anyone since I'd been little, but she deserved it.

"So I dated a lot of different guys, but none were great or even good. They were like the dancers—shallow and disposable."

"Ouch! Did you tell them that?" Avery reached out to clasp my hand.

"No, but I never dated anyone more than a couple months, then would try and go it alone and then back to the same cycle, again." Saying it aloud made me realize how true it'd been. "I never even felt close to love." Except with the one guy I couldn't love.

Oh no, I wasn't going there, so I thought instead of Frankie. "Then I met the main douchebag and he and I dated—maybe he had some help from my so-called 'friends.'" I did air quotes. "Long story to the point, I ended up here with too many bruises and a broken cheek." I sighed. "Now Delta is doing god knows what to make it better for me." I squeezed her hand. "You have to tell him to stop—I can dance other places." I couldn't let him risk death or kill for me. I wasn't worth that. "The guys wouldn't let me call him."

"It's not about you—"

"I'm the one he made the promise to, so how can it not be about me!"

Avery held up her hands. "It's club stuff now, but go ahead and call him, if that's what you need to do."

Chapter 19: Glory

I snatched Avery's phone and scrolled through it, noting all the biker names in there. When I spotted Delta, I hit the phone icon and it rang once.

"Pixie, is she okay?" He was breathless on the other end of the phone.

"Who is *she*?" I had a feeling he'd been checking up on me.

"Hey, Queenie, you doing okay?" He transitioned without a stutter.

"Better than you. What are you doing?"

"Just ran up 15 flights of stairs and beat Eagle." I could hear the satisfaction in his voice.

"Is it part of what you are...um...doing in Vegas?" I couldn't just blurt out killing the mob, besides I wasn't sure that was what he planned to do.

"Nah, just a thousand dollar bet—we have about a week to kill without much to do."

"So you race up flights of steps?" I didn't understand him. "Look, I called because you need to stop all this. Come home, call it quits."

A very sexy laugh met my words, and I wanted to reach through the line and choke Delta.

"Stop laughing at me."

"You aren't actually my queen—you can't give me orders." Humor still tinged his voice.

"Then I'll talk to Jericho! He'll call you off!" I was so angry. "This is because of me. I don't want you hurt or to hurt others."

"Going soft on me, Queen?" The low rumble of his voice made my stomach do butterfly somersaults.

"No!" Why did it matter to me that he didn't think I was soft? I was fine with every mobster dropping dead, but I just didn't want Delta or the club hurt because of it. "Look, I haven't ever hurt someone, but you have to a pay a price when you do violence. I don't want you paying that price for me! I can dance in LA or New York or somewhere else. I wouldn't ever forgive myself if you got hurt doing this!" I sucked in a deep breath. "Please, come home to me."

Silence met my plea. My heart thundered so loud I wasn't sure if I could have even heard Delta, but he didn't speak. And didn't speak.

I looked at the phone screen and seconds still ticked by. "Delta?" I didn't know what else to say.

"Be safe until I see you again."

"When…when will that be?"

"Ten days. I will see you in ten, yeah?"

"Yeah," I repeated. I looked back at the screen, but I already knew he'd hung up. His words had held a finality to them. Ten days. If he wasn't here in ten days, I'd be going to rescue him.

"I need to see Jericho!" I threw Avery her phone. "Will you take me?"

Avery frowned. "He's not exactly the friendliest guy…"

"And?"

"Fine, let's go."

I grabbed my purse and followed Avery outside to a bike—a motorcycle.

"You're riding pregnant?" I sounded like someone's mother.

"Now you sound like Rock! I am able to ride and be pregnant at the same time." She frowned at me. "You can ride bitch."

I stopped. "No, I can't."

She turned and stamped her foot. "I'm riding either way."

I swallowed the emotion blocking my throat. "I can't ride, now." I glanced away from her feisty expression, somehow ashamed by my injury. "They kicked me or something, here." I pointed to the V in my legs. "It's not close to being healed." I blinked away the tears threatening. No way in hell were they getting more of my tears.

"Goddammit!" Avery kicked the ground. "Let's take Mark's truck, but I'm driving."

I threw her the keys I'd pulled out of my purse and we climbed inside. But she turned toward the center of town instead of toward the clubhouse. "Where we going?"

"I can't just show up at Jericho's. Rock will kill me. First we tell Rock, then he freaks out, then we go."

"I don't understand this biker crap." And I didn't get it at all. "Lots of rules that you mostly break when you want to."

"Not so much—not many rules at all—and we never break them. But there are lots of expectations of respect. You can dis them if you want, but I don't want to."

"That's confusing!"

But Avery had parked so she didn't respond, just hopped out and hurried into Marked Man, the tattoo shop

Rock operated for the Brotherhood. I loved that Avery's kickass boutique had been rebuilt next to it. They looked perfect among the line of businesses on Main Street.

I followed her inside, not wanting to miss anything, and ran straight into Mark. I tried to move around him but he blocked me. "They need a private minute or two."

I heard the shouting from here. Spanish cursing, then *motorcycle*. Hell, they weren't even fighting about what I wanted. "Can you come with me?"

Mark tilted his head to the side.

"Follow or not."

Before he could decide what to do, I darted out the door. I needed to stop this manhunt in Vegas, and Rock needed to talk sense into my girl. Motorcycles and pregnancy didn't go together.

Thankfully, Avery had left the keys in the ignition, so I started the truck and had it in reverse when Mark opened the passenger door and slid into his seat. "Where we going?"

"I want to talk to Jericho. About the Vegas thing."

"Good." Mark nodded. "Avery told you he wanted the story from you."

I glanced at Mark, then back to the road. "No, I want to stop whatever they're doing in Vegas."

Mark's clear laugh rang out in the truck. It didn't give me any butterflies.

"Damn, girl, you haven't mellowed."

"Sure I have." Or maybe I hadn't. There hadn't been a lot in Vegas to rile me up, but Avery was usually around when I got riled. Maybe we fed each other. I was riled today, and that had nothing to do with Avery. Delta didn't need to do battle, or whatever, because of me.

Following Mark's directions, I drove past the clubhouse to a large ranch-style house back where MJ and the Old Man used to live. "This is fancy!"

"Jericho lives right." Mark sounded proud. "Um, you've met his old lady, right?"

"No, why?"

"She's intense—be nice or she'll hand you your ass without a second thought."

I nodded, although I doubted Mark's threat. I hurried out of the car and up the sidewalk to the front door.

"She's the one who trained Avery," Mark called from behind me.

Shit! She was a serious woman, or Domme. Without pausing to reconsider, I knocked on the door. Mark jogged up beside me as it opened.

Jericho stared down at me with his mismatched eyes and long curling hair—he was just the way I remembered—scary and intense.

"Thanks for bringing her, Sharpie." He stepped aside and we walked into one of the most comfortable homes I'd ever been in. It was a mix of leather, wood and deep, rich colors. Warm and lived in, it made me feel at home immediately.

"This is a wonderful home." I especially loved the huge stone fireplace.

"Thanks. Have a seat. Can I bring you a drink?"

"Water."

"A beer or whiskey." Mark sounded stressed.

"Like that, is it?" His old lady stood in the doorway. "Sit down, love, I'll bring in the refreshments." She was tall, black-haired and imposing. And sexy as hell, especially with her Irish accent. I wasn't into women, but I wanted to be into her.

Jericho sat in the huge leather chair that reminded

me of a throne a bit. "So, cousin, it's not my request that brings you here?"

That deep voice and penetrating stare almost made me stop before I ever began, but I remembered Delta. This wasn't about me, it was for him. "Not exactly, and Mark didn't know why I wanted to come until it was too late to jump out."

Jericho lifted a brow but didn't say anything.

"This confrontation with the mob—please don't do it. Stop. I'm not worth revenge, or whatever."

Jericho stroked his goatee. "You don't want the bastards who hurt you dead? That seems too bloodthirsty for you?"

His woman walked in then with four tumblers stacked atop each other in one hand and a bottle of Jameson in the other. "You the soft kind?"

"No, and no. I'd be happy with all of them dead." Anger seethed inside me. "They deserve it for what they've done to me and other women, no doubt!" I sucked in a breath to continue.

"Then let's drink to bloody deaths. I'm Marr and you must be Glory." Marr handed me the whiskey.

With a nod, I took the glass offered. "But it's not worth it to Delta or Thorn or Eagle or whoever else is doing the killing."

Marr started to speak again.

"Wait." I cut off the Domme who might do serious damage if I pissed her off. "I haven't ever hurt someone or killed someone." I glanced to each of them. "But it has to hurt the person who kills—take something from them."

Marr threw back her drink and poured another.

"I'm saying it's not worth *that* price. They don't need

to add any more burdens to their souls—their peace of mind, whatever—because of me. That's why I want you to stop this!"

"But then you can't return to Vegas," Jericho said.

"True, but I can dance a lot of places—"

"Ah, Pixie didn't convince you to stay, then," Marr interrupted again.

"No, we were on our way here, but she and Rock got into a fight about her riding her motorcycle."

Marr laughed and Jericho cursed.

"Tell me what happened," Jericho commanded.

"She showed up at my place on—"

"In Vegas," he said, cutting me off.

Oh, that. "I don't want to." I sighed. "But I owe it to you." I had asked them for help. "I was stupid and switched to the Remington from the Starlord. It's a long story as to why but let's just say Frankie, my ex, had someone I thought a friend help convince me." I couldn't believe I'd been so stupid. "Anyway, I ended up at the casino run by his uncle and the one he was next in line to run—and out of options." I sipped my whiskey. "I'm sure now that Frankie had picked that weekend to bring our standoff to a close. Delta stopped him for the night, but he kept after me. And he got my manager in on it, and I ended up in their porn studio with a needle coming my way. They weren't going to take no for an answer." My breathing was ragged and shallow thinking about it. I closed my eyes and breathed deep. I was in control. I repeated the statement until my breathing slowed.

I opened my eyes and continued. "I fought, kicking Frankie in the balls, he punched me in the cheek. I woke up in the hospital."

"You really kicked the guy coming for you in the

balls? You went down fighting?" Marr sat on the arm of Jericho's chair. He grabbed her waist and tugged her down to his lap.

"Yeah, I figured it was better to go out fighting."

Marr gave a nod of approval, and that warmed me. Why did I care what this woman thought? I didn't know how she'd done it, but already her approval mattered to me.

"I won't call it off." Jericho said the words with a casualness that made me do a double take. He really said that.

"Why not?"

Mark squeezed my arm. "That's not—"

"She's my responsibility," Jericho said smoothly, and Mark let go of my arm like he'd been burned.

I had no idea what had just happened here, but I hated it. "I'm my own woman. Thanks."

Marr lifted her drink in salute to me.

"In our club, you don't have that choice. And since you're my family, you become my responsibility."

"I never saw you at the family Christmas." My tone was sharp.

Marr laughed again.

"All the same, we're blood, so I will say this much to you." He steepled his fingers together and stared at me. But somehow in the past few minutes, he'd lost his scare factor. "Dammit," he mumbled under his breath.

"You're losing your edge." Marr bit his neck.

They must have noticed the change in me.

"Anyway, this isn't about you. It hasn't been since Delta and Thorn paid a visit to Frankie. This is about our club. So the price you talk about—it isn't because of you—it's because of this patch." He thumped the Brotherhood reaper on his cut that was over his heart.

More stupid club stuff I didn't understand.

"So Delta isn't about to kill people because of me, but because you ordered it?"

"Yes." Then he cursed again.

I smiled a cold smile. "He shouldn't kill for you either."

"He isn't. It's for the club, and every one of us would do it."

I saw the crazy in his eyes—the same I saw in Mark's eyes when he talked about the Brotherhood. I thought of it as cult mentality, but maybe it was more, or different. Because right then in Jericho's eyes, it looked a lot like love.

Chapter 20: Delta

Tonight we would finally execute the mission. Three weeks of planning had me itching for action. Straight-forward and simple had always been my motto, but that wasn't how this mission needed to go down. Thorn had considered a lot of plans, including one using the Raven Renegades, but he'd abandoned it because they weren't family.

We'd gathered in a run-down section of town on the edge of Vegas. In an equally run-down motel room, the eight of us listened to Thorn detail the objective and mission.

Zero and I walked the two doors down to our own room. Thorn had said to get sleep, since the plan would have us up for a solid twenty-four hours, but I couldn't sleep right now.

"So what do we do?" Zero sat on the bed with his knee bouncing. "No way I can sleep."

Good question. "How was she?"

"Better when I left. She and Pixie had made up, and she was starting to find her way." Zero grinned. "And did you hear about how she faced down Jericho?"

I hadn't, even though I'd talked to several guys in

Barden. "Tell me." If Jericho made her cry, I'd have words, make that fists, with him.

"She went to see Jericho, dragging poor Sharpie along! Man, he almost pissed his pants when she went all alpha on Jericho." He glanced at me. "Marr was there too."

Fuck. "She wasn't hurt?" You didn't show Marr disrespect.

"They got drunk together, so it all ended happily ever after." He spread his arms wide as if that were all that needed to be said.

I bit my tongue and waited on the ass to get on with it. Zero liked messing with others, and I wasn't falling for his shit. I could always call Rebel and bitch at him if I had to. He should have told me when we talked this morning.

"So she goes there." Zero gave me that shit-eating grin of his. "And get this, she demands that Jericho stop this operation and bring you home."

"That's not her business."

Zero nodded. "But she thinks it is—you're out here on account of her call, so she goes about demanding that you be brought home before you get hurt."

"She didn't fucking dis me like that." Anger rushed through me. I could take care of myself. Didn't she think I could take care of business?

"She didn't want you to kill—said it had to hurt the people who did it." Zero became more serious. "And she's right that there is always a cost to killing."

"One I'd pay a thousand times over for the club."

"As we all would," Zero agreed. "Anyway it was touch and go for a minute—like it always is when Marr gets her dander up. But they came to terms, and all got drunk together."

"What did Jericho say?" I didn't care about the rest.

"That this was for the club, not for her or him. But that she did bear some responsibility and she'd have to live with it, just like he had to live with it."

"What?" She wasn't responsible for any of this shit.

"She made the call and is guilty about what followed." Zero shrugged. "She made her choice, and we made ours."

The club was in this situation because of my reaction. What if I had handled Frankie differently? Had I made the best choice? Too late now—the bottom line was clear—we would solve the problem tonight. I anticipated my stay in Vegas while I sorted shit in the next few months. I didn't have anything keeping me in Oklahoma, and the idea of seeing Glory in Vegas excited me. I finally admitted that I wasn't done with her yet. I needed a few more nights.

"I've got to burn this energy." I changed into running clothes.

Zero did the same.

We started running south without a destination in mind. I'd run until this nervous tension was expended. I replayed the plan in my mind, visualizing each step over and over. The plan had to be so ingrained I didn't need to think. Every detail had to be precise, and it was my job to make sure all those details were absolutely right. The plan tonight was staged to give the Triad the credit. It had to be perfect so that the more the Triad denied involvement, the more guilty they became. Thorn figured they'd take credit and sweep in to the empty space we created. That's what we needed.

My mind quieted as I ran. The repetition of my shoes hitting the concrete road soothed me, and soon I found the peace I sought. Zero kept pace but for once didn't try and run his mouth. We ran a long time in quiet camaraderie before turning and heading back to our motel. After a shower, I dressed and loaded up with the arsenal of weapons Thorn had assigned me—only he carried more weapons than me.

At 21:00 we left the hotel and drove toward the compound, arriving at 00:17, three minutes ahead of schedule. The house was centered on a couple of acres away from other homes in the area—that worked to our advantage. The compound had a high wrought-iron fence with sharp points surrounding it. It was wired to alert if someone scaled it, but Eagle would disarm the security system before our entry. Then there were more than a hundred feet of empty yard to cross with little to no cover. But we all knew what to do, and we'd make it to our targets.

Thorn looked at each of us masked in identical ski masks. Yet each of us held ourselves differently, making it easy to identify my brothers. "This is it. Do it right." He wasn't a motivational speaker. We all nodded back, then the four teams of two deployed to our assigned entry points. Zero and I waited at the Humvee—one of two vehicles we'd brought.

"Will we see any action?" Zero had no military training, but he'd seen action in Brotherhood skirmishes. The guy was a natural leader, and he'd go places in the club. He was my opposite in many ways.

"Hopefully not." I motioned him to follow.

We moved through the gate team one had cleared and opened. "Two down." They lay sprawled on the green lawn. We cut the throats of the two dead men. That left sixteen, according to our intel.

"Four down." Eagle spoke next. He was part of team two.

That was good, we were still silent. The longer we killed without any noise, the better our odds of success.

"Two down." Mojo, part of team two, had entered the back. "No other guards. Repeat two missing."

Damn. I walked by the two Thorn had put down. Zero and I cut their throats and place two silenced rounds in them. One in the head and the other in the heart. We moved across the manicured lawn in a low run to check Eagle's kills. He'd cut the throats so we added the bullets. I was tempted to send Zero to follow Thorn, but I stuck to the plan. "We follow Mojo, and clean up."

Zero nodded.

"Hunting." This word let the other three teams know they should fully take out their target Triad style. I'd check each one before our team left, but we needed to account for the missing guards. I spotted the two Mojo had hit. Zero bent and sliced the throats. I searched the ground and spotted some cigarette butts. I moved over and continued toward the stucco pool house. I spotted lights there, but our intel didn't have anyone located there. I bet our missing guards were taking a break. I motioned Zero to follow. He was quiet despite his lack of training. I spied two guys through the window. They had porn on the big screen.

Zero grinned and gave me a thumbs-up before starting around me. I held his black jacket until he made eye contact, then pointed to head and heart. We couldn't afford any sloppy shots.

With another thumbs-up, he moved forward and through the door without any hesitation. I watched as the guy turned and Zero shot the first through the forehead, then the second fell to another precisely placed bullet. He stepped closer and finished the job with bullets to the heart and throats sliced. He wasn't bloodthirsty, but determined, efficient, and maybe trying to prove something to himself. He was my brother and had nothing to prove to me or the others. We accepted our brothers without question or reservation—it was what made the club work.

"Two missing are down." He spoke into his headset.

While we hunted, the count had increased to twelve, meaning only DeLuca and two guards were left. We made quick work, zigzagging through the yard to check the other kills. I had just checked the two in the front hall when the machine gun sounded. I brought up my machine gun, spraying bullets through the entryway and up into the ceiling. With two fingers, I indicated that Zero should set the incendiary charges. Scorched earth, literally.

I ran up the steps and surprised a guy leaving the bathroom—two shots and he was down. I slit his throat. Damn. There was a wild card and when there was one, there might be more. The machine gun sprayed again with its trademark *rat-a-tat-tat* rhythm. Three more doors opened and I started shooting with my machine gun. They got off a few shots.

"Six additional—do a full search." I spoke quickly as I shot my targets. Once all were down, I moved forward, slitting throats with quick precision.

"Copy that." Eagle and Mojo both spoke into my ear.

"All new targets down." There couldn't be any witnesses. I moved into the first room, checked the closet, the bathroom, under the bed. The second room was empty. The third wasn't—my gun moved automatically.

I lifted the Glock and squeezed off two shots before the guys moved their guns from their sides. Blood blossomed in the center of each forehead. Dead. I moved into the room to complete the ritual killings. I stared down at the targets—they were teenagers.

Fuck me, I'd just killed two goddam children. *Fuck. Fuck. Fuck.* I turned and jabbed the wall. Hitting it over and over, but the rage only built inside me. Eyes unfocused with tears I'd never shed, the sudden desire to turn the Glock on myself appealed. I could just end my misery—I didn't deserve to live after killing those kids.

With a dry laugh, I keyed my mic. "Two additional targets down." I might hate myself but I still had a job to do. Swallowing hard before I puked, I finished the job— another shot to the heart and two slices to the throat. My fuckups knew no bounds. My stupidity kept costing lives—I wish it'd claim my life, but I wasn't that goddam lucky.

Numb, I turned to see Thorn in the doorway. He gave me a nod and ghosted away. I finished the search then checked the main room. DeLuca, and two bodyguards I recognized from the Remington were laid out cold. I snapped the photos with the disposable phone we'd bought.

Each team reported their sectors of the house and grounds clear.

"Five minutes," Zero warned into the headset. I booked it out the door and met at the rendezvous point. Eagle started to lift his face mask, but I shook my head. "Keep it in place."

We were fairly sure we knew where all the cameras were placed, but Thorn had ordered us to keep our masks in place until we cleared Vegas.

"That's bullshit," he mumbled but put his balaclava back in place.

"Here are the shots you requested." I tossed Thorn the phone.

"See you on the flip side." Thorn caught the phone.

We'd each go our own way from individual drop-off points. Those of us heading back to Barden would meet up in Kingman across the border in Arizona.

The Hummer left and Zero and I sat in the Mercedes sedan favored by the Triad. The house's fire alarms sounded as the fire expanded. We let it blare for a minute, then peeled out, driving like bats out of hell down the quiet road. We hot rodded through town and into Triad territory. We parked in an abandoned alley, shed our outer layers of clothes, and stuffed them in the car before burning it. Now dressed like tourists, Zero and I walked with our canvas bags of artillery to a self-storage unit a block away. Zero hopped in the driver's seat and pulled the rental out of the storage space and drove south. Our bikes were stored at the meet-up point.

"Who were they guarding in the other rooms?"

I shook my head, not wanting to discuss it.

"What? Women? Lightskirts?" he pried. "It'll be on the news, you know."

Fuck. He's right, it would. "Two teenage boys."

"You did what? We don't kill—"

"Doesn't matter to the Triad." Their faces were burned into my memory. I might always be haunted by those faces.

"Shit. That's harsh. Man, I don't know what to say."

I shut my eyes as Zero drove on.

"Man, that'd fuck with my head bad."

"Not helping." I ground out the words. I'd killed for Uncle Sam. I'd killed for the club. But ending those boys' lives wasn't the same. Fury burned deep in me. I raged against myself for doing it and my club for requiring it. The loathing was all tied together, and I was afraid it would always taint my devotion to the Brotherhood.

Thankfully he shut the hell up. I didn't need his help. Those boys would be joining my two friends, who'd lost their lives under my command. I'd carry them with me forever.

Lars's face, battered and cut, filled my mind. He'd been beaten to death while investigating a murder on base. His partner, Mike, had been shot in the back. Neither one had ever received justice. Jojo and I had been pulled from the case, reassigned, transferred, and drummed out of the army on a Bad Conduct Discharge because we refused to let their murders go. It galled me that I'd never found their killers. Hell, the fucker had probably made general by now.

When I fucked up, I fucked up bad. And Thorn wanted me to train new recruits. No way. My judgment couldn't be trusted. First I'd fucked up in the army, then with Frankie, now two innocent kids were dead by me and because of me. At least my mistake hadn't put the burden of those kids on another brother. No, I couldn't be trusted with the next generation of brothers.

Chapter 21: Glory

After weeks of recovery, my thighs and unmentionables didn't hurt anymore. Thank God! I'd finally been able to at least relieve a bit of the tension through some quality alone time last night. I might not rip off anyone's head today because of those orgasms—not that they deserved such a title. The powerful way Delta could make me come was an orgasm, and the temporary relief of my vibrator was barely a ghost of that kind of pleasure.

And there he was again. All morning my mind had returned to Delta and our night together at my place because I'd used those memories when I'd masturbated last night. He had given me intense jolts of ecstasy that had crackled through me as if I'd been struck by lightning. Unfortunately there were no lighting strikes last night.

Was he ever coming back? I hadn't heard a damn thing about Delta since I'd stormed into Jericho's days ago. Even Avery was silent about Delta despite my many attempts to pry information from her. The Brotherhood had closed ranks at Jericho's command—that was the last thing Avery had said to me about Delta. Then she'd admitted she didn't know anything anyway because the brothers weren't even sharing with their mates. Her words still haunted me. "It's serious shit when they go silent like this. Stay out of it."

What choice did I have, anyway? I couldn't get into it because I didn't know what *it* entailed. Frustrated, I paced Mama's living room with no real idea how to spend my day. Now that I was healed, this inactivity was driving me crazy. I needed to do something or I'd start pounding my head against the wall. So I ran back upstairs and changed into running clothes. The month of inactivity would have taken a toll on my body no doubt. I'd have to bust my ass to get back into dancing shape. I wrote a quick note to my mom and left. I decided to jog from the house to the river and back—four miles in total.

Before I hit the city limits I was winded, but I pushed on because I wasn't a quitter. I'd set a goal and I'd achieve it. At a pitifully slow pace, I finally made the bridge. Huffing from the effort I rested on the steel frame and watched the water rush by. The sun warmed me and the smell of green grass comforted me. Spring was the best time of year—a time of new growth. I needed a new start myself.

I stared down at the rock outcropping where we'd spent so many nights as teenagers and even later. I left the bridge and climbed down the hill to party rock. We'd made so many memories here. I traced where Mark had carved our initials into the rock. Just a few feet away I remember Avery declaring her dream of running a clothing store. She'd made her dream a reality. And I'd taken a good bite out of my dream too. But I wanted more. That summed me up though—I always wanted more.

That thought got me off my ass, and I hiked back up the hill before setting out at a faster pace. Dreams didn't come true on their own. I had to work my ass off to get there—if I could even go back to Vegas. I pushed away that doubt and all the others as I pushed through the hurt to achieve that high that came from the run. Sweaty, exhausted, and exhilarated, I stopped in the front yard of my childhood home.

Avery's old truck sat in the driveway. It was in a lot better shape than a few years ago with a fresh coat of paint and a lot of new chrome. Avery and Mama were having lemonade and cookies at the kitchen table, just like we'd done a thousand times growing up.

"About time you got here. Where have you been?" Avery wrinkled her nose at my sweaty condition.

"A slow run." I hated my body's limitations. "I have a lot of work to do."

"You need to go get prettied up." Mama smiled at me. "Avery's taking you to a party."

"Is Delta back?" I rushed to her.

She gave a sad shake of her head. "Lila's having some people over to see little Rhianna. The baby is almost a year old."

"I'm not up for people." I needed Delta. I didn't need to be dragged into the Brotherhood world any more than I already had been.

"Lila says not to come without you." Avery gave me her puppy dog face. "I want to go, please go with me."

I never could resist that look and she knew it. "Fine."

"Oh, I brought you some new stuff from my shop." Avery jumped up. "Let's go."

New clothes always perked up my mood.

On the bed were five dresses in light cottons and knit. All easy to wear with sore muscles but still sexy. And with my bruises mostly gone, I wouldn't feel self-conscious in those shorter dresses.

I picked up a long knit dress that tied around my neck. "I'm wearing this." I hurried into my bathroom to shower and get ready.

Avery chatted the whole time I did my hair and makeup, telling me about the women I'd meet.

"We don't really do the nickname thing—that's for the guys." She laughed. "It's way too confusing that way."

"So Elle will be there. She's Rebel's woman, and kick ass in her own right." She ticked people off with her fingers. "Of course me and Lila. Then there will be Marr, who you met."

"Is that her real name?"

"Um, I dunno any other name. And I'm not asking." Avery shrugged. "She's—"

"The Domme who trained you, I know."

"Oh, and there will be Charlie, she's JoJo's woman. And JoJo is Delta's best friend."

"This feels more like a test than a party." I struggled to remember the names she'd told me.

"And there will be Angie, who works with Rock, Cheri, she's one of my friends in the club, and probably a few others."

"Why do I need to be there?" Apprehension made my stomach tight. "I will never be one of them."

"Because you're my best friend and Lila misses you. So what if it's a bunch of biker old ladies? Are you scared?"

"No, but you know I am going back to Vegas, soon."

Avery sighed. "Even more reason to come see everyone. Besides, little Rhianna has red curly hair, she's freaking adorable."

Fine. A baby was always reason to go, and I did miss Lila, although I wished it was just the three of us like it had been before I moved to Vegas. Life kept moving, even faster when you weren't around to watch it go by.

"Let's go already." I grinned at Avery.

"Finally." She looked me over and gave a wolf whistle. "Damn you look good."

Avery wanted to drive us both, but I took my mama's car, so I could leave when I wanted. Lila and Dare's house was just down the road from Jericho's and it was even bigger. I walked up to the door with Avery—we were the first ones here.

"Where's everyone else?" I figured we'd be late since I'd taken time to make myself up.

"Not coming for a bit. I figured we could use some time together before they all arrive." Avery gave me a wink and just walked inside. She didn't even knock.

"What?"

"She knows we're here." Avery rolled her eyes. "She texted me to come on in."

In the living room Dare held the curly-haired baby with a huge smile on his handsome face. I'd always thought of him as stern, but he looked damn happy right now. Wood floors covered the entryway and all of the first floor that I could see. Leather furniture decorated the huge living room.

Dare glanced at us then back to his daughter. "Red, get your ass in here," he hollered. From the living room, I spied a huge dining room with an open island that separated it from a massive kitchen.

Of course, Lila was pulling something from the oven. She hadn't changed that much.

"Hold our daughter a couple more minutes, then you can escape," Lila shot back. "Girls, come get a drink."

The oak dining room table was huge.

"You plan to have an army of kids?" There were ten seats at her table.

"No way, but we already run out of room on a regular basis," Lila said.

"Then be less friendly." Dare handed his daughter to Lila. "I'm out of here."

She took the chubby baby and leaned in for a hot kiss from her biker. Then he hurried out the back door without another glance.

Lila passed the baby to Avery and enveloped me in a hug. "I'm glad you're here. I've missed you." Her soft words warmed me and put me at ease.

Why had I worried about seeing her? Because I was crazy.

"And you too." We held the hug a long minute and it made me feel safe.

She and Avery understood me.

"So." Lila stood back.

Avery handed me a glass of lemonade.

"Which one is best in bed?" Lila asked.

I choked on the sip I'd just taken. "What?"

"Stop playing coy." Avery added her two cents. "Who's best? Zero or Delta?"

"Don't forget Mark," Lila added.

My cheeks and neck burned.

"There's a child here," I protested.

"And she wants to know too." Lila gave me that stubborn look I knew too well.

"After all I've been through, this is what you ask me." I tried to distract her.

"Yes," they both answered at once.

The baby cooed as if she was asking too.

We all laughed and I gave in, as if I'd ever had a

chance to avoid it. "Why do you even care?" I planned
to make them work for the intel.

"Delta and Zero have hot reputations for their skills,"
Avery quipped.

"Pussy hounds?"

Now Avery blushed.

"Exactly," Lila agreed.

"You two already tired of what you have and need to
live through me." I knew that wasn't the case, but they
deserved a little hell.

Lila just laughed. "I've got the king of pussy hounds,
so I am well satisfied. But…there is a small wager on
this."

Avery gulped. "Lila, shut it."

"You two…" I didn't know what else to say about betting on something like that. "Delta is the best—for me
anyway." He'd shown me pleasure like I'd never known.

"Pay up." Lila held out a hand.

Avery rolled her eyes. "Later. Really better than
Zero?"

I nodded.

"And so you're tapping that again? Soon." Lila made
it less a question and more a certainty.

"We agreed on once." I sounded certain. "So, no."

Now as long as they didn't read my mind…

"I'm sure you could renegotiate," Lila encouraged.

"And then when I live in Vegas and he lives here, how
do we renegotiate that?"

Avery opened her mouth but didn't say anything.

"Here, meet Rhianna. She makes everything look
brighter." Lila handed me her daughter. We chatted a
few minutes about life, catching up on everything, yet
there was no way to really close the gulf of information

I didn't know. And that was fine with me—the more I saw the happiness my friends had, the more their life tempted me.

In another year, two babies would be here and the joy would be tenfold. Their life tempted me, but down deep it wasn't my dream. Sure, the happy mother and wife part was my dream, most girls' dream actually, but I didn't want their lives in a small town amidst a nosy gaggle of bikers.

The doorbell rang and Lila hurried to the front room. I heard chatter and laughs.

"Come on." Avery dragged me and little Rhianna into the living room.

A parade of women entered over the next couple minutes, and other than the leather cuts, I wouldn't have been able to tell they were old ladies—well a couple fit my stereotype, but so many more didn't. These women were as diverse as the men I'd met in the club. And too late, I realized a critical mistake—I was holding the star of this gathering. The horde of women descended on me.

Desperate to escape, I tried to hand off the baby but both Avery and Lila were across the room from me. So I shook off the panic and met the horde with the manners Mama had instilled in me. And soon, the imposing Domme had taken the baby, letting me slide away to the kitchen. I needed a minute to regroup. I found another lady there and figured she had the same idea.

"Hiding?" I smiled to her.

"Sorta. These groups are intimidating, and I feel like the worst sort of pretender." She shot out her hand. "I'm Charlie, and I'm a cop."

I choked on my lemonade. I could see how that would be uncomfortable. While everyone swore the Brotherhood didn't do criminal stuff, its members could be considered sketchy, at best.

"Where's your cut?" I'd noticed a couple of the women hadn't worn one.

"Um, I haven't agreed to that." She grinned. "Not sure I can wear that and my shield."

"And if someone told me, I don't remember—do you have your own biker?"

She giggled. "I do. One of the bounty hunters—JoJo."

"So you know Delta. He helped me out, big time."

She nodded with another grin. "My man and Delta are best friends. Served in the military together."

So I'd been right that he was a military man. I bet he'd been handsome in his uniform and wished I'd met him then.

Chapter 22: Delta

We hit Henderson by early morning. Thorn was in the motel restaurant eating when we arrived. "Get some chow, then we'll be riding like we're fleeing hell."

A girl with boobs hanging out a halter and shorts that showed off her fine ass came by to take my order. I ordered steak and eggs with pancakes. I needed the extra fuel since I'd had damn little rest. The girl batted her eyelashes and dangled her boobs in my face but I was too exhausted to fuck. That was a first for me. I'd been too drunk but never too tired. Even if Glory strolled by, I'd have to pass. The thought of Glory's tiny waist and fuller hips made my cock stir, proving me a liar.

"We got time for you to take care of her." Thorn nodded to the retreating waitress. "Sometimes a good fuck is all that chases away the demons."

"Damn, when'd you go from badass to den mother?" I frowned at him. "You should take the damn recruits if you've got advice to spare."

"Fuck that." Thorn dismissed the idea. "You got the hots for another hot body."

"What hot body?" Zero sat down across from me. He'd been on the phone and came in after me.

Of course the bastard walked in right as Thorn was

razzing me. Like I needed two of them fucking with me. "Nothing."

"He's got it for Glory," Thorn said at the same time.

The waitress wandered back and took Zero's order, dropping off another pot of coffee. Zero flirted and the girl giggled. I only felt world-weary and ancient. The past few weeks had changed me.

Once the waitress flounced away, Zero turned back to me and waggled his brows and made kissing noises. "You should take her, bro." Zero gave me a wide, shit-eating grin.

"Not interested." I drank down my coffee and poured another cup from the pot on the table.

"He wants Glory," Thorn added. "But won't cop to it."

I flipped him the bird.

Zero laughed.

The waitress brought our food and we dug in, making quick work of the meal. As I finished up the last of my eggs, Zero shot me a quick smile and headed for the waitress. I threw bills on the table and stalked outside. I needed fresh air.

Thorn followed me out. "We got a few minutes to kill." He glanced to where Zero took the giggling waitress down to the room they'd booked.

I wished for a smoke or a bottle of bourbon, but I didn't have either.

"You need to talk." Thorn took a seat on the tailgate of the truck he'd driven down here.

Talking wasn't what I needed. And I didn't know what would ever ease the growing heaviness in my chest. I sat down next to him so I wouldn't look so damn suspicious while we waited for Zero to finish up.

"You can't keep it all inside—believe me." He stared off, thinking his own dark thoughts.

I'd seen his scars and I wasn't even close to holding in as much as he'd experienced. I could handle my demons just fine. "Man, I just need space."

Thorn nodded. He didn't say anything else. Zero came strolling our way twenty minutes later with a lazy grin. It took about a half hour to drop off the rental cars and take a rideshare to the storage unit where we'd locked up our bikes.

I needed speed and away from the two brothers trying too hard to help me out. I got their worry, and sort of appreciated it, but I had nothing to give back. I was bone dry, parched, and the holes in my soul too large to patch up. I'd likely be empty all my life—some shit you just didn't get over.

We sped out of town and headed south and blew through Flagstaff. I wanted to drive the 18 hours straight home but I got outvoted when we stopped for dinner in Albuquerque. So we stayed in a motel near I-40.

While we ate, our informants gave us good news—the Triad had taken credit for the hit and were already moving into the territory DeLuca had controlled. It was the best case scenario but I couldn't care less—all I saw were those two dead kids.

I lay in bed and stared at the ceiling. Each scene with Glory replayed in my mind. The hot way we fucked filled my brain. I could almost taste her when I closed my eyes. I needed another taste, but I was afraid one more taste would addict me. She was walking heroin and I should stay the hell away before she controlled my life. Then I fast-forwarded to her in the hospital, and a dark, hateful anger engulfed me. Every single person involved had paid with their life, and still the anger ate at me.

Those boys came back to my mind and I wanted to shoot myself in the fucking head, again. The mission was completed, so I could take the easy way out. I didn't deserve easy, and I didn't deserve someone clean and innocent like Glory. I was the worst kind of killer—the kind I'd put away when I was in the army. I'd wiped out two kids, and those boys' deaths weighed on me. Darkness surrounded me and I wasn't sure I'd ever feel the clean again. The taint kept spreading, coloring my future, my commitment to the club and even my desire to wake up again. The weight of those two crushed my chest, smothering me.

After a fitful night of dreams, I woke up at daybreak. At six, I pounded on Thorn's door to find him already awake. Zero wasn't awake or alone. After too much pissing and moaning, we finally were on the road at seven. I set the pace because we needed to make up time. Each mile that passed brought me closer to my obsession, and the one thing I dare not take. Glory deserved a better man than me, even if I wanted to settle down. But I didn't want to settle. I didn't want a relationship, and I wanted Glory Ann Atkins. I was totally fucked.

I revved my bike and focused on the road. The speed blew away all my thoughts, and I found the Zen of the road. I could always rely on the high riding brought me.

When we stopped at a truck stop to eat about halfway there, I called Rebel to let him know when we'd be back and to have Glory there. While I should stay away, I needed her tonight.

Chapter 23: Glory

Two days later a truck I didn't recognize stood outside Mama's house. I'd just walked back from Avery's store, Black Label, where I'd helped her put away a new shipment of merchandise. She'd tried to talk me into a tattoo, but that wasn't happening. I showed too much skin as a dancer and tattoos weren't welcome. Inside, I found Jericho eating cookies with my mom in the living room. The fierce man looked out of place amid her lace doilies and knickknacks. He was wild and untamed, and Mama's house was a study of Southern charm with Queen Anne furniture and porcelain figurines on every free surface.

"What are you doing here?"

"Glory Ann, that's no way to speak to your cousin and my guest." Mama's chest puffed up like a hen.

"Sorry, Mama."

Jericho smiled and stood. Relief flashed on his face. "I need you at the club."

"Why?" Hands fisted on my hips I stared up at the man who'd shut me down just a few days ago.

"Delta is on his way home, and I thought—"

"Give me twenty minutes and I'll be ready." I turned and rushed up the stairs before he could protest. I was sure the idea of twenty minutes with my mom wasn't on his agenda, but I wasn't seeing Delta without full armor, and that meant looking my best. What should I wear? I didn't want to look like shit but I sure didn't want to appear like I'd dressed up for him. Decisions, decisions. I finally pulled on a pair of jeans and one of the shirts I'd bought at Black Label a couple days ago. I slipped on some wedges and grabbed my bag.

I was downstairs in fifteen minutes, a personal record for me. Jericho gave me a harassed look.

"Ready?"

"Yeah." He almost ran toward the door, trying to get away from my mom.

I hauled my ass up into his big truck. He backed out of the drive and drove out of town.

"Your auntie scare you that bad?"

He scowled at me. "She asked me to dinner Sunday night. And told me to bring Marr."

I burst out laughing, imagining those two in my mama's fussy house. Then I sobered. "Don't hurt her feelings. She's trying to see beyond the past."

"I ain't stupid, but I didn't commit to dinner, either." His hands tightened on the wheel. "I don't know if it is better to go or not. Shit, you bring all kinds of complications."

"I think MJ is the one who did that." I crossed my arms. "You should go. She's your only family in town."

"My brothers are my fucking family." He whipped those words at me.

"She's family too." I refused to budge on that fact. "And *you* are her only family in town now."

"Yeah," he sighed. "I get that." He slammed his hand on the steering wheel.

I jumped and cursed the jitters that still plagued me. Would I ever be normal again?

"Shit was easier when the town hated us."

I snorted. "Well, that's the past."

"If I go, you and Avery come too."

"You aren't the boss of me." I wasn't one of his minions.

"You'll come."

And I would. Hell, I could charge admission to that dinner. Both bikers and Mama's friends from town would pay top dollar to see that dinner play out.

I remembered the reason I'd agreed to come with him. "Is he okay?"

"He'll survive."

Worry shot through me, leave me feeling sick and unbalanced. "Did he get hurt?"

"Not so you could tell it."

"What the fuck?"

"Forget I said anything." He glanced over at me. "He asked me to have you at the club. That should tell you everything you need to know." Then he clamped his mouth shut.

"That doesn't tell me jack shit," I fumed. "How did the mission go? Was he injured?"

I waited but Jericho didn't say anything.

Stubborn ass. I wanted to shake him. Dammit, he was a frustrating man.

We pulled into the club parking lot before I could badger him more. He hurried out of the truck like hellhounds nipped at his heels, and disappeared inside the club before I'd even gotten out of the truck.

I followed him inside the clubhouse to a hive of activity. Guys were moving the scarred, mismatched tables and a band was setting up on the small stage. Two guys were carting beer to the bar in back. Hell, they were getting ready for a party. This was the last place I wanted to be. I started backing out and bumped into someone. I turned and saw Marr.

"Pixie's in the kitchen. Go find her." She pointed to the swinging door, although I knew my way to the kitchen.

"I think I should go. This isn't my scene."

"Delta says different." Marr frowned down at me. "You need to be here. Get me?"

No. I didn't. "I have no fucking idea what you mean. No one tells me shit." Anger felt damn good. It was so much better than the fear and uncertainty.

She tskd and shook her head. "Pixie said you were smart."

"I am," I protested. "What has that...?" I was talking to no one. She'd walked away.

Dammit. I needed answers and the Brotherhood wouldn't help. That meant staying until Delta arrived. But I needed transportation too. I had heard about Brotherhood parties, and I had no plans of staying here. Why hadn't I thought to drive my mama's car here? Jericho, that's why. The man rattled me.

I spotted Mark in the crowd and zigzagged through the tables and people until I stood toe-to-toe with him. "I need your truck again."

He stared at me a long, awkward moment, and I worried he wasn't going to give them to me. With a sigh, he tugged the keys from his pocket and dropped them into my outstretched hand. "Think carefully before you act tonight. Don't do that Glory thing, yeah?"

I wanted to protest but I knew damn well what he

was talking about. I tended to end up in a snit where I acted first and thought way later. I could go from happy to pissed in a second, and I'd let my tongue run loose too many times.

"I'll try." I closed my hand over the keys, already more calm. "I know this isn't my turf."

"And Delta isn't going to take your shit." He chucked my chin and turned away.

I didn't want Delta. Our deal was once and I planned to keep it that way, no matter how bad my baser parts craved him.

My body had healed and the need to make love was powerful. All my fantasies centered around the biker who was bad for me.

Stop fooling yourself. You want him. You fantasize about another night. You can pretend you'll say no, but you know better.

I hated when I argued with myself, and lost.

I was determined to be on a plane home on Monday. Surely I could hold strong for four days. If Vegas wasn't an option, I'd to go to LA. There were lots of dance options there, and I'd fight for my place. I wasn't ending up on the back of some small-town biker's ride, no matter how tempting he might be.

The sensuous way he'd kissed flashed through my mind. I could see his penetrating gaze eating me up. I'd never felt more desirable than when Delta had made love—no, he'd fucked me. My stupid heart couldn't confuse mind-melting orgasms with emotion. Not that I wanted him emotionally involved because that'd be so much worse. We were oil and water, black and white, ice and fire, and I couldn't forget that. We could never be happy together.

"Hey, girl." Avery bumped me with her hip. "You look serious over here."

"I'm tired of waiting, tired of not knowing, tired of everything." Tired of resisting these bikers. Tired of being disappointed by men. Just plain tired.

"Sweetie, Delta took care of everything." She patted my shoulder.

"So I can go back to Vegas, pick up the pieces of my life?" I wrung my hands together and made myself stop, then dropped them to my sides. I wasn't some country girl who couldn't control her own fucking body.

"I... I just don't know that." Avery bit her lip. "We know it was successful, but that's not very specific."

"Exactly." I sighed.

"You didn't used to be so..."

"So what?" I tapped my foot.

"Serious, angry, unhappy." Avery threw her hands in the air. "I want my old Glory back."

"So do I, but I'm not sure that's possible." I hadn't admitted it to anyone, but I was scared. I was scared I'd never find the old me, the carefree, confident girl who'd tackled Vegas with a wink and a grin. "I miss me too."

Avery gathered me in her arms and held me tight. I wished her hug made everything better, but it just didn't. Nothing made it better, and I was scared nothing ever would.

The door to the clubhouse opened. I stepped away from Avery. Zero strode through, then Thorn, and the door began to swing closed. Where was Delta?

Then he was there. Blond hair all messy, eyes downcast, and he was different. I couldn't pinpoint what was wrong, but something was definitely wrong. What had happened to him?

What had my stupidity made him do?

Without thinking, I moved toward him. I couldn't stop myself. I had to touch him, look into those piercing blue eyes and see what was wrong. The closer I came, the more off he felt. I hated it. I needed him to be the same cocky bastard I'd met in Vegas.

He'd barely made it into the room when I launched myself at him. "Delta." His name was only a whisper on my lips, but he glanced up and caught me in a tight hug and swung me around so we both faced away from the crowd of bikers.

"Queenie, damn you look good." He inhaled deeply. "Peaches."

I think that's what he mumbled before his mouth crashed into mine. His kiss branded me in a way none of our other kisses had. I was his. Emotion flared between us. I curled my arms around his neck and pressed closer, surrendering everything I had to him. I gave him my heart, then and there.

The kiss changed, growing deeper, yet softer all at once.

When my mind fired again, I heard hoots and whistles and I tried to pull back. He held me tight, then lifted me up and turned and took a step. My legs awkwardly dangled in the air, but his hold was tight and his kiss only grew fiercer.

Fuck it all.

I wrapped my legs around his middle and let him carry me from the clubroom. He kicked open the second room in the hallway and walked inside. He didn't drop me to the bed like I thought he would. He sat on the bed, cradling me in his lap.

When he finally broke the kiss, he looked at me. "You healed up?"

"Yeah. I'm better." I ran fingers down his stubbled cheek, loving the rough texture of his new whiskers.

"You can go back to Vegas to the Starlord again, if you want it."

Something shifted inside me, and the jagged pieces that had hurt so much fell back into place. "You're serious?"

"Yeah, I made it good." He gave me a ghost of a smile.

Relief washed through me, and hope blossomed for the first time since I'd turned in my resignation all those weeks ago. "You made it good." I smiled the first real smile in a long time. "You made it good." A bubble of laughter escaped. Then I kissed him. His lips first, then his cheeks, chin, tip of his nose, each eyelid, and kept showering him with kisses until he moved and claimed my mouth in a slow, passionate kiss.

Oh hell yeah, that was exactly what I'd been missing.

I held him tight and kissed him with all I had, pouring my own passion into what was brewing between us. Had it been an hour ago when I'd decided to hold strong? Four days? I hadn't lasted four freaking minutes.

I would give him all he wanted because I couldn't say no, and I didn't even want to. I only wanted to help him, give to him, and maybe he could find his way back. Because of him, I thought I might find my way back to that Glory that Avery missed.

His calloused hands slid up the back of my tee and unhooked my bra before sliding across my ribs to my front. Shivers chased down my spine. I pressed into him, feeling his hard erection. We were both on the same page, and I wanted to move to the good stuff, pronto.

A knock sounded on the door and I pulled back but Delta just followed me, not even slowing.

"You're needed in the council chambers." Thorn's voice boomed through the door.

"Goddammit." Delta did this smooth move that had me on the bed and he stood up. "Fuck, I hate to leave right now." He ran a hand through his hair. "You stay here. When this is done we're going to my place. Get me?"

With just-kissed lips and smoldering blue eyes devouring me, he was the sexiest man I'd ever seen. I'd say yes to anything he wanted. "I'll be here."

He gave me that smart-ass half grin of his. "You better be." Then he walked out the door.

Chapter 24: Delta

I rearranged my hard-on as I walked down the hall to the council chambers. I didn't want to see the leadership or talk about the shit I'd done for this club. Killing those teens had broken something in me, and I feared it had ruined my connection to the Brotherhood. When I thought of my club now, the anger boiled in me. Would that go away?

Inside, the leadership team sat around the table. I looked up at them since the table was set on a platform for just that reason.

Jericho nodded to me. "Thank you for the work you did in Vegas. That shit isn't ever easy." He looked at Thorn. "Thorn's already given us a report, but we have a couple questions for you."

I glanced at Rebel, my boss, who seemed worried. In fact the whole group was uptight.

"Did I do something wrong?" Why did I ask that? Everyone knew I'd done bad shit, and I knew I would never be the same.

"Fuck, no," Thorn barked.

"You kept us whole and we know what you sacrificed. It can't have been easy to take out those boys." Jericho said the thing I'd been trying to ignore.

Rage blasted through me. He'd been the reason I killed them. They all had. I saw their young faces devoid of life. The easy way the knife sliced through their throats. Fuck. I couldn't escape those memories. Glory had made them go away, but I didn't deserve her or deserve any respite. I'd killed those kids and now I had to live with it.

"Delta, you okay?" Rebel looked at me funny.

"What?"

"I said, you need anything?" Jericho had the same worried look on his face. "Maybe talk to someone."

"Fuck that. I ain't some wet-behind-the-ears whelp." I met the gaze of each of the council members. "You sent me to take care of it. I did. And that's all there is to it."

Jericho nodded. "Thorn said he talked to you about Vegas. You okay being out there from time to time to make sure things are going smooth? We haven't really talked that through yet."

"Maybe have you do the bail work out there? Or whatever you want, really," Rebel said.

"Whatever you need—I'll do it." I met Rebel's gaze. "I'm fine with what went down." That was total bullshit on my part. I was far from fine.

"I know, brother." Rebel nodded.

My skin itched—it was like I no longer fit in myself or in the Brotherhood. I'd changed and I wasn't sure I'd ever really fit again.

"Let's party, then," Rock said. "Thank you for taking care of Glory."

"Anything for the club, brother." I gave him my two finger salute. "But I'm going to pass on the party. Glory and I got business."

I booked it away from them before they came up with

any other ideas, but Thorn still caught up to me outside the door to where Queenie waited.

"When something eats at you, it don't stop. Not ever." He spoke low. "You got to purge that shit or it'll leave you a shell."

"I got this." I clapped him on the back. "No worries."

I didn't have myself under control and I sure as shit wasn't right with killing those kids in Vegas, but whining to Thorn or the council wasn't going to help get me right in the head. I figured I'd ignore it until it went away. It'd always worked for me before.

I slipped inside the room and locked it behind me. Glory lay atop the bed bared for me. Her golden skin called to me, and her deep blue eyes were pulling me under.

"You're too far away." She lifted her arms above her head, and her beautiful tits poked straight up.

I stepped forward and kicked off each boot. She beckoned me forward with her finger. I stripped off my shirt and unbuttoned my jeans.

My queen sat up as I shoved the pants down—she leaned forward and sucked my cock into her mouth. Fuck. Her hot mouth slid down my shaft, taking me all in. She moved up and down faster and faster. I tangled my hands in her hair and held on as she rocked my world.

The weeks without a woman was playing hell with my control. I tried to hold out, pull back but she wouldn't let me.

"Queen," I panted. Then I pushed ahead, as the climax built in my knees, rushed up my thighs and shot out of me. I'd held back too long, and the sweet relief almost stole my strength as my knees shook.

With a satisfied smile, she lay back on the bed. "Ready to go to your place?"

"In time." I stood and stepped to the end of the bed. I grabbed each ankle and pulled her toward me until her ass rested on the edge of the mattress.

She'd switched the order up, but I still planned to make her beg me to stop. I needed to satisfy her in ways she didn't know she needed. That was what I did, and normally, after making a woman scream my name all night long, I was done. But Queenie was different—I couldn't get enough of her.

I bent my head and ran my tongue along her seam. Her sweet cream tasted like perfection. With her hips rocking, she tried to anchor herself by wrapping her fingers in my hair but it was too short. I focused on her, feeling every nuance of her arousal and letting it feed mine. I coveted every groan, every breathy sigh, and every whimper.

Like the imperious queen she was—she pushed up on elbows to stare down at me. "Fuck me. I need—"

I nuzzled her clit in that way I had, and her words turned to a scream as her body quaked. Others might consider this the end, but for me, it was only the beginning.

She writhed on the bed, trying to find a deeper release. Orgasms crashed into her faster and faster until her body shook.

"Fuck me," she whimpered. "Fuck me, now." She tugged my arms but I didn't budge. I was feasting.

She leaned forward dangling her tits over me and raked fingers up my back. "I need that big cock buried deep, pounding me hard. Give me what I need."

Her begging turned me on. I'd give her what she wanted, in time.

Then she hit it—the peak where reason left and pleasure was all that remained. She pumped up into my mouth while she chanted *fuck me*. Her nails dug into my back. I had to see how I'd unraveled the queen. Her tits were magnificent and I had to taste them.

She moved her hand lower until she stroked my cock. "Fuck me, please. I need to explode around you, right fucking now." She snarled the command. Lucky for her, I recovered quickly, especially after what the women at our sex club had taught me about control.

With that wicked grin, I met her gaze, stood and with a jerk positioned her before plunging deep into that hot, ready pussy.

Within seconds her body shook harder than before. She arched up and clawed me to her. I thrust harder, faster, needing to own her as she fell apart under me. There I saw her as she truly was—and her beauty was unmatched. The passion and intensity stole my reasoning and I felt myself follow her, coming again. But this wasn't just sexual fulfillment—it went deeper. She was mine, and when I was with her she made me feel whole and right again. Holding me tight to her, I loved the fierce way she'd fucked me and I still needed more.

I settled next to her and let her snuggle into my side— something else I never did. I had never been a cuddler, but as Glory drifted to sleep beside me I started to understand the appeal. She fell asleep beside me, and I wasn't impatient to move, wasn't ready to move on. I could stare at her forever.

Chapter 25: Glory

"You joining us?" A pounding on the door woke me with a start.

Delta mumbled curse words and chucked a boot at the door. "Go away."

"Fuck that." An Italian biker strode through the door.

I should care that I was naked, but I was too exhausted.

"What the fuck?" Delta sat up and threw a cover over me. "Get the fuck out, JoJo!"

"Man, that's not a sheep." The biker sounded confused.

I had the urge to baa but that required too much energy.

"No shit! Get the fuck out of here."

"I come from OKC, and this is the welcome I get," he growled at Delta.

"I didn't ask you to come. Did I?"

"Where else would I be after the shit you went through." The guy stepped forward and hugged Delta, who was stark-ass naked.

I was sure Delta would deck him, but he didn't do anything. I saw his shoulders droop, and I realized he'd needed this just as much as the intense fucking we'd just finished. I wasn't the smartest girl, but even I could see something bothered him bad.

"Trying to sleep here. Take it outside, boys." I wasn't tired anymore, but maybe it would be the push he needed to talk to his friend.

Delta flashed me a grin and stepped into his pants before he walked out the door.

I wished I could follow him, maybe turn into a fly to hear what they said. But I'd have to pry it out of him the hard way. I lay in bed but I couldn't go back to sleep—that train had left the depot. So I pulled up my hair and stepped into the shabby but clean shower and washed off the sweat and fluids from our fun.

After I dressed, I walked around the room for only a minute or two before I got bored. Voices carried from the main room, and I decided to investigate. The club-room was now filled with bikers and girls. Some were old ladies but others were definitely the party type. Were they sheep? I spotted Avery and Lila across the room and made my way there.

"I wondered if he'd ever let you go." Avery gave me a huge smile and squeezed me in a tight hug. "I walked back to find you, but the sounds coming from your room were scalding hot—"

"Perv." I pushed my friend back a step. "Don't you get enough on your own? Have to listen to mine?"

She laughed her high-pitched tinkle that I absolutely loved.

"She's a desperate woman," Lila agreed.

I laughed. "I need a beer."

The girls walked me to the bar, where I got a vodka tonic instead of a beer from the cute kid who worked the bar.

"I get off at ten tonight." He winked and handed me a drink.

"I already got off."

"She's with Delta," Avery said at the same time as me.

The kid ducked his head and found something to do at the other end of the bar.

I turned to Avery. "Who says I'm with Delta?"

"I do." His deep rumble sounded behind me.

I glanced over my shoulder and grinned. "Well then, I guess that works for me." To the red-faced kid, I yelled. "Another vodka."

He brought me another vodka and handed Delta a bottle of Southern Comfort.

I pulled him away from the girls. "I want to dance."

"Lead the way, Queen." His gravelly voice made me wet.

"I thought that was the man's job," I quipped.

"Not when they dance with you." He arched that eyebrow and downed his whiskey.

"When did we dance together?"

"At your place—the first night we met?"

"That doesn't count—that was foreplay dancing." I remembered the way he'd moved with an understated grace.

"It's the only kind of dancing I do." He smirked and took another swig, then set his bottle on a table filled with bikers.

I downed my drink and set the glass next to his bottle. He clasped my hands and led me into the handful of dancers moving in a makeshift dance floor in front of the stage. A band played Southern rock covers. I tried to move back but Delta held on to me.

"I ain't letting you go, Queen."

With a slight jerk, he sent me stumbling forward into his arms. And then the man surprised me, again. He began a fast two-step that moved us around the room. A perfect base step for the song. As we moved, I improvised, adding more steps and sways to our dance. He followed my lead. A smile broke out on my face as we twirled around the room, moving faster with more flourish with every step. The song ended and Delta dipped me low, kissing me. The dance had been fun, but the kiss was dark and intense, filled with passion and promise.

The next song started and we moved in a sway and grind to the gritty song. Despite the fact he'd come twice in the past hour, the man was hard again. Could I ever fuck him until he didn't pop back up? Suddenly, I wanted to try. As if he read my mind, he ground into me and gave me another passionate kiss.

Fuck, he wound me up. Songs played and I worked up another sweat with my clothes on. I leaned forward to speak into his ear. "I need a break and a drink."

With a lazy grin, he led me off the floor. With a casual grace, he reclaimed his bottle and we moved through the crowd to the bar. "We need to make a decision. Go to my place and drink and fuck, or stay here and drink and fuck."

I gave him what I hoped was a saucy smile. "Do you have a band at your place?"

"So we stay." He threw his head back and laughed.

Shivers ran through me—his laugh was sexy.

"I guess we do." I couldn't believe it. I'd just agreed to stay at a biker party—to do everything I'd said I despised for years. Who was I and where had Glory Ann Atkins gone? I knew what happened. That proud, surefire girl had gone and fallen for Delta.

I shook my head, trying to dislodge the thought, but it wouldn't go away.

"Delta, the prez wants a word." Rebel joined us at the bar. "Bring Blondie, it concerns her too."

Delta gave a two finger salute. "Alright, boss."

The biker in training behind the bar handed me another drink. "Better make it two." Delta winked at me. "You need to get fucked up before I fuck you again."

I glanced at the bartender, who was grinning wide. Talking about me like that should've pissed me off, but I chose to laugh instead. These guys had no sense of privacy, and it really didn't make any sense to get pissed off about it.

"So you do have a funny bone." Delta gave me that panty-wetting smile of his.

After I collected my second drink, we meandered outside with Delta stopping every chair or two to talk to another guy. So, I knew they were all bikers—duh, we were at a damn biker party—but they didn't look anything alike and definitely not the stereotypical hairy, beer-bellied biker you see on the news. There were a few big guys, but they were country-boy, brick-shithouse big. Some were thin, others, like Avery's man, were muscle-bound. But most looked like normal guys, like I'd see at a bar on any Friday night, except they wore cuts.

I'd let myself build this stereotype of doom about the Brotherhood members, and the more I was around them, the less true it became. And that fact seriously compromised my few remaining defenses. I wished I could reclaim my sense of superiority. It'd be better than the longing I felt right now.

Delta had made his way to where Avery and Lila sat with their men, among a bunch of other bikers—they were the core group, I think. Avery's stories were always vague on detail and big on laughs.

"Pull up a chair." Jericho nodded to us. I had trouble reconciling the gritty biker at home among his family with the way he looked in my mom's dining room.

Delta sat in a chair that materialized via another biker-in-training. He sat and pulled me onto his lap. I didn't understand the lap fetish these men had. It was like a woman couldn't be trusted with her own chair. That afraid we'd leave?

Marr raised an eyebrow at her Jericho.

"Stay, all of you." He glanced at me and the other women.

And there was another reason not to fall for the stupid man under me. These macho boys didn't let girls into their club, not in the ways that mattered most.

"The Vegas situation is escalating, and we need boots on the ground, ears on the strip." Jericho cocked his head to the side.

"I can ride tomorrow." Delta absently rubbed his thumb up and down my thigh.

The delicious touch distracted me. But, if he was going to Vegas, he'd be taking me home too. "And me," I piped up, even though I suspected women were supposed to be seen, not heard.

"Works for me." Jericho froze halfway through the nod. His face got that weird look he'd had in Mom's dining room. "Monday is soon enough." He narrowed his gaze at me. "You two are going with me to this dinner I was roped into."

The big bad biker was scared of my mama. I snorted, then laughed. "Really? You got a solid foot on my mama, she's not that mean."

"She's sweet." Avery piped up. "Rock likes her."

Jericho's gaze turned black when Marr joined my laughter. "He's a baby—all men are."

"We're all going."

"How'd I get—" Delta snapped his mouth shut at the dangerous set of his president's mouth. "Fuck," he mumbled and drank down more whiskey.

I finished my two drinks as the guys gave each other shit. Rebel pulled up a chair and he and Delta talked bounty-hunting shop. That wasn't any fun. All the women were glued to their men, rubbing, touching, kissing. While it presented a sexy scene, it bothered me. They were all swallowed up with their men, and part of me wished I was too, but that rebellious streak balked at the idea of being anyone's pleasure piece. I leaned into Delta to whisper in his ear. "Going for another drink, I'll be back." I stood up and the booze went straight to my head, but at least I didn't stumble.

Before I'd taken two steps, Delta was beside me.

"What?"

"Queen, I'm not letting you out of my sight. Besides, those old guys are boring." He winked at me. "We need to dance and drink."

"And fuck." I gave him my most sassy look.

He stopped and pulled me to him. His kiss pulled me under in seconds. I loved the way his touch made me feel. When he let me go, I stumbled back, but that had nothing to do with the alcohol, it was all Delta's sex appeal.

He grasped my hand and tugged me forward. "Let's go, Queen." He wrapped an arm around my waist. "You're so fucking hot."

An icy shiver chased down my spine and coiled low in my stomach. Damn, he could turn me on with a whispered word. I was in so much trouble. We wound through the bikers until we reached the bar. He grabbed a bottle and two glasses from the kid behind the bar. "It's time to make our party private."

I ran back upstairs for the twentieth time in two hours. Mama was in a tizzy about her nephew coming to dinner today. This time I pulled out Grandma's tablecloth—the one Mama saved for the most special occasions—and hoofed it back downstairs to reset the dining room table for a third time.

My night with Delta had been scalding hot even though we never made it to his house. I'd eaten breakfast at the club Saturday morning with him and a few others before taking Mark's truck home. Delta had offered to take me on his bike, but I'd evaded that particular trap. I didn't want to know what it felt like. A good decision, it turned out, since I hadn't heard from him since then. Twenty-four hours of silence, and I cursed myself for my own stupid dreams. Why had I imagined another night of animal sex would make him call me? It hadn't the last time.

To make it worse, he'd be here today, and I had no idea what to do with that. We weren't dating, maybe we were friends, but he'd definitely saved me. What exactly was the protocol for having Sunday dinner with your hero?

"Oh that's exactly right!" Mama touched the antique lace tablecloth. "Your grandma always hated that she had a grandbaby she couldn't love on." She sighed. "MJ ripped our family and this town asunder." She took off her apron. "But I'm done letting that stand." With a smile, she patted my cheek. "Perfect, as always. You'll turn that young man's head." Mama had touched my still healing cheek with its red line. Yet she gazed at me with the same adoration she always had despite that imperfection.

I bit my tongue to keep from reminding her of all the times she'd made me swear to not date one of those bikers.

"He rescued you, and that says a lot right there." She gave me her Mama-knows-best smile. "I'll just freshen up before our guests arrive. Go ahead and arrange the savories."

I carried the trays of finger foods to the table, arranging the deviled eggs, cheese tray, olives, veggies and dips. This could fill us up, but Mama had heaping dishes for the main course and her famous five-layer chocolate cake for dessert. I stacked the small china plates and petite forks Mama insisted we use for her savories.

The doorbell rang and I hurried to Mama's room. "We have company."

"Then why are you standing there, girl. Go get the door," Mama screeched. She hated rudeness, and me hoping she'd answer the door was an offense in hospitality.

I rushed to the door and opened it with the slow grace of a Southern lady. A gaggle of bikers stood in front of me—they'd all arrived together. How had they coordinated that? Jericho and Marr entered first, and Mama walked out, making an entrance. She had that kind of theatrical timing.

"Oh, Isaac, introduce me to your friends." She smoothly bypassed the fact that none of the women were wives.

Jericho cleared his throat and a tinge of pink touched the badass's cheeks. Mama embarrassed him. I caught Delta's eye, and he glanced away, not even giving me a smile. What was that about?

"Mrs. Atkins—"

"You call me auntie or Aunt Violet or Vi, but none of this Mrs. Business—none of you!" Mama scolded him.

Jericho cleared his throat again. "Aunt Violet, these are some of my best friends."

Marr stepped forward. "I'm Marr, Jericho's old lady. Pleasure to meet his people." Her Irish brogue had Mama grinning wide.

Mama stepped forward and embraced the Amazon dressed in jeans and a T-shirt instead of her normal leather. "He needs a good woman." Mama patted Marr's back. "Welcome to the family."

Jericho glanced everywhere but at his woman and his aunt. Avery caught my eye and we stifled the laugh we both felt. Mama had the iron will of any Southern lady on a mission—she planned to adopt these bikers whether they wanted that or not.

I glanced back at Delta and wished things were different, but obviously he wasn't interested in me or being here. It wasn't like I'd tricked him into meeting my mama. This wasn't a bring-him-home-to-the-parent moment. He was here because of his precious freaking club, and I didn't appreciate his attitude.

"You know Avery and Rock," Jericho ground out.

Mama let go of Marr to embrace Avery. "Girl, you keeping that bundle safe?" She patted Avery's still-flat belly. Then hugged Rock. "I've been trying to get Avery to bring you by for weeks now."

Rock's tan cheeks turned red too. Mama was in rare form—making bikers blush took talent.

"Yes, ma'am." At her stern look, Rock amended that to a mumbled, "Vi."

"And you haven't met Delta. He was the one who helped Glory in Las Vegas."

Mama brightened up and set her sights on Delta. Before the poor guy could step aside or do anything but glance my way with panic in his eyes, Mama had scooped him into her embrace. "You saved my little girl. God bless you, son."

Now heat rose up my neck, and no doubt red stained my cheeks.

Delta stepped back and shoved hands in his pockets. Annoyance flashed across his face and he turned away. Mama watched him before turning to the group. "Please, enjoy some snacks before dinner is ready." She turned to me. "Glory Ann, bring in that tub of beer. On the back porch, now move it." She shooed me toward the kitchen.

The next few minutes were awkward as Mama hawked her beer and the bikers stood around, not sure what to do. I drew Avery and Rock aside because I wanted to discuss all things baby. Avery bubbled enthusiasm. Rock stayed quiet but joy surrounded him. He was just as stoked as Avery. They were too cute.

While I tried to ignore Delta, I couldn't. Like I'd developed Delta radar, he stayed fixed in my peripheral vision. He leaned against a wall alone drinking the Miller that Mama had supplied. He probably needed to be rescued since Mama was bearing down on him, but I was done with him—totally done.

"So you two a thing now?" Avery nodded Delta's way. Rock gave me a silent, intense stare.

"Not even. He's a biker who lives here, and I'm not staying here." That was the simplest reason although I had lots more reasons why we'd never work out.

"He'll be in Vegas most of the next year." Rock dropped that bomb like I should know that.

My skin prickled as cold and heat hit me at once. In Vegas. A year. That was bad news for me. I'd planned on distance being my number one defense against my unreasonable attraction to him.

I crossed my arms. "He didn't tell me." Translation: he didn't want me to know. Didn't want an attachment. When Jericho said he needed to go to Vegas, I'd assumed it was a quick trip and that I could hitch a ride, but after the fuck-me-and-leave-me routine, I'd decided I'd rather take a plane. Hell, I'd rather take a bicycle to Las Vegas rather than go with him, now.

"Glory Ann."

I jumped at Mama's voice. Busy working myself up over the jerk, I'd missed her coming up to us.

"You need to go talk with your friend."

"I'm talking with friends." I ignored her implied meaning.

"I raised you—"

"Yes, Mama." I tried to head off her lecture on manners. She wanted me to go rescue tall, sexy and brooding with entertaining conversation. I'd rather shove Mama's appetizer forks under my fingernails, but her disappointment was worse than any torture I could imagine. I winked at Avery and crossed the short distance to where Delta held up the wall.

"Thank you for coming today." It was a lame start, but what did I say to him?

"Not here for you." He tipped back his bottle.

"Pull your head out of your ass. I'm not here for you either, but Mama expects me to be kind to even the biggest assholes." I gave him a sweet smile. "And right now, that's you."

His mouth twitched up. "Watch that sass, girl."

"No need, I'm aware of everything I do."

"Really?" His blue eyes sparkled with mischief. Damn, he was so sexy. "Yes, I'm in control."

"I can remember some out-of-control moments."

"Moments I chose."

"That's not how I am remember it."

"You'd had a lot to drink."

"Not so much. Maybe you overestimate the benefits of control—sometimes you need to turn yourself over to more competent hands."

"If I'd ever met someone I could trust."

He tossed his head back and laughed.

My body tingled as pleasure slid through me hearing his full laugh. I loved when he laughed, and he didn't do it near enough.

A bell rang in a high tinkling sound—Mama's way of announcing dinner. "Please join me at the table, everyone."

I left him standing there with a smile on his face.

Chapter 26: Delta

Glory swished that fine ass away from me, moving straight to the kitchen. I didn't move and contemplated how much trouble I'd be in if I booked it out the door. I didn't do family, relationships, or people, really.

Jericho walked my way, as if he'd read my thoughts.

"Let's get this done." He looked as uncomfortable as I felt.

"Why are we here?"

"She's family."

"Make that why am I here?"

"You want her." He glanced to where Glory placed two dishes on the large dining room table.

"And I had her." So I was done. That's how it needed to be, even if my body wasn't yet on board with the decision.

Jericho cocked an eyebrow. "Go eat."

So much for escape. I followed orders and sat next to Rock and Avery. Violet sat next to me at the head of the table and Glory sat opposite her at the other end— far away from me. Jericho sat across from me and Marr next to him.

Bowls of food were passed around the table, and I

heaped on ham, potatoes, green beans, baked beans and some salad that had Jell-O. I took it all.

"Let's say grace." Violet smiled at us. "Glory Ann, please lead."

She gave a nod. "Dear Lord, thank you for your blessings. Please watch over all at this table and provide your loving hand to help each and every one of us. Bless the strong, bless the weak and bless the promise of the next generation. In Jesus's name, amen."

"Amen." I'd expected a rote prayer, not the heartfelt prayer she'd uttered. Obviously Glory believed. Why did that surprise me? I had trouble reconciling the girl sitting at her mama's table with the showgirl I'd met in Las Vegas.

"So do you live here in town?" Violet asked, adoration clear on her face. Tears had come to the woman's eyes when she thanked me. It had made me want to flee, but I'd mumbled the right words and stayed put. I wasn't used to mamas liking me, or attending Sunday dinner as if I were the favored son.

"I live in Ardmore, but I'll be in Las Vegas a lot this year."

"Oh, good. I feel so much better knowing Glory will have a real friend there."

"Mama, I can take of myself."

"Right. I saw how that went." I regretted the words instantly.

Glory turned bright red and fury burned in her eyes.

Rock frowned and Jericho rolled his eyes.

That had been a dick thing to say.

Violet nodded. "He's right, dear. You're tough, but you aren't a match for every challenge." She beamed at me. "Glory is talking about taking a flight out soon.

When will you be back in Vegas? I'll feel so much better if you're there when she goes back."

"I'm leaving tomorrow." I took a bite and hoped eating would stop her from talking to me. "Jericho, when are you jumping on the baby train?" It wasn't smooth, but I was tired of being cornered.

Violet winked at Marr but kept her steely focus on me. "You should go with him, Glory Ann—that way you wouldn't need to fly."

"I'm taking my bike, it's a hard ride."

"I can fly." We spoke at the same time.

"You two should totally go together—you can show Glory her new place!" Avery clapped her hands.

Fuck. Glory didn't know I'd secured an apartment and had her possessions moved to the new place. She wasn't going to be happy about that. I shot Rock a warning glare. He'd been too free with information.

He ducked his head and squeezed Avery's hand, but she ignored the warning.

"Glory, you're going to love it! Rock showed me photos."

"That's interesting." Her words froze the air. "I haven't seen photos. And I have two appointments this week to see new places." Her cool words dashed Avery's excitement.

Wide-eyed she glanced from me to Glory and back again. "No one told you?"

"What the bloody hell? This is Glory's life." Marr smacked the table.

"Well, I think that's sweet. A woman needs someone looking after her." Violet smiled at me.

That would only bring me more trouble. The other women scowled at me, and Rock swallowed hard.

"You screwed the pooch." Jericho laughed.

Glory stood and turned to walk away.

"Glory Ann Atkins, remember your manners." Violet spoke with authority.

The queen froze and then returned to her seat. With one of the coldest smiles I'd ever witnessed, she turned to Jericho. "Tell me, how is my auntie MJ?"

Violet sucked in a breath, and mother and daughter glared at each other. Damn! That was serious attitude going between them.

"I wouldn't know since I kicked her and the old man out of the club and out of this town." Jericho spoke conversationally but his eyes narrowed at Glory. His actions had transformed our club. After he'd taken control, our club had exploded with growth—new members, new businesses, and new opportunities.

"You're such a smart boy." Violet patted Jericho's hand.

Conversation struggled through the rest of the meal and I needed to escape.

Glory stood. "Excuse me, I'm not feeling…well." She stared hard at me, then walked toward the front door.

"Glory Ann don't be rude."

The door slammed on the last word. Shit. I'd created this mess, so I stood too. "Thank you for a delicious dinner."

"She's headstrong, my girl." Violet sighed.

I hurried after my queen, trying to figure the best way to work through the clusterfuck I'd created. One glance at the fuming woman on the front porch swing, and I knew I had to let her spew the venom inside her. Some women might let a mad go, but not the queen.

"Let's go." I jogged down the five steps and walked

across the yard. She'd follow because her temper wouldn't let her stay behind, not when she had so much to say to me.

"What gives you the fucking right to—to order my life?"

"It needed done."

"I'm an adult. Been taking care of myself awhile now."

"That went well." I provoked her.

"You fucking bastard. I'm very capable and don't need you holding my hand. You need to let your guilt go. How far are you willing to go, my tarnished knight?"

I smirked at that. "I'm done."

"You sure?" She purred the words. "You might need to pity fuck me again. Or maybe move in and make sure I get to work all right or maybe marry me 'cause I'm so damn helpless."

"Pity fuck? I don't pity fuck anyone." I moved in so we stood inches apart. "What's between us is hot, real, and necessary." I kissed her hard. I'd wanted to kiss her pink lips since I'd walked in the house. She pushed against me and I let her go.

Breathing hard, she stepped back as soon as I released her. She glared at me with hands fisted on her hips. "You—I can't—oh you're so damn irritating." She spun and stomped away from me.

I followed slower, letting her settle.

"I figured you wanted your things, and I needed somewhere to put them, so I found a place in that apartment building where we stayed in Vegas." I shoved my hand through my hair. "You want something else, get it."

"No way I can afford that place, and I'm not ever having another roommate." She pointed her finger at me. "You're too much. What am I supposed to do with you?"

Glory strode forward until less than an inch separated us. "You save me, make my home safe to return to, find me a place, save my stuff and fuck me better than anyone ever has—what the hell am I supposed to do with that?" she shouted while tears ran down her face.

I'd fucked her better than anyone. My chest swelled in pride.

She bit her lip and wiped her cheeks.

I pulled her into my arms. She clung to me, and a sob shuddered through her petite frame. She'd been through hell, and my surprise hadn't helped her a bit. I inhaled peaches and thought about what she'd said. I had no idea what either of us were supposed to do. Stroking her hair, I held her until her sobs quieted.

She sniffed and peeked up at me. "So much for the strong woman, huh. I'm just as weak as Mama makes me out to be."

"Bullshit. I saw you at your worst and you were *not* weak. You're strong, feisty and determined." I chucked her chin. "A true queen—you rule everyone around you."

"Except you," she whispered and looked away.

If only she knew how much she consumed my thoughts and how hard it had been to stay away from her. "Look, I'm going to be in Vegas for most of the next year, and I'd like us to be friends, yeah?"

"Why?"

"I like you."

"No—why will you be in Vegas so long?"

"Club shit." She was the last person I wanted to explain that to. Even if I could, I'd hate to admit that I'd been caught in the aftermath of my screwup. She didn't need to know anything about it.

She nodded. "Another reason we aren't a good match."

"What's up with you and our club? Hell, even your mama likes us." I didn't get why she despised the club even after we'd saved her ass.

"That wasn't always the case. You might've caught on that MJ is her sister, and she hated the club for years. But that's not my problem." She crossed her arms and bit her lip.

"And the problem?" I wanted to hear this shit.

"You'll laugh, or worse, think I'm a bitch." She blew out a breath.

I cocked a brow and waited.

"I'm not settling, and picking any man in the Jericho Brotherhood would be settling."

Was she too good for us? Really?

"I want the man I love to put me first—definitely not second to the club. Maybe I'm selfish, but I deserve to be the one he loves the most."

I stepped forward. "You deserve that and more." I kissed her forehead and traced her jawline. "We could have some fun until you find what you need."

"I'll think about it." She cocked her head. "And how much is the rent for my new place?"

I wasn't going there when I'd just calmed her down. I'd paid the rent at her place for the year, and she'd be pissed off again, for sure. "Want to go for a ride?"

She shook her head, then stared up at me. "Yes. I'd love to."

Crazy woman. I held out my hand. "Let's jet."

At my bike, I gave her my helmet since I only had the one with me. She strapped it on and I double-checked it before I stepped on my Harley Street Glide. I revved the bike and then we took off, heading down Main Street toward the highway.

Her hands around my waist scalded my skin. I was too aware of her touch as we rode. I'd never had a woman on my bike, and it bothered me that Glory had found her way inside me and onto my ride. But I was tired of fighting my self-imposed rules. Fuck those rules. Right now this is what we both needed.

Queen was the only one who kept my demons subdued. When I was with her, the boys didn't haunt me—I didn't see their deaths over and over again.

I revved the gas and we raced down the street and out of town. Moving off the main highway, I traced the curvy asphalt roads that snaked between here and Ardmore. It was past time I took Glory home.

Chapter 27: Glory

After a glorious night of sex at Delta's place, he dropped me back at home the next afternoon. Delta was a persuasive S.O.B., and I'd agreed to let him take me home to Vegas. He'd been happy to win that argument, but more, he needed me, even if he didn't say so. I could feel the turmoil churning in him. And I owed him, and I wanted a little more time with him.

So I spent the rest of the day packing then took it to the UPS store in Ardmore to ship home. I wasn't fitting much on Delta's bike. He'd given me a tiny backpack and said to pack all my shit in there. I'd stuffed an extra pair of jeans, three tops and two pairs of underwear in the bag along with my mascara, eyeliner, blush and lipstick. It wasn't easy but I was ready when he arrived at nine the next morning. With a hug and kiss to Mama, I hopped on the back of the bike, ready to be home again.

Delta and I rode into Albuquerque, New Mexico about six that night. My body didn't ache at all, and I felt lighter than I had for weeks. Riding was its own type of release and I'd always known it might addict me, which was why I'd stayed far away from these two-wheel freedom machines. All my life, I'd fought against my attraction to motorcycles and the dark men who rode them. The

Brotherhood bikers had always been the sexiest men in Barden, but the price had been too high.

And it was still too high. I needed to remember that.

We drove through Albuquerque into the Old Town. This section of town had an ambiance that made me want to live here. Delta parked his bike and helped me off the back, storing my helmet on the seat next to his. I shook out my hair and glanced around.

He clasped my hand and we walked across the street to a small adobe-style restaurant. Restaurant Antiquity was discreetly tucked into a row of businesses. A couple exited the door dressed in a suit and dress. We weren't dressed that way, and I wondered what Delta meant to do. He held the door open, and I walked into a small space filled with round cloth-covered tables. Very intimate. Delta stepped around me and greeted the person at the hostess stand with a big smile and handshake.

"Ah, Mr. Delta, so happy to see you again, your table is this way." The man led us to a corner table away from the door and the kitchen—a prime spot. Delta didn't even look as others glanced our way—his cut created an impression.

Once we were seated, he smiled wide. "They prepare the best steak I've ever tasted."

"When—" I couldn't get my thoughts together.

"I called this morning for a reservation. I never pass up the chance to have the chef's steak."

A younger man hurried over with a bottle of wine. "So nice to see you again, Mr. Delta."

I would never have expected him to drink wine.

"Are you having steak too?"

"Yes, sure." I was still trying to catch up to what was

happening. This biker was on first-name basis with the staff at this fine dining establishment.

"Two steaks, medium rare—Tony can pick the rest." He glanced up at me. "No food allergies?"

"Not even." I waved the question away.

Once the waiter left, Delta focused on me. "Damn, I'm hungry." He cocked a brow. "And I'm having you for dessert."

I smiled back. The idea of Delta in my bed was never a bad idea. I'd agreed to this fling idea of his, after all. Straightforward sex the way Delta did it was exhilarating.

The wine came first, and Delta waved away the formal tasting process. "I know it's good."

And Delta was right, the merlot was tart without being too dry.

"Why dancing?" He leaned back and swirled the deep red wine. The sconces created bright blond highlights and shadows that danced across his hair.

I pasted on my pageant smile and prepared to give my pat answer, but something in his eyes made me stop and reconsider. "I love it. Always have. My first memory is twirling in the center of a big stage. Maybe I was three—people clapped as I danced, and that was perfection. It's just what I'm meant to do."

"Then you're in the right place. You deserve that dream."

"Deserve? Not even, but I'll claw and fight for it because that's me too." I sipped the wine and considered him. "What were you made to do?"

"Nothing."

"Everyone is meant for something," I teased.

Darkness fell across his features, and a chill settled

into me. "I'm good at getting people killed, letting them down, fucking it all up."

Ouch. His words hurt me, but it was the first of his pain he'd verbalized. I forced myself to stay calm. Upbeat.

"Well, that's not nothing!" I forced a smile. "We both have our talents."

He glowered and I wondered if he was going to lay into me or leave, but then he shook his head and laughed. It wasn't a good laugh, but he didn't look like he was going to bolt anymore, so I held up my glass in toast. I didn't want to mess up the new peace, so I stayed quiet and we enjoyed a silent toast.

I steered conversation to lighter topics, not wanting to see that darkness again. The steaks came in a few minutes with baby potatoes and green beans artfully arranged around the steak.

I sliced the first bite of pink steak. The aroma was divine, but nothing compared to the delicious taste of the tender cut. I moaned my appreciation. "This is better than I have words for."

He gave me a genuine smile. "I'm glad you agree. You're the only thing that tastes better than this steak."

Heat rushed to my cheeks. No one had ever worshipped my sex like Delta did, and I'm not sure I'd ever be the same.

The next day we rode on and then we turned south, instead of heading north toward Nevada. Part of me was annoyed but another part didn't want to rush him because I'd made a decision in the wee hours of the night wrapped tight in his embrace. This affair was done when we reached Vegas. I needed to be a realist and protect myself. He wasn't mine, and I wasn't one of them. What might be didn't matter because the reality of our situation killed all possibilities for a future.

Navajo reservation signs dotted the road. What was he doing? We drove on until we came to a Hopi reservation sign. He turned onto a gravel road then turned onto a blacktop. Obviously he knew his way around this country. Why had he been to the reservations before? The longer I was with him, the less he made sense. He had layers and layers and no desire to share beyond the surface. He stopped at a roadside café with a faded painted sign that read Café.

"Let's get breakfast." He wrapped me close to him, guiding me with the hand now snug against the small of my back.

Inside were a few tables that looked more pathetic than the oddball collection at the Brotherhood clubhouse. We sat down, and a large Native American shuffled out from the kitchen.

"What can I get you?"

"The special and directions to the local fair."

The guy took a few more steps our way. "You missed it, it's—"

"The *local* fair."

"It's over three towns in Falls until about noon. You'll need to book it to get there."

The guy went back to the kitchen and came out in just a few minutes with two plates that smelled delicious. He set down two glasses of water with barely any ice and then two heaping plates of food. An Indian flatbread was folded beside a mixture of eggs, sausage and peppers. I took one bite—it was amazing. I started scooping it in as fast as I could.

"What are we doing today?" I asked between bites.

"The Hopi Indians have the best fairs—full of color and light. I thought we'd explore it and the reservation for a while."

"You like Indian art?"

"Yeah, you got a problem with that?"

"Not really...just seems like...not your thing."

"You don't know jack about me or my thing."

That was too true. "So tell me, then."

"Like I'm giving you that kind of ammunition, Queenie."

"Trade you...morsel for morsel. You ask then I ask, if you dare."

He cocked his head and arched an eyebrow. "Why Vegas? Why not LA or New York?"

"I'm Vegas material—flash with the right curves. I don't have the training to be a dancer in New York, and LA is about beauty and acting. Vegas is for me. It's where I belong—the white trash cousin to New York."

"Ouch. Hard on yourself much?"

"I'm a realist, and I don't lie to myself. I'm good with Vegas, good with dancing—it satisfies me in a way nothing else ever has." I considered him and then asked my question. "Why the Brotherhood?"

"I fell into the club, I guess. I wanted the army, and JoJo followed me there. When that was done, well, I wasn't in a place to make decisions about anything. JoJo joined and I did too." He stared out the window of the diner. "They accepted me, accepted us, and I never thought much about it..." He just let the words trail off and stared into the middle distance.

I wished I could read his mind, see what troubled him.

With a shake of his head, he met my gaze. "Why ain't you married?"

"No one ever asked me. I haven't had that many boyfriends. This face scares away more than you'd think."

"Right." He chuckled. "'Cause you're so hard on the eyes."

"I'm too easy on the eyes for many guys' confidence, and I pick the worst of the worst, apparently." I glared at him, thinking about how much I liked him. Too damn much for my own good. He was another asshole who'd hurt me if I let him, so I wouldn't let him.

"Who did you kill in Vegas?" There, I'd asked the question I wanted answered most of all. What had he done in order to let me come back to the city I loved?

He didn't even look at me, just scraped back his chair, dropped a twenty on the table. "Let's jet." He turned and left me still sitting there, fork halfway to my mouth. Well, I'd ended that game.

After I caught up to him and strapped on my helmet, he took off like the demons of hell were on our tails, and maybe they were. Maybe I'd set them loose when I asked my question.

I'd expected him to head north toward the highway since I'd obviously pissed him off, but he turned onto another small road that wound deeper into the reservation. In a few minutes, a few houses dotted the road and we slowed. Across from us, there was a sign. Market Open. He came to a stop and parked. Behind the sign was an old building that in its heyday might have been a store or restaurant, now it was as decrepit as the cars parked along the road.

We walked inside, and six different booths were scattered through the space. There were katsina dolls the

Hopi were known for, colorful rugs, paintings and pottery. A wrinkled crone sold herbs in a far corner, and she had a line. The others weren't as busy.

Delta walked straight to the rug dealer. "Kotori, how's it hanging, brother?" Delta and the large man clasped hands and did a back-slapping hug.

"Hanging low, brother." The big guy shook with laughter, then looked to me. "And your friend?"

"This is Glory, she's in the market for some new stuff for her place. You need to hook her up." Delta winked at me.

The brightly woven rugs called to me most. But I loved the pottery and paintings too. The little dolls they were famous for didn't really do much for me. I only wished I could afford it all, but there was no way I could.

"Go find things you want and bring them back here. Kotori and I will haggle the price." He tried to shoo me away.

"No."

He stared at me as if he didn't know the simplest word in the human language. "Get shopping." The two words held traces of meaning I couldn't even begin to decipher.

"No," I repeated.

He turned fully to me and guided me out the door by the elbow. "What the hell?" He spoke as soon as we'd cleared the door.

"I'm not your charity case." I couldn't be plainer than that. "And I don't have the extra money to spend now."

"I am buying you shit, so get in there and pick it out." He spoke with low menace, but I wasn't about to back down.

"No, dammit." I stomped my foot. "You got me a new place, moved my shit, are taking me home, and that's all too much. Too much on top of too much. You already did too much when you did whatever you did that you won't tell me about, so I could even go back home," I groused. "I will never be able to repay you for all you've done for me. I admit you've been my hero—my knight in fucking armor—but enough is enough."

He grinned at me. "Done now?"

The irritating man grinned.

"Get your ass in there and pick out shit, or I'll do it for you!" He smacked my ass.

"I said no! You rode in, saved me, killed people so I could go home, and now you're fixing everything, like… like I'm yours." I willed the tears gathering in my eyes not to fall. "Stop it!"

Chapter 28: Delta

Glory stood with anger shining bright, and I'd never been more turned on in my life. I loved her riled up and ready to fight—it lit me up.

And she thought I was some kind of knight? Boy was she wrong.

"I fucked up, and I'm just making shit right." I hated admitting it, but I saw no other way to get her stubborn ass inside and doing what I needed her to do.

"You didn't fuck up anything—that was all me."

"No, it wasn't. Sure, they tried to make you pay for rejecting their boy Frankie, but that retribution was over with the beating they gave you." I had hoped I wouldn't have to cop to how much I'd fucked up her life. "Our response—my response—to Frankie fucking with you is what caused the blowback. I took it too far, and DeLuca was going to pay me back." I stalked toward her but she didn't back away from me.

Rage built and the emotion from all those kills, all those mistakes, poured out of me. "I fucked up, and I am trying here to make shit right. You *are* going to let me do that for you."

Her eyes narrowed and she stepped right into my

space. "You didn't fuck up, you saved me. And don't you forget it." She poked me in the chest.

Her arms snaked around my neck and she pulled me down to her and kissed me hard. There wasn't an ounce of soft in her kiss, and I gave back what she dished out. And she took it all, standing toe-to-toe with me, she didn't waver once. Emotion, lust, need poured out of me and she took it and turned it back into our connection. Heat blazed between us and I knew right then, I was a goner. I loved her, and there wasn't a damn thing I could do to change that.

The kiss broke and we both stood panting. I wanted to drag her behind a building and fuck her now, and I had a good shot at getting her to agree.

"Let's go buy shit." She winked at me and strode past, leaving me dick-hard and panting.

I'd never met a more glorious woman than my queen.

I took a minute to calm my racing heart, then I followed her inside. In the time I'd left her to shop, she'd already picked out four colorful rugs and stood in front of the art booth.

"What's the issue?" I noted the wrinkle between her brows.

"Can't decide between these two. I like them both but I don't think both will fit in the space."

"We'll take both. Put one in your bedroom, in the john—if you like them, then buy them."

"You aren't helping." She shot over her shoulder as she moved on to the pottery.

In just a half hour, she picked out a good selection of art that all blended together, but didn't have that arranged feel, like it was too matched. I'd paid the bill and arranged for Kotori to ship it all to her apartment in Las Vegas.

"I'll be back." She followed one of the women out the side door.

"Where are they going?"

"Mina has a large rug almost done and Blondie is looking it over." Kotori watched after them. "You keeping that one?"

"She's not a stray animal." I didn't want to think about forever.

"She's in need of a home, though."

"What do you know?"

The big man just stared right into me and sent chills down my arms.

"Stop that spooky stuff." Just because he was the tribe's shaman didn't mean he needed to practice on me.

His deep laugh filled the emptying shop. Our visit had kept the small market open longer than normal, but our purchases would keep them fed for weeks. Rez life was good and bad—just like life everywhere—but it was definitely slower here. Time was one thing everyone had in abundance, and hurrying just didn't happen.

Glory strolled back inside with a wide smile. "Add Mina's rug to the list. She'll ship it in a couple weeks." She sashayed her hips and didn't stop until she was right in front of me. "Thank you, Delta. I love these treasures." Then she kissed me. Sweet and slow. We hadn't shared a kiss like this before—one without the fire I'd come to associate with her. Damn, she tasted perfect all sugar with only a hint of spice.

We rode away from the Hopi reservation a little after one in the afternoon, and all too soon the guilt seeped back. It was like a cancer consuming me in every quiet moment. I'd tried whiskey, my bike, and only Glory in my arms blocked the visions of those two teens falling from my gunshots. I saw the surprise and then the expressions went blank—life gone by my hand.

I remembered the trickle of dark red blood as I cut their throats, smelled the metallic odor of their blood, and I knew I'd never escape the memory, let alone the guilt that weighed on me. Hell, I deserved that guilt and a thousand times worse.

I had nothing good in me. I brought death with me, and I was done trying to run from it. I'd get Glory home, then I'd spend my days suffering, letting it eat me from the inside out. I had no idea what to do about it, and honestly, I didn't deserve a reprieve. Those boys weren't waking from the worms, so I'd have to wallow down there with them.

The only good thing besides Glory was being away from the club. My mistakes had soured the club too. The Brotherhood I'd cherished felt like additional weight now. The club was tied up in my self-hatred, and no matter what Thorn, Jericho or anyone said, what I'd done wasn't right. And I'd done it for the club because I hadn't realized what I was doing. When I'd seen those boys die— my connection to the Brotherhood had become forever twisted in my guilt. Another thing I'd spoiled.

My mood darkened faster than the sky as we drove into the evening. I need a bottle of whiskey or three and some hard fucking. I didn't deserve her, didn't deserve anything good, and sure as hell didn't deserve to be considered her fucking hero. That's what she'd called me. If only she knew how wrong she was.

I stopped at a motel just past the Nevada line. We went inside and I booked two rooms for the first time. I was so done with people, with her. The clerk passed me two keys and we went upstairs to the adjoining rooms. I flipped open my wallet and pulled out two hundred and tossed it to the bed before striding out and into my own room.

"You fucking asshole." Glory yelled behind me, but I didn't care. "What are you paying me for now?"

I spent maybe five minutes staring at my wall in my room before I left, again. I needed a bar and whiskey and maybe someone who wanted to start shit. I drove maybe half a mile before I spotted the kind of bar I liked—a dive with a few bikes out front. I parked next to another Harley and headed inside.

A bleached blonde with a huge rack smiled wide when I sat at the end of the bar. "What can I get you, handsome?" By the way she said it I knew I could fuck her, and maybe I would, but first I needed the whiskey.

"Southern Comfort, in doubles, and keep them coming. Give me a stout ale, and keep those coming too."

She gave me a wide smile and set down the bottle, a tumbler and a stout.

I slid her two twenties. "That's for you."

She folded the bills and tucked them in her bra, giving me an even better view of her tits.

I drank the whiskey, sipped my beer and brooded. I needed to figure out my next move. I could go nomad, ride free and stay away from the club I considered home. I didn't deserve a home or brothers after the death I'd caused. At least none of my brothers were dead, yet. I hadn't screwed up enough to cause that kind of damage, like I had in the army. But I'd done shit that was wrong, against every code I ever held. How could I not hate the men I'd protected when I'd killed those kids? Already I felt the hate coloring everything—I hated myself, and soon that would be the Brotherhood too. Maybe I should just leave the club. That idea tore through my chest—pain scorched me. The Jericho Brotherhood was the only home I'd ever had. And I didn't deserve a home anymore.

I reached for the bottle of whiskey but it was empty, and so were the four beer glasses in front of me. Hell, I wasn't even drunk. The regret and guilt swirled in a bitter storm in my core. "Give me a bottle to go." I slid a hundred to her.

She cocked her head at me. "Fingers?" She held up two.

"Two."

She took the hundred, and it followed the twenties into her bra. "I get off in two hours, you want to wait for me?"

The girl was hot and my type, but I wasn't interested in fucking anyone but the blonde who had been on the back of my bike for two days now. Just another sign of my bad fucking luck—I only wanted a woman who didn't want me.

"I'm not in that kind of mood tonight."

Just as I spoke, an idiot swaying on his feet lurched to the bar. "You must be one of those fake bikers then—all bark no bite." He guffawed at his own joke and didn't even see the punch I threw—he ended up on the floor, out cold. Nobody dissed my cut.

The bartender gave me a smile and slid me my bottle. "You know where to find me."

"I do at that." I took my bottle to the bike and stored it in the saddlebags before driving back to the hotel. Back in my room, I shed my clothes down to my boxers and turned on the TV to some true crime show before I opened the bottle of whiskey. Only a few sips into the bottle, a knock sounded on the connecting door—I ignored it. She stopped.

I kept drinking. Now my brain slowed and thinking was harder—staring into nothing and not thinking was almost easy. Peace. Damn, I missed this quiet.

The door clicked and then opened. "Don't need anything."

"You need me." She sauntered in, and man was she right.

Every time I saw her, she took my fucking breath away.

"You need to share that whiskey." She plopped down on the bed beside me, ruining my peace.

Now all I could think about was fucking her, again. I passed her the whiskey. She drank but didn't talk. She handed me back the bottle and we sat there sharing what was left of my bottle. She smelled wonderful—I loved her fresh peach scent just like I loved her.

Fuck. That was another reason to drink. I tipped up the bottle and nothing came out.

"Finished it." She stared into me. "Wanna talk or fuck?"

"What do you think?" I never wanted to talk.

She slid her shirt up her peach skin and I was hard—damn, she was fine.

In seconds, her tits bounced and her ass tempted me. "Get naked." She bit her lip and watched me strip off my boxers. "You have a great cock—good size and you know how to use it." She bent low and sucked my cock into her mouth, taking all of me and then sliding back up.

The physical pleasure mixed with the fog created from too much whiskey shrouded me in a haziness I craved. All too soon I felt the haze clear as need shook through me. I would claim her, fuck her until nothing remained to haunt me. I'd sacrifice all my demons to the lust that always blazed between us.

Then Glory wiggled that ass and took me deep. As she came back up, I caught her under her arms and pulled her up until I could smash my mouth into hers. I let the wild loose, biting her bottom lip and plundering her sweet mouth.

"Going to fuck you hard," I growled. "Ass up, Queen." I smacked her ass as she scrambled into position. "Not taking it easy on you. Need to be rough, you with me?"

She tossed her hair over her shoulder and met my gaze. Hunger burned in those baby blues. "I'm with you."

With a quick jerk, I lined her hips up and pushed into her. With singular focus, I pumped into her and let the sensation cut through me, ripping away the loathing, regret, and guilt. She purged my darkness and filled me with her perfection.

"More." She massaged her plump tits. "Close."

I ground into her, and she moaned.

So much built inside me, behind the walls I'd created to keep all that rage and shit buried.

"That all you got, boy?" She panted the challenge. "Thought you—" Her words turned to a scream, and she squeezed me tight as her orgasm racked her.

Where was that sassy mouth now?

I held tight and pounded her, her whole body shook, then I was gone—the wall broke and it all flooded out of me as I bellowed. She'd brought me over faster than I'd figured possible, but damn, it was just what I needed. I rode the sweeping pleasure and lay wasted.

Body quivering and mind quiet, peace stole through

me. So sweet. I pushed her down to the bed and collapsed over her back, holding her to me.

Sweat dripped down my face and for the first time since that damn night in Vegas, I felt hope.

"Move already." Glory jostled me.

Had I passed out? I rolled onto my back and looked down at my Queen.

"That was hot, right up until you tried to smother me." She arched that perfect brow. "You trying to kill me?"

My mind was muddled, so I shrugged. Words were too hard right now. She stretched and pushed that ass straight up in the air. My cock twitched. *Don't even think about it*, I warned it. *Ain't got more in me now.*

Glory rose and padded to the bathroom. A few minutes later, she came out of the bathroom and stared at me before coming over and climbing into bed beside me. "Scooch down and hold me."

I did what she said, loving the way she fit against me. Her hand traced circles on my chest. Her peach scent tickled my nose.

"Tell me about it." She didn't look my way.

"We had sex, really fucking great sex."

She rolled to her side and her full tits distracted me. She had pert nipples, and I needed a taste.

"About what you did in Vegas," she said when I'd finished tasting her tit.

"You don't want to know."

"You need to talk. Believe me, I know." She sat up and pulled her knees to her chest. "You're eating yourself up because I made you kill those people. I deserve to know."

Deserve? That pissed me off. Who the fuck did she think she was? Besides, she'd hate me if she understood how far I'd gone.

"Get this straight—whatever I did wasn't for you." I spewed the words, feeling the rage behind them. "It was for my brothers, my club. I don't owe you shit."

"Then there's no reason not to say it." She glared at me. "Unless you're afraid of telling me? Ashamed of your actions?"·

Ashamed, hell yes.

Afraid, never.

I'd walked through hell and had the scars to prove it. Maybe it was time to prove to Queenie just how dark my life was—then she'd leave me in peace. No way she'd want to be around me once she knew I was a kid killer. It was for the best she understood just who I was.

"You can't handle my truth." I gave her one last out.

"I can handle it far better than you are."

"Really? Here it is." I sat up as adrenaline pounded through me. "I killed two kids. Shot them without even knowing I'd killed kids until...until they were fucking dead."

She sucked in a breath.

"Yeah. And, when we were done, seventeen were dead. I slit every single one of those throats, pinning it all on another gang." Hatred ran through my veins. "You got something smart to say now?"

"Who were the kids?"

I glanced up, that wasn't what I'd expected to hear.

"Sons of one of the mob guys. And they were there, so they were popped."

"And it's eating you alive." She stared at me with cold eyes. "If you're such a badass, why is this even bothering you? Was it the wrong call? What?"

I shook my head, trying to make sense of the shit coming out of Glory. Where was the outrage, the shock, the revulsion? None showed on her face. Just this cold curiosity that fed my anger.

"I didn't even think about it, just did it. And if I had? If I'd registered they were kids, they would've still had to die."

Chapter 29: Glory

I wanted to cry for him. Pain had carved lines in his face, and I hated seeing it.

"What bothers you most?" I steeled myself and forged ahead. "That you killed them without knowing, or that you couldn't have done it if you'd known."

"Fuck!" he bellowed. "All of it! That what you want to hear? It bothers me to have done it, and it bothers me to know that if it hadn't been me, it would've been another brother. And it just eats me up that this scum has ruined the purest thing in my fucking life."

"What did it ruin?"

"I fucked up! Get me. This was all because I took it too far with fucking Frankie, and I paid, we all fucking paid because I got carried away. Costing people their lives—that's what I'm fucking good for. That's all I'm fucking good for." He ran fingers through his messy hair. "I kill people, get people killed, I'm fucking poison. And now I'm spreading that poison to you."

"You're a good man." I ran a hand over his cheek. "With a conscience and a definite idea of what's right and what's not." I loved him, and I wished I didn't because every road I saw from here ended with my heart broken and Delta gone. "You are right to feel bad, but destroying yourself isn't helping anyone. Not you or those kids."

"What do you know? Death for death—that's what's right."

"Not even." He was so buried in guilt and I needed him to see light or what he said would come true. I couldn't bear a world without Delta in it. "You owe those kids a long full life—one you live clean and bright." I poked his chest. "You should live for not only you but for them."

"You don't fucking know anything." He pushed up and fell back as the whiskey and sex took their toll.

I palmed his cheek and he jerked away.

"I don't need your fucking advice."

"But you need my fucking." I caressed his cock.

He exhaled with eyes closed. He stole my breath with his devastating beauty. I pushed up on my knees and kissed his closed eyes, moving down to his cheek before capturing those perfect lips. With slow deliberation, I moved down his neck to his chest.

"Make me forget again." The words were a low whisper.

"I can do that." I caressed his cock and guided him inside me. I moved in slow circles. He had tried to fuck me so hard he'd exorcise his guilt. It hadn't worked, so this time I'd try soft lovemaking. Each stroke, each soft circle, I felt the need build, the love I felt budding between us.

He groaned and held me tight. "Yes, my Queen. Make me forget."

We wound each other up with slow, sexy touches. Each one more addicting than the last, and when we climaxed together, I'd given him my heart—he'd tattooed my soul. And if it only comforted him for those minutes, it was worth the price.

After that night, our relationship changed. Not in the hearts and declarations of love kind of way, but we were one—a unit. He'd come to me with this haunted look and we'd fuck it away. We stayed in that little town another day, just being together.

On the fourth day of our trip, we saw Las Vegas ahead. I'd vowed to end this affair when we reached Vegas, but I couldn't do it. Delta didn't have forever in him—at least not the way I wanted forever—but I wasn't ready to say goodbye. He needed me right now and I didn't have the strength to end it, yet. I'd just have to ride it out and trust I'd know when it was time to move on. More likely, he'd get tired of me and take care of leaving without me doing anything. I had too much on my plate anyway. The Brotherhood had gotten me rehired at the Starlord, so I'd need to bust my ass to practice so I'd be in performing shape.

We pulled into the apartment complex, and excitement made my pulse race. A new place that was only mine— well, mine and Delta's for however long that lasted.

"You ready to see the place?" He gave me one of his rare smiles.

"I am. And I'm ready to soak this body. I'm sore from riding today." Or more likely all the sex we were having.

"I can work those kinks out."

I grinned. "I thought you liked my kinks."

"Let's get a move on, Queen." He pulled me after him.

The apartment was on the ground floor, a rare find in Vegas. I walked in and squealed. He'd had someone unpack and arrange things. Of course, I'd need to fix it up, but at least there weren't a thousand boxes. In the middle of the living room five boxes sat still packed. I moved to them and saw an Arizona return address. "My Hopi stuff." I did a little dance before I ripped into the first box.

It was my pottery pieces. I took out the bright blue vase and circled the room, finding the perfect place for it. Delta plopped into my recliner with a satisfied grin stretched across his face.

I went about placing my treasures while he flipped between channels. He'd give an opinion if I needled him, but I could tell he liked watching me decide where to put everything. I started with one of the smaller Hopi rugs and attached it to the wall, making it the centerpiece of my dining room. I put two rugs in my bedroom. One by my side of the bed and one at the end of it. I loved the color. Then I hung one of the paintings on the wall in the bedroom. I placed a couple small pieces of pottery on a shelf I hung in the bathroom.

The rest of the pottery went in the kitchen. The big bowl went on my table and the other pieces decorated the bar between the kitchen and dining area. The apartment only had one bedroom, but the living area was spacious. I loved it.

Eventually, the last Hopi box was empty and the place had character. It was home.

"I'm going to take a bath."

He gave a nod.

The tub was a huge whirlpool affair. I began running the water and undressing. Delta had taken care of everything, and that should rub my feminist bone the wrong way, but it didn't. He'd needed to do it, I think. And I needed him to feel better. I loved the way light flooded the space from the glass block wall beside the tub.

I slid into the steaming, sudsy water and shut my brain off, just letting the aches wash away. The door opened and Delta stood staring at me. The hunger in his gaze ignited my need, not that it took much.

"You joining me?"

He pulled off his tee in answer and soon padded toward me naked. Water sloshed over the edge when he joined me. I should care, but I couldn't look away from the heat of his stare.

He pulled me to him and settled me on top of his lap before he lavished kisses on my neck and breasts, stealing my breath and feeding the crazy addiction I had for him. When I couldn't stand the touches another minute, I moved up until I was centered over his cock and slowly I lowered myself, taking him in inch by inch. The water caressed us, our bodies moved, and I fell harder. How was that even possible?

Without ever talking about it, Delta just stayed. He didn't tell me why or how long, but he was there when I got home from work most nights, and when he wasn't he texted. I liked having him near because I felt safe and strong with him in my life. I could almost ignore the seed of fear lodged deep inside me. Pretend I didn't flinch when a man who wasn't Delta walked too near me. Pretend I hadn't woken up in a hospital just a few months ago.

In Delta, a darkness lurked, and it was growing stronger as days passed. It didn't scare me because that darkness wasn't aimed at me, but at himself. Whiskey bottles began to pile up in my trash and I needed to do something, say something, but what did you say to a man whose demons you understood, whose love you needed, but whose heart was locked away?

Nothing. I just used my body to give comfort and my smile to give him a bit of cheer. I was the worst kind of coward.

After a hard night dancing, I came home after midnight and wanted a bath, my man and sleep, in that order. The place was dark and I worried Delta was gone again. He'd been away a lot more recently.

I unlocked the door, dropped my bag and kicked off my heels inside the door. Delta sat in the recliner—two empty bottles of Southern Comfort on the floor and a third to his lips. That was ten bottles in the trash this week and it was only Wednesday. This couldn't fucking continue—he'd kill himself.

I stalked forward trying to figure out what to say. What to do?

"Hey, sexy, you partying alone again?" That was lame and weak.

He didn't even look my way.

I climbed up on his lap and bent for a kiss. He latched on and kissed me like I was his only hope of salvation. And my heart broke for him. Killing those teens was eating him up.

"Thought you'd never come home." His words slurred, he clumsily pulled me close. "You make it stop."

"Make what stop?"

"The thoughts—the voices telling me how bad I fucked up. The faces, I see their dead faces all the fucking time." He drew me down in another kiss.

I broke the kiss and tugged his hand. "Let's go to bed, love."

With a lopsided smile he struggled out of the chair. Damn, he was drunk, more so than I'd ever seen before. We made it down the hall and he flopped into bed, fully clothed. I pulled off his boots and undressed before heading to the bathroom to remove my makeup and get ready for bed. The bath would have to wait. Delta needed me. Honestly, he needed so much more than I could give him.

When I came back into the bedroom, his eyes were closed. I lay down next to him and he drew me to him, holding me so tight I could barely breathe. His grip loosened and I stretched out to grab my phone. I hit Avery's contact to text her.

Send me Thorn's number.

A second later, she replied. Why?

I typed furiously. Delta is fucked up about shit that went down in Vegas, and I'm scared. He needs more help than I can give him. Do you think Thorn could help?

My thumb hovered over send, instead I deleted it. Delta would've reached out if he wanted the club to know, and my message felt like a betrayal.

Instead I typed back a simple response. I need it.

The baby kicked today! I am sooooooo excited!

You will be a wonderful mama!

Avery sent the number and told me goodnight. I stared at the number and tried to decide what to type to Thorn.

Have you called Delta? Too little.

He's killing himself. Help Delta. Too dramatic.

How can I help Delta? He's hurting. Wrong too.

I slipped out from under his arm and moved into the living room. Before I lost my nerve, I hit call on my phone screen.

"Yeah? Glory, you okay?" Thorn's deep rumble answered.

How did he know it was me? "I am, but he isn't."

"How's he doing? He hasn't talked to me in weeks."

"He's finished off ten bottles of whiskey in four days, and that's been going on awhile now."

"Fuck me. I warned him. I'll take care of him."

He clicked off.

That was one of the strangest conversations I'd ever had, yet I was relieved. I had no idea how to help Delta through this mess, but my intuition said Thorn knew a whole lot about surviving shit. The weight I'd been carrying the past few weeks eased some as I walked back to bed. I curled up next to my broken man and willed sleep to come.

The next morning, Delta woke me with kisses to my breasts before he moved low between my legs. He knew my body so much better than he did when we met, and he built my need to new heights today, showing me just how intimately he understood me, body and soul. He ravaged me with orgasms, stealing my breath and making my body shake with ecstasy.

"Please, need you, now." I all but wept the words as he began another campaign on my overstimulated sex.

He glanced up at me with suppressed need of his own. "When I say you're done."

Moans, gasps and screams came from me as he played my body with absolute expertise. I held on to him, and prayed for more, for the release I wanted most of all.

But he pushed my body higher and higher until it

crashed with yet another orgasm. As I shook with the power of it, he plunged inside me, hard and rough.

"Yes!" I chanted over and over, digging fingers into his shoulders.

He met my eyes and fierceness possessed him. I gave every bit of that back, moving to meet him with my own frantic thrusts. Orgasms fell one after another as he finally gave me what I'd begged for. I loved him. Needed him. Reveled in the fierce way we fucked.

"Ass up," he growled and turned me over.

I scrambled to comply. He smacked my ass hard, and a thrill chased through me, revving me up yet again. I'd never met a man who understood me like Delta did.

"That's it. Fuck, I love you." He pushed into me.

He'd said it. Then he consumed me and thoughts escaped, thinking gone, I soared with him and we both came together. His bellow of release matched my own and we collapsed down to the bed with him lying atop me.

Panting to regain my breath, I lay sweating and spent. He'd possessed me so completely, I barely knew my name, but I understood one thing—we loved each other. I should tell him that I loved him. Did he even remember telling me?

Seconds ticked past, my breathing slowed, and the window to share my heart closed. We lay wrapped together until my alarm sounded and reminded me it was time to start my day. With one last kiss, I rolled off the bed, giving Delta my attention. The heavens moved when we were together today, yet words were always hard for us. Not having any words to say, I padded quietly into the bathroom to shower and get ready for dance practice.

When I came back out almost an hour later, he was

gone. I hoped he was making food for us. I dressed in my yoga pants and top before exploring the rest of the condo. Delta was gone. When had he left? I checked my phone, but he hadn't messaged me and he rarely did.

I grabbed my bag and decided to have breakfast at the casino. As I opened my door, my phone pinged. I clicked the message from Delta. Heading back to Barden. It's been fun.

A laugh escaped at the message I'd received. Of all the ways I imagined our affair ending, this hadn't occurred to me. A fucking text? A tear slid down my face as I dropped my phone back into my purse. There was no response needed—none I was capable of anyway.

Chapter 30: Delta

The wind blowing on my face and the sun hot as hell did nothing to improve the hangover raging through me. I was heading back to the one place I had no desire to go—the clubhouse. But Thorn had sent out a call for help, and I would never ignore that, despite the fact I'd ignored his calls for the last three weeks.

My last morning with Queen replayed through my mind. She embodied perfection to me—strong, sexy, and she gave no quarter. I loved her fire and it was all that had kept me halfway sane the past few months. This morning I'd tried to show her how much she'd meant to me, to thank her in the only way I knew how, and I think she understood me. The woman could fuck like no other, and she'd given me every ounce of her passion, even when she didn't want to. She'd tried to hold some of herself back, but I'd kept after her until every bit in her was mine.

When the call came from Thorn, she'd been in the shower. It would've been easy to walk in the bathroom, but I'd been a chickenshit pussy who'd bailed without seeing her. Hell, she was probably glad I was gone. I'd seen the worry and the way she hurt for me, and it only made me want to drink deeper. Hell, she probably had felt too sorry for me to kick my drunk ass out. No. A clean break was best, and I promised myself I would not go back. I could never go back to her because if I did, I wouldn't be able to leave her again. She deserved a helluva lot better than me.

The trip back to the Brotherhood was nothing like our trip out to Vegas. I drove straight through, hitting Barden sixteen hours after I left. Glory and I had taken four days traveling to Vegas—magical days I'd always remember. But that was my past, and this was now.

Head pounding and eyes burning I rode into the Brotherhood compound after midnight. Thorn hadn't said what the situation was, but I needed a job, something to forget the shit slicing me up.

I walked inside and found Thorn at the bar with Jericho and Rebel. What the fuck were those two doing here after midnight? They had women at home. I know if I had Glory as mine, I sure as fuck wouldn't be here when I could be with her.

"You made good time." Thorn nodded for me to sit. Jericho held up a beer.

When I inclined my head, he stood and grabbed one out of ice on the other side of the bar, then slid it down to where I sat.

"You've done good in Vegas," Jericho said. "Job looks done to me. The Triad took up the slack. You smoothed over the few rough spots with the Renegades." He sipped his beer. "Glad they got a piece of the action."

"Nice that the Remington is under new, legitimate management." Thorn grinned. "How'd you arrange that?"

"I put word out that the 14K didn't want any competition. Eagle helped me spread rumors in the Vegas underworld. And none of the smaller mob groups wanted to share DeLuca's fate. The Remington never had enough to attract the big family." Vegas operated like any ecosystem with small predators living in fear of the alpha predators. As long as the 14K Triad laundered the money, the alpha group had no need for a small-time casino.

"Smart move." Jericho lifted his beer in toast. "We need that kind of leadership at home." He grinned at me. "Ready to take on that challenge? Rebel needs you. We need you."

Fuck. That was the last thing I needed. While I'd been in Vegas, the club hadn't been real. But when I talked to Thorn or saw Eagle, I'd be fucked-up for days with a foul mood and a need to escape. It's why I'd stopped returning Thorn's calls. It's why I'd cleaned up the Vegas mess so quick—I hadn't wanted to deal with my club.

"Not many brothers would do what you did for the club. It's time for you received your reward." Dare nodded to me. "We have two open spots in our leadership team. We want you to take one. We are creating a new VP position—I've got too much shit to do."

"This position would deal with logistics, making sure we have the shit we need, figuring out how to grow the club into new businesses, that kind of gig." Jericho met my gaze. "Right up your alley."

"Or you can go back to the bounty business. Rebel needs a number two who handles Texas businesses. You'd be over like fifteen bail bonds operations," Thorn offered. "Rebel would be here but he and Elle are closing on a new business in Amarillo. Rebel is going to stay here and manage the biker component and Elle is operating the company on a large scale. We have forty bail bonds locations now."

"What about JoJo?" That brother was the guy they needed.

"He's operating five locations in OKC, but he doesn't want more." Jericho frowned. "Why don't you know that?"

I didn't answer. I hadn't talked to my best friend since I'd left Barden. I couldn't tell him what was eating at me because I didn't want to burden him with it all. "I'm not really leadership—"

"Bullshit," Dare growled.

"I'll email you some stuff on both roles—take a few days and decide which you want. I'll announce it this Sunday at church." Jericho stood and moved down to me. "Be good to have you back here." He smacked me on the back.

I had three days to decide which shit job to take. Hell, anyone else in the club would be glad to be promoted, but it was a death sentence to me. Jericho and Dare left before I figured out what to say. How did you turn down a leadership role?

Already I felt wrong being here. The club was closing in on me. I had to get out of here.

"So which one you taking?" Thorn glanced at me.

"I'm heading home." I stood and almost raced out of the clubhouse. I needed space.

I headed to Ardmore and checked into a hotel. I'd let another biker use my place while I was gone and I didn't want to surprise him at one in the morning. And I didn't want to be in my house.

I checked my phone as I lay in the bed, unable to sleep. All the hatred surrounded me—I'd killed those boys and nothing would change that. I'd done it for the club and now the club wasn't my home anymore. Glory was my home, but I hadn't heard from her. But then what did I expect after that chickenshit text I'd sent.

At ten in the morning my phone pinged. It was Thorn. In Ardmore. Let's get food.

He'd just keep after me until he saw me, so I agreed to meet him in thirty. I took a quick shower and headed over to the restaurant I used to love for breakfast. Now it didn't even sound good. Nothing in my life was good anymore. I hated being back in Oklahoma.

Of course, Thorn was already in there with coffee and food. He was the last guy I wanted to see. He'd have questions, and I didn't have answers or the patience to pretend I did.

I ordered a steak and eggs. Thorn grunted and kept eating. Once his breakfast was gone, he scooted his plate back and stared at me, or into me. He had always been able to read me too fucking well.

"See you've fucked yourself up. Congratulations."

"Fuck off. I don't need a nanny."

The waitress set my plate down. I sliced off a bite of steak. Damn, it tasted good. No wonder it did, I hadn't eaten since sometime the day before yesterday. I'd definitely been guzzling too much booze.

"Those two deaths will kill you if you let them."

I stuffed food in my mouth and tried to ignore him.

"She called me because you scared her. She's afraid of what you're becoming."

Glory had called him? Fuck. I had screwed up. And I'd been past due to leave.

"What the fuck is up your ass? Spit it out—that's a fucking order."

I glanced across the table and laughed. "You can't order me to get over this shit."

"I fucking wish I'd killed them," he muttered.

"I'm coward enough to wish that too, and that eats at me right along with the deed." I pushed away my half-eaten food. "You were trained to kill. I wasn't—you can't begin to understand how that fucks with my head."

"I'm a master at being fucked in the head."

"Right. I know my shit is nothing compared to what you carry. Nothing as bad as many of our brothers carry. Yet, it's still eating me alive, and I don't have a fucking clue how to make it stop. Maybe it won't stop, and that's fine with me. I don't deserve for it to stop because I took those fucking lives for the club."

"The club is the kicker, right?" Thorn just kept pushing.

"Fuck yeah. I did shit for them. Shit that I can't undo and don't feel right about."

"What does feel right?"

"Nothing feels right. Nothing is good. Nothing! I deserve nothing."

"Poor Delta, feeling all bad and sad," Thorn sneered. "Man the fuck up."

I stood and dropped cash on the table. I was done here.

I hadn't made it two steps out the door before Thorn was in my face. "You need to let that shit go—we're rewarding you for what you did."

Rage burst out of me. Rage at them rewarding me. Rage at Glory being scared. All of me burned in rage. I put all my power into the left hook and followed with a right.

Thorn laughed. "You got more than that?"

I punched again and again, then he got in a swing and knocked me to my ass.

"You blame me?"

"No, it's me. All me!" I got to my feet, the fight gone.

"The club, then?"

I opened my mouth to deny it but nothing came out.

"What's the club mean to you?"

"My life. My best friend."

"That's JoJo, but he's got a new life now. What does the Brotherhood mean to you?"

I had nothing. Felt nothing. The kills in Vegas had poisoned my connection to the club.

"I don't know," I finally admitted.

He poked my chest. "Figure that shit out or get out. If I was you, I'd get the fuck out."

Was he kicking me out? Now the club didn't even want me. "Is that from the top?"

"Nah, you're golden with the club. The top wants to reward you. I told them to wait and give you time. Jericho wanted to call you home a month ago." Thorn shook his head. "Nah, man, that's my advice—get the fuck out and don't look back." Turning his back on me, he headed to his bike.

Anger built and I had nowhere for it to go. I got on my bike and drove away, with no destination in mind. I needed time to think, time to figure out what I wanted.

I pulled into the Brotherhood lot at 10 a.m. Saturday morning. I'd asked Jericho to call a special council meeting today. He'd assumed it was so I could announce my decision, and in a way it was. I walked inside and noticed how full the place was. Over seventy bikers crowded into the main room eating breakfast. Nods and smiles greeted me, but I kept moving. I had business with the council today.

When I got to the council door, I knocked twice and

strode inside before anyone had even moved from the table where they conducted business.

Jericho smiled at me. "Come on up here and join us."

I shook my head. "I'll stay here."

Jericho frowned. "So what did you decide?"

"I need out. I want to retire." Lots of guys retired after a few years. I'd been part of the club ten.

"What the fuck? You could be up here with us." Jericho stared at me.

"I hate to see you go," my boss, Rebel, said.

"Why?" Jericho broke in.

"I can't stay."

"Why?" Thorn was going to make me say it.

"I'm done. Those deaths in Vegas ruined this for me. I ruined this for me." I dropped my head.

Silence met my announcement. "I move to retire Delta with honors from the Jericho Brotherhood." Rock's voice surprised me.

"I agree," Thorn said.

"Vote," Jericho announced.

No sound followed so I glanced up. Everyone had a thumb up. It was done. I was out. Numb and not sure if I'd made a good choice, I knew it was the only one for me. It was time to be on my own.

Chapter 31: Glory

Two months and no word from Delta. It sucked less every day, but I still missed the bastard. Of course, I hadn't contacted him either. A girl had her pride, and I used mine as a blanket wrapped tight around me on all the lonely nights in Las Vegas.

"Glory, I need a minute." My boss pulled me into his office. "I'm posting the new chorus line tonight, but I wanted to talk to you first."

Shit, I didn't make it. There were four spotlight dancers who stood on pedestals during part of the act, they were the stars of the show, and I'd tried out again.

"I wanted you to know I appreciate the hard work and extra practices you've been putting in here. I see your dedication."

Yada yada...but you're not good enough.

"So I'm happy to say you got one of the spotlights." He smiled wide.

Had I heard him right? "What?"

"You got it, girl. You did it."

"I did it." I whooped and gave him a hug. "Damn straight I did."

That night I made it home later than normal since a few of the girls and I had gone out to celebrate my new position. I'd made it! Hit my damn goal and I'd celebrated, but not so much I was drunk. Even all these months later, my lessons from the Remington made me cautious. I was okay with that. I parked and walked toward my apartment. I noticed his bike first—the sleek black Harley stood proud right in front of my condo.

Excitement danced inside me. I tried to remind myself I should be pissed, but honestly, I just didn't find it in me. He wasn't outside the door and that ticked me off a bit. It was my place and he'd just let himself in. Of course, I knew he had a key and I hadn't changed my locks. Hell, I'd even fantasized about him being inside my place when I came home from work.

And now he was.

A huge bouquet of red roses was on my coffee table and a trail of petals led to the back bedroom. The pissed-off I'd been trying to work up fizzled at the sight of the flowers. I followed the trail to my room, where my biker lay sprawled on my bed staring up at the ceiling.

"And who's been sleeping in my bed?"

He glanced to me and I froze. So much emotion swirled in his eyes and I crossed to him. I had to be sure this wasn't a dream. He was back and I had to touch him, kiss him and be sure this was all real.

I climbed up on the bed and he enfolded me in a hug. Safe. I felt safe for the first time in two months.

"I couldn't stay away." He spoke into my ear. "I tried, but I couldn't stay away."

I just squeezed tighter, not trusting my words right then. What if I said the wrong thing? I had no idea what this meant. Hell, I didn't even know if I wanted him here. Well, of course I wanted him, but did I want him if it was only a couple more nights and then he left again?

He sat up with me and scooted back, meeting my gaze again. "Why aren't you pissed?"

Good question. But somewhere along the way I'd lost my temper in my sorrow and missing him. "I dunno."

"You should be pissed."

I nodded. "Totally."

"You didn't text me."

"I didn't." God, all I could do was repeat him. Where was my brain tonight?

"You probably know I left the club?"

"What the fuck?"

"Or not," he chuckled.

"Why did you leave?"

"The shit in Vegas—it was too much."

"When? Why didn't you come back?" I wanted to snatch that question right back.

"You didn't need a mess, again." He ran hands through his hair. "And I needed to make peace, and then I was going to leave you be because...hell, because I was stupid." He laughed again.

"And you got smarter?" I inched closer, touching his leg, needing that reminder he was really here.

"You wouldn't let me be—in my dreams, my memories, everywhere."

I laughed now. "Yeah? You were haunting me too."

"I found myself here, and I couldn't leave again."

"Again?" A spark of anger came to life.

"I've been here in Vegas three times, but made myself leave. I couldn't leave again." He squeezed my hand. "I think I fucking love you and I don't know what to do about that."

"Leaving ain't it," I shot back.

He gave me a smile. "Figured that part out."

Then it hit. He said it. He loved me. He fucking loved me.

I jumped forward and kissed him hard. He fell back with me wrapped tight in his arms. The kiss felt right and suddenly I understood he was it for me. No one had made me feel like this, and no one ever would. He was the man I loved.

"About time you figured that shit out." I swiped his nose. "I love you too, in case you hadn't figured that out."

"Yeah?"

"Yeah." I kissed him again then pulled back. "Welcome home."

Epilogue

I hardly recognized the scene in front of me. What the hell had happened to the badass bikers I'd called brothers? They were all docile dads now, and I couldn't be happier for them. Glory and I sat at a table at a Brotherhood party—kids shouted and chased each other—people laughed—Glory's mom was at the center of a group of old ladies. She'd become the club grandma, helping all the families with little ones.

Queenie leaned over and kissed me. "This isn't like the first biker party I attended."

"Not even close." I laughed, remembering the way we'd drank, danced and ended up doing it in the back rooms. She still rocked my world five years later.

"You missing your cut?" she asked me again. I knew it worried her that I'd given up the club, but I didn't miss it. I missed the brotherhood, but not the structure. I didn't want to owe anyone but my wife allegiance. My last mission in Vegas had tainted my love for the club. It had been a poison I'd had to eradicate or I would have died.

"Auntie Glory, show me how to dance!" Four-year-old Evaline tugged at my wife's hand. The kid had Avery's eyes and knew how to use every ounce of her charm.

Glory laughed and let herself be dragged to where a band played. Ten little kids surrounded her. She organized them in a line and began helping them learn another move in the dance she'd been teaching them.

Thorn sat next to me and stared out at my wife. "You're a lucky bastard."

"I know it." I looked over at my friend. "The luckiest."

He nodded. "You doing good?"

He'd asked me this on a regular basis over the past five years. In fact, he'd connected me to a veterans' group in Vegas who'd helped me work out the last of my demons. I'd never be good with the deaths of those kids or my buddies, but they haunted me less now.

"I am good. When are you joining the married mob?"

He gave me a sad grin. "Maybe one day. Not all of us are made for happy endings."

"Bullshit, brother." I punched his arm. "You just got to be brave enough to grab hold of what you need."

"Well, I'm no coward." He looked away, lost in thought. He shook his head and refocused on me. "What about you two? Ready to retire back home?"

I'd embraced my love of poker and it had made us wealthy enough to retire. "Not even. Glory loves her new job managing the chorus line, and we aren't made for this kind of living anymore. And I have my veteran project—it's only in its infancy."

I'd created a nonprofit to support veterans who were damaged in service—physical or mental trauma. They formed a group with a veteran as the officer in charge of each house. Our nonprofit offered counseling, job training, and other services for them. In two months, I'd open the third house, and ten veterans would have a home, help, and brotherhood to help them through the hard times.

"It's good work." Thorn sighed. "I miss you."

"I need someone to serve as the house leader for my newest project." I had asked him to join us before. "You could go nomad and take the job."

"It sounds better all the time," Thorn admitted.

Avery bounded over. "Your wife needs your help."

Glory always figured a way to involve me in her messes. I loved that about her. "Of course my queen needs me."

I stood up and walked toward where she was trying to teach them how to dance together.

"When are you two adding to our tribe of kids?" Avery was not subtle. She was convinced I was keeping Glory from having kids.

We had decided not to have children. Our lives were busy and Las Vegas wasn't where we would choose to raise children.

"Not anytime soon." I gave a chin nod to Jericho as I passed him and Marr. "You pester Jericho about this shit?"

"Yeah. Because it's my job." Avery grinned wide. "I want you both to be happy. You're both happy?"

"You know we are." I laughed. Happy was something I'd never thought I'd feel again, but Glory had shown me true happiness.

"Finally." Glory clasped my hand. "My perfect partner." She leaned up on tiptoes to kiss me. Giggles and groans sounded as we kissed.

"Let's show them our best moves." I spun Queenie in a circle and dipped her low before snapping her close to me.

"We'll need one of those bedrooms for that," she whispered in my ear.

"Damn, I love you." I was the luckiest bastard on earth.

* * * * *

Reviews are an invaluable tool when it comes to spreading the word about great reads. Please consider leaving an honest review for this or any of Carina Press's other titles that you've read on your favorite retailer or review site.

To purchase other books by this author visit jadechandler.com

Author Note

I have been writing about the strong, sexy bikers of the Jericho Brotherhood for five years. These six books have taught me so much about writing. *Get Away* allowed me to revisit some of my first hero and heroines. Dare and Lila, Rock and Avery, and Jericho and Marr from my first three books (from the Jericho Brotherhood series) all make an appearance in this one. I enjoyed catching up with those characters again.

Acknowledgments

I want to thank Harlequin, Carina Press, and Angela James for seeing the potential in the Jericho Brotherhood and Brotherhood Bonds. My editors have all been wonderful and I appreciate learning from each of them. I want to give a special shout-out to my agent and cheerleader Jessica Waterson for all her advice and guidance through this process. Thank you to my friends, family and especially my critique partners who have helped me as I wrote each book and made me a better person.

To my readers, I give the biggest thanks of all. When you read my books, they come alive and the characters live again and again. There is no greater joy for a writer than to share her stories with others, so thank you for allowing me so much joy!

Now available from Carina Press and Jade Chandler.

From the moment she walked into my tattoo shop, she was going to end up in my bed. Tied up, moaning my name and begging for more.

Read on for an excerpt from
Enough,
the first book in Jade Chandler's
Jericho Brotherhood series

Life offered new chances all the time, and today was mine. Nothing matched the optimism of the first day. I've always loved the potential of these days—new school years, new jobs, new opportunities.

"Today, I *will* kick ass and take names," I told myself with a confidence I didn't feel.

Hell, I couldn't even convince my reflection.

I swiped a coat of gloss on my lips before I grabbed my red hobo bag and headed to my first day of work.

I hurried down the narrow wood stairs and around the corner to the tattoo shop's side entrance, literally mere feet from my apartment. I hit the four-digit code to my new home away from home.

Astringent and wood scents greeted me as I flipped up a row of switches and lit the workroom. My steps echoed across the worn wooden floor, and I approved of the way the brick-colored walls accented the chrome and black motif of the stations.

"Anyone here?" I raised my voice, and it echoed through the huge room. Apparently not. I wish I knew who would be meeting me, but all Jericho had said was "one of the guys will be there at eleven."

The hall split in two directions—the left led to the

front, my domain, and the right to a closed door marked Staff Only. I itched to dig in to the inventory. Instead, I moved to the front so I wouldn't miss my mysterious guide who was now...oh, who'd now be just on time. Right, I'd come early, unable to wait anymore.

Besides, the front belonged to me. The green walls, huge old wooden counter and 1950s retro cash register shouted attitude and style. The shelves under the oak counter held the leather-bound appointment book and the ledger Jericho, the guy who'd interviewed me, said I should use to track sales and expenses.

There really wasn't a freaking computer. Who did business like that?

The Jericho Brotherhood. Unease made me move, I needed to do anything besides think about the barely legal motorcycle club who owned the shop.

I grabbed the window cleaner and polished the print-smudged glass covering the old counter.

I erased the drink rings coating the two end tables before I tackled the door and two huge plate-glass windows. Hands on hips, I surveyed my work—the waiting area gleamed.

I took a quick look at my watch to reaffirm what the huge metal clock on the wall said—eleven fifteen. Now Mr. Mysterious was late, and my nerves started to eat my stomach lining since the cleaning hadn't helped my anxiety. I stowed away the cleaner before I walked outside to see my handiwork.

The tattoo shop, the Marked Man, stood at the west end of Main Street with boutiques, small businesses, the only bar and two of Barden's four restaurants. The hot Oklahoma sun beat down, with the temperature above ninety, according to the bank sign cattywampus from the shop. Sweat popped on my brow in seconds, and white light bounced off the windows, almost blinding me.

"Hey," a deep rumbling voice called from behind me. I steeled myself to not react, no matter how scary or intimidating the biker might be. I mean, the boss guy, Jericho, gave me the willies with his cold, bi-colored eyes.

"Hey, Red," the man repeated.

I wasn't a fan of my curly red hair that refused to do anything I wanted. Seriously, it was like a temperamental cat lived on my head. Give me Medusa hair any day over this stuff.

I turned but only saw a white-outlined silhouette in the bright noon sun. Tall, blond and the owner of a seriously sexy voice.

"Dare," he greeted me, before he opened the door.

I walked into the dimmer light of the reception area.

"Did ya find your way around?"

When I turned toward him, I almost swallowed my tongue.

He stood in front of me dressed in leather chaps, motorcycle boots and a tight red T-shirt almost painted on his wide chest.

His strong chin was bare, even though I thought beards were a biker requirement. Full lips tilted in a sexy, sarcastic smirk. Aviator glasses slid off, and he assessed me with the bluest eyes I'd ever seen.

"Hey, I'm Lila." I held out my hand, glad it didn't tremble.

He clasped it in a firm but not crushing handshake.

Tingles shot from my fingers up my arm and raced down my spine. I was in serious trouble. My attraction meter shot past interested into the red zone.

"Glad you're here to fix the chaos."

His wide smile lit up his face, adding a hint of adorable to his charm.

No bikers, no men, period, I chastised myself. *I don't want trouble.* I liked the empty apartment above my lust-filled head. Hadn't I just run from one loser as soon as I landed this job?

I stepped back into the counter. "Doesn't look like it's in too bad of shape." I bit my lip and suppressed the moan I wanted to let loose thanks to the six feet of sexiness standing in front of me.

He leaned forward, his breath brushing my cheek. "Yeah?" With his hands planted on the glass top of the counter, his scent, a mix of outdoors, leather and citrus, surrounded me.

Delicious.

When he tugged at one of my auburn curls, I froze with my knees resembling Jell-O.

"Love this hair."

I'd been too harsh on my hair all these years. His lips inches from me were a perfect bow of temptation. I prayed he'd step away, so when he gave me space, the prick of pain in my chest made absolutely no sense. Stupid brain.

"Jericho says you've done this before." He moved down the hall.

Dazed by our encounter, I stood planted in place.

"You coming." Command clear on his face and in his short tone.

I jerked like I'd been shocked to life before I hurried after him to the workroom.

"Yeah, this is my third tat shop. I was office manager at the last one in Texarkana. I told Jericho to call anyone about my work, but if you need my—"

"Enough, Red." His lips curled up on one side.

"My name is Lila Braham, did Jericho forget to mention it…?" My words trailed off into this half squeak, half whisper. I think it sounded like the death rattle of one of those squeakers in dog toys.

He arched an eyebrow and stared at me a long time, like an hour, although I know in real time it could have only been seconds. He pointed to the two stations right next to each other. "Weasel and Angel work there. Angel does piercing only. If she ain't here, most of us can pierce too, except dick or pussy hoods, those are tricky and all Angel."

I desperately wanted to write this down, but like an addled idiot, I'd left the legal pad I'd found under the counter. I contemplated making a run for it, but he didn't appear the patient type. My memory would have to do.

"This is Zayn's space." He pointed to the opposite side of where Angel and Ferret—no that wasn't right—Angel and Weasel worked. "He'll be here most of the time. Rock is up here across from my station. If you have questions and I'm not here, you ask either of them." He moved over to stand in front of a work space, the one closest to the back door and my apartment.

"I work when I got appointments or when we're real busy or when I get a wild hair."

The word *hair* brought my attention back to his hair perfection. Shoulder-length and the color of sunshine, it appeared silky soft, and I wanted to confirm my suspicion.

"You book appointments, and unless it's marked out up front, you schedule it, and the artist will call the customer back if it don't work."

I nodded. "Got it."

"What do you have, Red?" He drew out the name I hoped he'd quit using.

"I book appointments, mostly toward Rock and Zayn unless someone asks for you or Weasel. Angel for piercings." I bit my lip.

Dare's energy changed in a flash and he devoured me in a way I knew too well. My pulse raced and moisture spread at the apex of my legs. Yeah, there was some serious energy between us.

Ignoring my own traitor of a body and his whole sex vibe, with monumental effort I focused on the job. "Do I order inks and supplies?"

He strode past me without a word, so I followed when he opened the door marked Staff Only and gestured for me to go inside. The room was small, with shelves all organized with supplies: art books, inks, needles and piercing supplies. They were well set up, and it was neater than most supply areas I'd seen, at least before I'd enforced my brand of neat-freak on them.

Turning, I bumped into his hard, muscled chest, which caused me to stumble back in surprise into the nearest shelf. The shelving unit shook and I worried paper towels were about to rain down on me. They wobbled but stayed in place. Good paper towels.

He gripped my upper arm. A nuclear-level heat washed through me and flamed persistently in my core. If more moisture accumulated in my panties, I might have to go change them. My nipples joined the act, not that I could see if they'd decided to flaunt their happiness unless I obviously stared down at my chest.

"When we need things," his voice purred close in my ear, "you just ask me before you get what you need."

I sucked in a breath but wasn't about to let him get the

best of me with this flirty, dirty innuendo. It was nothing new, except how much it affected me.

I glanced up through lowered lashes. "And you'll always get me what I need?"

A full smile spread across his face. "Count on it, Red."

His words sounded like a promise instead of the flirty game.

But I decided to play a bit more. "I will, Dare." I drew out his name almost the same way he'd done with mine.

His eyes closed for a second too long before he removed his hand from my arm. I squeezed past him out of the closet, waiting for him in the hall unsure if my instruction was done and I could ask my questions.

He moved past me, so I hurried to catch up.

"What else should I do?" A lame question but it had burst out over all my more intelligent questions.

He stopped and turned to me. "I told you. Do the paperwork shit, don't keep me waiting and make sure shit runs smooth." He started walking again.

While not the most eloquent answer, I understood the bottom line—don't bother him with small stuff and keep the rest quick and simple. This job was the same as the one I'd left when I kicked my no-good ex in the balls and stormed out of his tattoo shop. This time, I wouldn't make the same mistake of falling right into the arms of the first guy I stumbled across.

"I like *oral* reports Red, so don't hand me any fucking papers. Also, call me, never text, I hate that shit." He continued moving to the front.

Good thing he didn't look at me then. My cheeks heated and I'm sure I blushed, not from embarrassment, at least not embarrassment from the comment, but defi-

nitely from imagining my mouth on his cock—a plea-
surable fantasy.

*No, Lila. Stop falling before you've even landed on
your feet. New start, no old mistakes.*

I heard laughter before I walked into the reception
area.

Dare slapped the back of a young guy, who couldn't
be twenty-one, in the same leather vest with floppy black
hair.

"Zayn meet Lila." Dare's attention felt like a physical force to me.

Oh my god, he'd finally used my name, we were making progress. "Hi, I'm the new office manager." I held out
a hand, but the enthusiastic guy pressed me into a hug.

"Thank God, I'm so glad you're here." He smiled
wide. "They've been making me straighten up and shit
so you wouldn't run away in the first hour." He cocked
his head at me. "I must've succeeded."

I laughed. He was too cute, like a puppy you knew
would grow up into one of those huge scary dogs. "Yeah,
things are in great shape."

With a nod, he moved to the appointment book.
"We're busy today. Shit, I got two, and you have three
appointments at one, six and eight."

Was I supposed to tell Dare his appointments when
he came in? Was I supposed to tell everyone? I needed
to start a list of questions because my brain turned to
lust-filled goo near Dare.

"Yeah." He nodded to Zayn. "Come back and see the
art I created for Mark. He's my first customer." Dare
strolled down the hall beside Zayn without a glance my
way.

I straightened and pulled my shit together. I never

picked good men, I think the part that picks out the right man was broken in me. How could it not be after all the years with my horror-show father? Tony, my ex, had taught me the dangers of dating the boss. He was the owner, and with our breakup, I'd ended the job I loved. Worse, I'd had to pretend for weeks he wasn't a cheating bastard, until I could line up a new job. Funny how he could control me, put me down, make fun of me, but cheating pushed me over the edge. I guess I should be glad he did, but it still stung that he went somewhere else for the one thing no one ever complained about.

My body purred in a familiar way—the hum of attraction lit me up. Goddammit, my sense always flew out the window when my body voted for sex. Whatever inside my head controlled my sex drive had declared it was in charge, but not this time. I'd sworn to take charge of my own life without the aid of a man.

The front door jingled and a guy strode inside. "Hey." He flashed a boy-next-door smile. "I'm Mark, here for—"

"You're scheduled for Dare. Nice to meet you. I'm Lila."

He gave me the nod.

"He's here, head on back."

Less than thirty minutes after Mark disappeared down the hall, I resumed obsessing about Dare and the day, which led to thinking about his club, the Jericho Brotherhood.

When Jericho interviewed me, he'd made it clear Dare would be my boss. But he hadn't made clear who he was. Was he Dare's boss?

I'd been ecstatic when Jericho offered me the job during the middle of the interview. So ready to leave Tony, I'd gushed out my acceptance.

Then things turned strange. Part of managing a shop was doing the bookwork, paying invoices, depositing the day's earnings and making sure the accountant had all the information needed, plus a hundred other small jobs. When Jericho explained my office work duties, a chill had run down my back; they were nothing like what I did at Ink Masters in Texarkana. I remember wondering why he even called the job an office manager. The duties were simple but made me slightly skeptical of the club's legality. I paid myself in cash or check, taxes optional. I opted for the legal tax version of payroll. I did the bookwork, entering expenses, revenue and profit, but I did it in an old ledger, all by hand. Nobody did business that way in the twenty-first century.

After doing the bookwork, I bagged deposits for each day separately and stored them in the safe. A guy, Stork, would be by every day or two to collect invoices, credit card receipts, and the cash and check deposits, which was another odd bit because no one accepted checks anymore. But the Brotherhood did, along with other questionable practices.

I'd volunteered to do the deposit drops, but Jericho swept away the suggestion, saying the bank was in Ardmore and no need for me to make the extra trip. Most bosses were all about others doing the grunt work, but then they didn't have an unknown numbers of bikers at their beck and call.

When I'd asked about how to get more cash for the registers, he'd told me to call the number taped to the desk, and Stork or one of his guys would bring it to me. I'd nodded and planned to ask more questions, when Jericho distracted me with the salary and free apartment that was part of the position.

The need to escape my previous life had trumped my vague unease about the Brotherhood's operations. Now my gut twisted like it had during the interview. What had I agreed to do? Did it matter if everything I did was legal if I worked for a dirty business? Despite my inner apprehension, I had no sense the business was a cover for anything else. In fact, the shop had lots more appointments scheduled than the last place, and the quality of the operation, from ink to artists, was the best I'd ever seen. Despite the extra overhead of quality product, the shop turned a very respectable profit, according to the ledger I'd flipped through.

"Lila, come see this," Zayn yelled from the back.

Happy for the distraction, I hurried to the workroom. Dare focused on Mark's shoulder, inking the outline of the piece with a steady hand. A man with an ink iron always caught my attention, and I almost tasted his sexiness—spicy with a touch of sweet.

Zayn showed me the tribal pattern Dare had drawn. A complicated set of markings like the tats on The Rock's arms—he'd made tribal artwork crazy-hot.

I flipped through the art book Zayn handed me. A Chinese-inspired dragon impressed me. Wow. The dragons chased each other in a circle, destined to be frustrated for eternity. The center held a yin and yang on backgrounds of fire and ice.

"Beautiful." The word escaped and I clamped my mouth shut.

"Dare's a fuckin' artist." Zayn smirked. "He can draw anything."

I'd noticed the *Z* and *D* in the corners of some drawings. Dare's art had a fantasy flair while Zayn's was darker, sort of gothic. They were two of the most talented artists I'd met.

When the buzz of the needle stopped, Dare gestured me over with a nod of his jutting chin.

"Hey." He cocked his head. "What do you think about some deep red accents?"

Did Dare want me to comment? I grinned at Mark, a guy about my age, who assessed his work in the mirror.

"Show me where," Mark said.

Dare grabbed my hand, using my finger to trace Mark's skin in the area Dare proposed adding the crimson accent. A zing of electricity shot from where his hand touched mine and ricocheted through my body in a distracting, haphazard path, but it managed to hit all my important bits.

Both guys gazed toward me.

"What do you think?" Mark's boyish smile gave him just the right combination of sexy, not that my bits responded to him, at all.

Nope, my body lit up like a winning pinball machine for Dare. *Not going there*, I reminded myself.

"It'd feel more like a fighting piece with the red, so it depends on the vibe you want." I struggled to keep my words steady despite Dare's distracting touch.

He still hadn't released the finger he'd hijacked.

"Badass—that's the vibe I need." Mark traced the same place I had a moment before.

I attempted to shake off the spell Dare created. "I would go for the red, then. You'll be a total badass."

Dare's mouth twitched in a hint of a grin, and I imagined kissing his seductive lips. Sucking in another breath, I moved away before I lost my impulse control.

It wasn't a problem he appeared to share. He finished

the outline with a quick precision I respected. Mark waved away the offer of a break, so Dare started filling in the design. Intense concentration lined his brow and tightened his lips. He rarely spoke, working faster than any other artist I'd seen. The front door jingled and woke me from my trance.

"That'll be Mary." Zayn waggled his eyebrows. "She's wanting a boob piece, you can come watch me."

"She might want privacy." I rolled my eyes at him. "And your undivided attention."

"Well, that's true." He followed me to the front and welcomed his client.

As I thought, she batted long lashes at Zayn, dressed in tight-fitting jeans I wished I could wear and full makeup. She was angling for more than good customer service, and by the spark in his eye, she might just get lucky.

The rest of the day was on fast-forward between the clients and trying to figure out how the shop ran. I only saw the guys a few times as they brought customers to me for check-out.

Dare appeared next to me before closing time. "Lock the door." Dare surprised me. Why did he want me to lock up early?

I frowned up at him, pausing from counting my drawer. "We've got twenty minutes until close."

He stood arms crossed, waiting for me to do as told, I guess. I strode over and flipped the sign before turning the two dead bolts on the door.

"Closing is simple, we clean our areas before we go, you make the front decent, close the register, lock up the deposit, and you're done."

This was much easier than my last job where I'd had

to do the final sanitizing on all the stations and clean the floors. I understood why shops had to be more sterile than hospitals and hadn't minded the work of sanitizing, but not being responsible for the workroom was a huge relief. I'd be out of here in minutes, not hours, which was great tonight because the first day kicked my ass. Totally.

"Z is already at Blue's drinking beer, I'm headed over. You joining us?" The words were totally innocent, but his sexy undertone asked an entirely different question.

"Not tonight." I laughed. "I feel like I've been run over."

He frowned and parted his lips.

"It's good, I just need a day or two to get the routine down and let my brain catch up. "But, I'm ready to hit my bed tonight."

The worst thing to say, ever.

A grin spread with a slow sexiness that hit me hard right in my already overstimulated parts. Dare might be a walking sex god who would enchant me if I didn't leave fast. I hurried to the safe with the deposit, hoping he wouldn't see the blush burning my cheeks.

"Next time," he called to my back, a laugh in his voice.

I trudged up the stairs, tired from the ten-hour day. I hoped I wasn't expected to work all the hours the shop was open. Why hadn't I asked Dare? Instead, I'd almost invited him to my bed. *Way to hold strong, Braham.*

Inside, I kicked off my boots, undressed and slipped between the covers of my fifty-dollar blow-up mattress from Walmart. The mattress welcomed me like a million-dollar bed tonight. I fell asleep in seconds.

The next morning my alarm blared, and sun hit me in the face. *Shit. I don't want to wake up.*

I groaned and smacked the alarm. My body ached,

not from work yesterday, but in sexual frustration. All night, I'd dreamed of the sexy biker, but dating the boss was one screwup I planned not to repeat. Too messy. My job was too good to lose for a nice ass and the bluest eyes on earth.

I stepped into the hot shower and steam enveloped me.

Dare pulled tight on the knot binding my ankles. He'd created a maze of ropes across my torso, firm but not tight. When I moved, the ropes slid across my skin, my nipples. I arched back, unable to resist the sensations. He positioned me with my ass in the air and secured my hands to the bed in front of me before he fingered me.

In the shower, the images played over again in my mind while my fingers traveled to my pussy. The hot water beat on my sensitive breasts, my fingers plucked with purpose, and I climaxed, remembering the intense orgasm from my dream. Panting, I leaned against the wall. One day, only one day, and he'd invaded my dreams.

Between the long shower and fitful night, my morning routine took longer. Unable to speed up despite three cups of java, I managed to take almost an hour on my normal thirty-minute routine. I'd just picked up my trail of clothes from the night before when I glanced at the clock.

Damn. It was five minutes until noon, I was beyond late by my standards.

I almost ran out of the apartment and down the stairs, hurrying to hit the code and get set up for the day. Thankfully, our first appointment came in at two.

I walked in to foreign voices, and stopped a minute before I called out, "It's Lila, the new girl."

"Damn, girl, thought we'd have to open. You always

late?" A gnarled guy well past thirty stared at me with beady eyes—snake eyes.

"Weasel, lay off the new girl, you old goat." A Hispanic-looking guy with bulging muscles leaned against the doorway. "I'm Rock, the ornery one is Weasel and his old lady Angel is piercing a chick now."

"Lila." I frowned, worried I'd messed up already, missed an appointment, not even two days into my new job. "Great to meet y'all."

Weasel growled and turned back to the work area, so I moved up front, and Rock followed.

"Don't mind Weasel and Angel, they're always sour." Rock laughed. "I got enough sweetness to make up for them both." He winked at me.

I laughed and scoured the books. "Did I miss the appointment?" I bit my lip.

"Nah, Angel called me this morning saying a girlfriend of hers needed a piercing, so I came in with them." He still grinned. "You settled in?"

About the Author

Jade Chandler lives in the Midwest with her family and pets. She has always loved romance books, and now gets to follow her passion of writing romances, too. When she isn't at the computer, typing new stories, she is enjoying life and creating memories with her family and friends. Be sure to visit her at jadechandler.com.

Get 4 FREE REWARDS!

We'll send you 2 FREE Books <u>plus</u> 2 FREE Mystery Gifts.

Worldwide Library books feature gripping mysteries from "whodunits" to police procedurals and courtroom dramas.

FREE Value Over **$20**

ReaderService.com has a new look!

We have refreshed our website and
we want to share our new look with you.
Head over to ReaderService.com
and check it out!

On ReaderService.com, you can:

- Try 2 free books from any series
- Access risk-free special offers
- View your account history & manage payments
- Browse the latest Bonus Bucks catalog

Don't miss out!

If you want to stay up-to-date on the latest at the Reader Service and enjoy more Harlequin content, make sure you've signed up for our monthly News & Notes email newsletter. Sign up online at ReaderService.com.

RS19